Dark River

A Novel of Suspense

Heather Buchanan

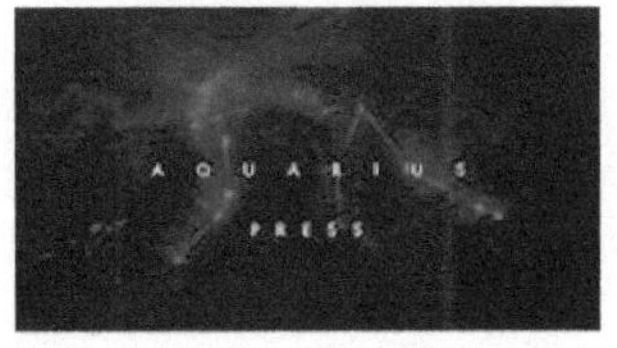

AQUARIUS PRESS

Detroit, MI

Dark River
A Novel of Suspense
2nd Edition

(c) 2025 Heather Buchanan

ISBN978-0-9985278-9-5

Disclaimer: This is a work of fiction, but several historical facts have been incorporated into this novel. To protect and preserve the rich French-Canadian heritage of early Detroit families, however, Fontaine Street and the Fontaine family line are fictional. Usage of the term "Indian" reflects colloquialisms of the 1700s -1800s and is in no way meant to defame Native Americans and the First Nations of Canada.

Printed in the United States of America

Praise for *Dark River*

"A suspenseful tale of love and deceit. . .*Dark River* combines real history with romantic suspense in a tale that will draw you in and keep you on the edge of your seat!"

~*Sylvia Hubbard, Editor, Michigan Murder & Mayhem*

"We recommend this book!"

~*Ella's Book Club*

"*Dark River* was a very good book. Excellent. This one should be sent to Oprah!"

~*Christine Miller, Veteran's Administration*

"I really loved the book . . . I read it in two sittings!"

~*Dr. Glenda Price, Marygrove College*

"Lyrical."

~*Tonya Hogans, Romance Writers of America*

"Highly recommended."

~*Circle of Life Book Club*

"I finished your book last night and absolutely LOVED IT! Once I started reading it, I couldn't put it down. It reminded me of *Wuthering Heights*. What I liked most was your historical accuracy of old Detroit. There aren't many books that I've read that moved me like this one."

~*Brenda Cornish, Playwright*

DEDICATION

This book would never have been possible without the help of the following people:

Sharon Stanford, thank you for your excellent editing skills and for always being the first person in line; to Sylvia McClain, thanks for teaching me about perseverance; to Karen White-Owens, I still have so much to learn from you; to Barbara Pattee, you never miss a thing; to Dr. Debraha Watson, thanks for asking about the book over the years; to Jocelyn "Eagle Eyes" Delaney, thanks for everything.

To the "First Group," my first critique group, where the idea was born: Karen Williams, Natalie Dunbar, Aubery Vaughn, Karen White-Owens and Mike Leslie, thank you all so very much for showing me a whole new world.

To my family, thanks for supporting all of my endeavors, and especially Moe, who has to read everything. To my husband, Royce, your love for the city of Detroit inspires me.

To the city of Detroit: *We both continue to rise from the ashes.*

TIMELINE

1701—Antoine de la Mothe Cadillac arrives at Detroit from Montreal and begins building what will become Fort Pontchartrain. French settlers bring their black and Indian slaves with them.

1712—Indian raid on Fort Pontchartrain, most of fort destroyed; *birth of Celeste Fontaine.*

1736—Record of death of first known black inhabitant, an unnamed female at Ste. Anne's Catholic Church.

1760—Detroit under British control; slavery in empire does not end until 1837.

1787—Northwest Ordinance bans slavery.

1796—Detroit under American control; census lists 300 slaves.

1805—Great fire destroys most of Detroit.

1807—"Woodward Ruling": All slaves living on May 31, 1793 and in the possession of Detroiters prior to July 11, 1796, must continue to be slaves for the rest of their lives. Children of slaves must either continue to be slaves until their 25th birthdays or be immediately set free, depending on their date of birth.

1818—Steamship, *Walk-in-the-Water*, becomes first steamship on the Detroit River to provide regular passenger service.

1825—Erie Canal opened; Detroit becomes leading commercial power.

1833—Blackburn riots—black Detroiters arm themselves to protect a black couple, Ruth and Thornton Blackburn, who had been seized as runaway slaves. Daring escape of the Blackburns to Canada.

1836-1839—Cass Farm Company riverfront development debacle.

1837—Michigan earns statehood.

PROLOGUE

Fort Pontchartrain du Detroit, 1736

"Unknown Negress, October 1736." Evangeline mouthed these words slowly as she struggled to read the small headstone. She had not come this close to crying in forty years. For Evangeline, this "unknown" woman was the closest thing to a daughter she ever had.

"Everyone knows who you are. Sleep, Child, and forget about us all."

Evangeline muttered prayers and curses in the chilly October air, her labored breathing making icy puffs of air. Her ankles were cold, but she was only concerned about getting to the buggy and back home. Slipping off from the house, Evangeline left a dying Sieur Louis in his room; maybe he would make it through the night, maybe not.

Celeste was gone, and their twilight world was plunged into an endless midnight. In the darkness, Evangeline did not want to hear that sound again, the sound that comes from the river. Hearing footsteps in the grass, then a sigh, she did not bother to turn around with her lantern.

The sigh came from everywhere at once. She knew he would come here. Her heart beat faster.

"Go away!" Evangeline shouted, crossing herself.

He was back, the sad man who had lost everything.

"Celeste," he moaned. "Celeste, my love."

The voice grew more demanding as it chased Evangeline. She made for the road. Choking on a silent scream, the old woman ran the rest of the way. Silas, who had driven her here, was at the ready. Evangeline scrambled into the buggy and they took off down Rue de Ste. Anne at a full gallop. Her hands over her ears, Evangeline felt so sorry for him back there, but she could not help him.

No one could.

This hallowed land was early Detroit. First came the Indians, then Cadillac and French settlers with their Black and Indian slaves. These early Blacks were French speaking Catholics with French names. History recorded that our first Black inhabitant was an unnamed female given the last rites by Father Daniel in 1736.

~~Historical marker in modern-day Detroit

CHAPTER ONE
Detroit, 1836

"Are you his forever? The river will tell."

These last hateful words filled her ears before the rushing water. Her lungs about to burst, she let herself sink with the heavy rock tied around her ankles. Her long skirts dragged her in a downward spiral. At last, her troubles would be over. In vain, she raised one frail arm towards the moonlight dancing on the water's surface. As her life drained away, she wished her beloved could be there with her in these final moments. As if in answer to her prayer, he suddenly appeared just inches above her, his floating body eclipsing the moon. Relieved, she reached up for him, then pulled back in horror. His once beautiful light brown eyes were now two gaping, empty hollows in his head. Her screams filled the dark abyss of their shared tomb.

~   ~   ~

Isabelle Fontaine awoke from her familiar nightmare. Rubbing her eyes, she remembered that she was on a ferry. Gasping for air, she fought a powerful urge to run and leap overboard. Taking deep breaths to calm herself, she looked to see if anyone had noticed her distress. An old woman seated next to her was fast asleep. Getting to her feet, Isabelle stumbled over her skirts and slipped on the wooden floor.

Reaching the ferry's railing, Isabelle's legs were weak. Staring down into the dark depths of the Detroit River, she finally calmed down as she felt the steady, reassuring rhythmic hum of the UNITED's motor beneath her feet. She shivered. *It was only a dream*, she reminded herself. This was the last ferry out of Windsor, and the sun was already kissing the river's horizon. The orange light glittered on the crests of calm waves, hiding the river's deadly undertow.

Isabelle felt eyes upon her back. Turning, she noticed a brown-skinned man in a fine tailored suit watching her. There were only a few people on board, but she did not remember seeing him. He was in the seat opposite her own seat. He appeared mildly amused. His silver-handled cane reflected bits of the sun's orange light. A gentleman, he tipped his tall hat to her.

Embarrassed, Isabelle quickly turned back to the water, clenching the rail. This awkwardness made her irritable. Pulling her black velvet trimmed fur mantle closer about herself, she winced as a familiar pain coursed through her left hand.

Where is my self-control? she thought. Isabelle's cheeks were flaming hot as she thought about how foolish she must look: dozing, stumbling, then almost jumping overboard as if the Devil was chasing her. She watched the countless steamships, sailboats, and canoes going to and fro. A tap on the shoulder startled her.

"Are you well, Miss?" a deep voice inquired. She knew it was the man with the cane. He sounded American.

"I'm perfectly fine, thank you," she answered crisply, turning to face him. Isabelle had to look up, as he was tall. He had to be in his middle thirties. She was immediately lost in the rich brown color of his eyes. "I—I just had a bad dream, I guess, and well, I didn't know I had fallen asleep!" She'd said the last with more force than intended. Her defensiveness appeared to be lost on the stranger, who still looked amused.

"It's easy to drift off on a boat, but that's a bit difficult on one such as this. They say the UNITED's engine sounds like the last wail of a lost soul. Some say her engine can be heard clear across the water from the opposite shore. Only people who are truly exhausted could sleep through that," he added. His amusement turned to concern as he studied her face.

Isabelle blinked in surprise. How did he know that she had not been sleeping well? She cringed inwardly at the thought of dark circles under her eyes.

"Well—" The blare of the ferry's horn was a welcome intrusion.

The man looked out towards their destination, the city of Detroit. His eyes turned hard, like coal. "Home," was all he said. He tipped his hat to her with a blank expression, walked back to his seat and grabbed his bags. He had a slight limp. Perturbed by his abrupt departure, Isabelle did not realize the ferry had docked and she almost lost her balance when it came to a sudden stop. By the time she retrieved her own bags, he was gone.

The minute her boots touched Detroit's wooden dock, Isabelle marveled at the odd feeling she was returning home after a long time away. She paused to look back at her native Canada, nestled across the river. *What am I doing?*

she thought as she turned away.

"Miss?" A young Negro boatman held out his arm to guide her. They climbed to higher ground, another boatman lugging her two bags. Curious, Isabelle looked around for the handsome stranger from the ferry. He was nowhere to be seen.

They walked for some time up the incline. She marveled at the buzzing people walking about, the horses and buggies going in every direction. They were docked at Griswold Street. The boatman signaled for a waiting four-wheeled carriage with whinnying horses to pull forward. When he told the coachman where Isabelle was headed, the coachman turned pale.

"The Fontaine Estate? That's where I'm to take her?" he asked, incredulous. "Fine," he said after a moment, visibly upset. "The only reason is because I was paid in advance." He turned to Isabelle, but before she could open her mouth, his eyes narrowed.

"But no *coloured* will ride in my fine coach!" he sputtered. His voice trailed off as his scowl turned into a questioning gaze as he reassessed Isabelle's fair complexion, light green eyes, and wavy black hair under her bonnet. She knew that "coloured," a Canadian term, meant descendants of slaves with white fathers. Back home, Isabelle would not be denied service, no matter her looks. But she was in America now, and the rules here were gravely different. Mother had warned her about this.

Isabelle did not cower. Unafraid, she met the coachman's gaze. She knew that a slave would never have the audacity to look a white man in the eye. The coachman, visibly shaken, jumped down and hastily opened the door for Isabelle, loading her bags up top. She climbed up into the coach and settled into the plush blue velvet interior. The coachman paused before he closed the carriage door. She heard him muttering under his breath as he closed the door.

Isabelle listened to an erratic *clip-clop* of the horses' hooves as the carriage swayed down the road. The attorney who contacted her about the house explained that the Fontaine was the last of the ribbon farms deeded to French settlers by Antoine de la Mothe Cadillac, the illustrious founder of Detroit. The Canadian shoreline seemed to run alongside her on her journey into the unknown. How many times had she wondered how Canada would look from the Detroit side? Isabelle never dreamed she would have the chance to find out. Yet here she was, in the flesh, under sad circumstances.

It was dinnertime, but the last of the daylight was nearly gone by the time they took Atwater Street eastward. Crossing Orleans, they took the smaller road, Fontaine, south. The road ended at a paved walking path. The coachman shouted "Fontaine Estate!" when they pulled to a stop. Anxious, Isabelle alighted from the carriage without the coachman's help. He tossed her bags onto the ground and did not wait for a tip. Absently, Isabelle heard the horses depart at a high gallop as she took the path all the way up to the porch steps.

Maison Fontaine was a large Georgian Colonial painted white with black trim. Taking a deep breath, Isabelle climbed a dozen wide steps. The front door was paneled with rectangular glass just above it and flattened columns on either side. To either side of the door was a series of windows, two to the left and three to the right. There were six windows across the top.

She rapped the main door with a brass knocker. After a moment, the door opened slowly. Through a narrow crack, Isabelle was greeted by a pair of large, inquisitive eyes. They belonged to a boy who looked no more than five years of age.

"Hello," Isabelle began. "I am—"

The boy turned to run before Isabelle could finish her introduction. She watched him from the doorway as he ran to a tall black woman who was rushing her way. Wearing a plain white day dress with her graying hair pinned neatly at the nape of her neck, the woman looked wary.

"Hello," Isabelle began again. "This is the Fontaine Estate, correct?" she asked.

Staring, the woman twisted her mouth in realization of some bizarre irony.

"Please forgive me, Miss. I apologize for staring," the woman began, stepping aside to allow entrance into the house. "I know you are Isabelle Fontaine, but you favor someone greatly. Come in. Welcome, welcome."

Unnerved, Isabelle stepped through the doorway. Just past a cast iron plant stand against the right wall was the dining room with a low-hung brass and glass chandelier with multiple candles, complete with a limestone fireplace. She peered in, noticing a broad landscape painting of early Detroit River wilderness, flanked by two candleholders. The table and chairs were also of smooth oak, with curling trim. Three large windows lined the front, but their burgundy brocade draperies were closed with gold tassels. Across the hallway was a parlor, with an upholstered Louis XIV settee clustered with two high back chairs. A large embroidered rug lay on the floor. Tabletop whale oil lamps cast bright light. Two windows lined the entire front of the house, but like the dining room, they were covered.

"Leave your bags here, Missus?" The woman let the question hang in the air.

"It's 'Miss,'" Isabelle answered. She forced a half-smile.

"Follow me, then. My name is Josephine, but you can call me Josie."

Isabelle followed Josie down a central hallway of pine flooring. Beyond the dining room was a large bright kitchen. A grand oak staircase stood in the center of the house, with fleur-de-lis carved into its newel posts. Directly across was the double set of doors leading to what looked to be the ballroom Mr. du Roy mentioned. Passing a cozy library with a nice leather chair, Isabelle set her eyes upon a music room, where an ebony upright piano stood waiting. Drawn to it, she paused in the doorway, then pulled herself away. She wasn't yet ready.

Josephine pointed out that the kitchen and her own room was just beyond the staircase.

"The bedrooms are upstairs," she said. "I'll let you get settled in. Supper will be ready shortly. You can leave your bags, and Marie will get 'em."

The stairs led to a second floor hallway. Isabelle saw three bedroom doors to her left, a center hallway window, and two rooms to her right; there was a dim light from underneath the second door. The hallway walls were painted a pale color. Small whale oil lamps were perched between two doorways on little oak tables. Behind her was a doorway and a set of stairs leading to the attic. Beyond the attic stairs was a padlocked door. Forcing herself to ignore the temptation to see inside, Isabelle returned to the front. She entered the first open doorway on the left, presuming it was her room. A girl of about sixteen jumped at Isabelle's entry. The little boy who had opened the door downstairs tried to hide behind the girl's legs.

"Welcome to the Fontaine," the girl said flatly. She had long, shiny black hair braided in a long rope down her back, ending in a worn red ribbon. Isabelle knew from the girl's rich coloring that she was an Indian. The girl's dress was very plain and worn, as were the clothes of her little boy.

"I am Marie," the girl said, smoothing the front of her apron. Her face was blank. "This is my son, Ben." The boy simply stared. "I just finished making the bed," she continued. "You'll find fresh towels. I will put your clothes away for you. Is there anything that you require?"

Isabelle perked up a little. She liked this "lady of the manor" treatment.

Despite her mother's pretensions, they only had a maid come in one day a week. Isabelle's dearly departed stepfather did not leave behind as much as Mother would have liked. Isabelle did most of the chores at the house, but that didn't stop Mother from telling friends that, like them, she had trouble keeping her household staff in line.

Isabelle smiled at Marie. "No, thank you. That will be all." Marie did not smile in return, but took Ben by the hand. Ben looked back several times as his mother closed the door behind them.

Isabelle liked her bedroom, which had hardwood floors and carved closet doors of solid oak. The sheer curtains over the window were parted slightly; she assumed someone had been watching her arrival from up here. The four-poster bed had an elaborately carved headboard of cherubs. Jacquard bed hangings hid the bedposts. An oak tallboy took up the wall behind the door. The room opened out into another smaller one containing a porcelain stand on which to place a bathtub, and a commode with folding top and chamber pot underneath.

Dipping her hands into a porcelain washbowl on a baroque mirrored dressing table, Isabelle splashed her face and dried it with a small towel. Looking into the mirror, Isabelle thought she saw something, a quick movement. She looked harder, waiting. Whatever it was, however, was gone as quickly as it had appeared. Shaking her head, she hurried from the room.

Lured by the tempting aromas coming from the dining room, Isabelle sat down at a place setting of fine silver and porcelain dishes. Josie entered with silver serving trays. She fixed Isabelle's plate, piling on steamed green beans, potatoes and roasted chicken.

"I'm in charge of household affairs," she said as she set the plate before Isabelle. "I worked for your grandpa Charles, takin' care of this place. I still do," she said with a pointed look. "I love the Fontaine. You met Marie, the part-time help. You have yet to meet Mr. Alders, the groundskeeper. He comes 'round early in the day."

"You've been here a long time?" Isabelle asked. "Did you know my grandfather well?"

Josie looked sad. "My sister and me was runaways from Virginia. We was on our way to Canada when we heard 'bout some jobs for domestics, but we was warned it was somethin' strange 'bout the house. My sister was scared, but I didn't care—we needed to eat. My Granny always told me I had the 'sight,' you know," she said proudly, "the ability to discern things from the great beyond." Isabelle stopped chewing when she heard that comment.

"Your Granddaddy was good to me," Josie continued. "My sister met a nice rail worker up here and got married straight away. I stayed on here—nothing out there for me. Charles was good enough to get Mr. du Roy to make up some free papers for me. In Detroit, everybody born a slave before 1793 is a slave for life. That reminds me," Josie went on, "Mr. du Roy posted your bond at the clerk's office already."

Isabelle's left hand flared up. She thought about how insulting it is for all free Negro visitors to have to post an unholy $500 bond to come to Detroit. She had also been warned about slave catchers grabbing free people of color and selling them South. Isabelle felt bad for making her mother worry so much about her coming to Detroit; even though Rosalie was self-absorbed, Isabelle could tell that her mother at least cared a little.

"Negroes with status or property in this city have it hard." Josie had not stopped talking yet. "After the Blackburn situation a few years ago, Charles couldn't get good seasonal workers to come pick the grapes. There were riots for two days, but Mr. Blackburn made it to Windsor. That was one time us Negroes stood together. My poor Michael, though. . ." her voice trailed off. "They jailed some of them that helped Mr. and Mrs. Blackburn escape, and Mayor Chapin threatened to expel all Negroes who didn't have no free papers if they protested further.

"Charles was up in age," she continued. "He caught pneumonia durin' the spring, and just went down over the months. He was under stress, tryin' to keep the house up. It's too dangerous for Negroes to be livin' in a house such as this, but I'm goin' to hold on.

"I didn't mean to go on about the riot," she said. "Wit' you bein' born free 'n all cross the river, you don't have to worry 'bout all that," Josie said.

Isabelle did not miss the resentful tone in Josie's voice. *Josie would be amazed at what I know about 'all that'*, Isabelle thought. Rather than correct Josie, though, Isabelle decided to let her ramble on about the house; after all, this was why she had come all this way.

"That happened three years ago," Isabelle countered. "With that unpleasantness over, it seems you could get more hired help now," Isabelle said, trying to get Josie back on the subject of the house.

To Isabelle's surprise, Josie went quiet and began to fix her own plate. Sighing, she said, "There are other reasons why some won't come here to work."

Just then, Ben rushed into the kitchen, startling Isabelle. The boy was still watching her hard, his shiny black hair neatly cut to frame his round face.

"You want somethin' to eat?" Josie asked him, smiling. There was no trace of her earlier discomfort. The boy nodded and climbed into a chair next to Josie. His seeming avoidance of Isabelle irritated her. She was good with her neighbor's and friend's children back home. *Yes, I am a stranger to Ben,* she thought, *but this boy watches me with such intensity!*

"It's been so lonely here without Charles," Josie said. It was obvious to Isabelle that the other topic would be dropped for now. Ben munched happily at the plate offered him, oblivious to the conversation. "We were at a loss about what to do when he passed away. You know there was men from the city just waitin' for him to die, so they can take this place. Charles asked Ned du Roy to try and find his daughter one last time. We didn't know about you. Your mama never wrote us, or anything. But Mr. Ned tracked you down like a hound dog," Josie laughed, slapping her knee.

"He came to one of my concerts in Amherstburg a few weeks ago," Isabelle said. "I wasn't very good that night, I'm afraid. He was gracious enough to give me a compliment besides," she looked down at her plate as she remembered her left hand tightening on her as she played, unbeknownst to the audience. She'd finished the piece, but it took great effort.

"He told me you played beautifully, that you had a true gift," Josie said, reaching out to pat Isabelle's arm. "You won Mr. Ned over that night, and he knows a good performance when he sees it. He often goes to concerts here in the city."

"He's kind," Isabelle said, unconvinced. "Tell me, he knows my mother's secret then, knows our history?" She glanced sideways at Ben, hoping he was not listening. He was still busy with his meal.

"He knows your mother had you without benefit of marriage, yes," Josie continued. "He knew her as a baby, watched her grow up into a beautiful, willful young woman. Then she ran away," Josie added, softly. "Mr. Ned wanted to see her after he found you, but he is leaving that to her to decide if she wants to renew the acquaintance. He knows she's respected as a widow where she lives."

Isabelle nodded, embarrassed. She knew the torrid story of her mother following her love to Canada where he could earn a decent living as a musician, only for him to run off with another woman. Even though she married a well-to-do older man who died shortly thereafter, Isabelle knew that her mother still loved Isabelle's father. Isabelle relived the memories through every pained look on her mother's face at her concerts. Mother and daughter had an unspoken agreement; Rosalie would not be involved in Isabelle's blossoming music career. It was lonely for Isabelle to continue in this profession, but making music was in her soul. At least it had been.

"The du Roy family has served as the Fontaine family's attorneys since this land was deeded as a ribbon farm, Mr. Ned tells me," Josie said. "His family swore an oath to the Fontaines after they saved one of them from an Indian raid. The du Roys helped negotiate deals with the local Indians and protected this property from British takeover when those bastards moved in."

Isabelle was amused at Josie's condemnation of the Brits; she spoke as if she had known them personally. "Your grandfather inherited the Fontaine, fightin' many battles over the years, but the house is his by blood, and by paper. There's nothin' those men in the city can do 'bout it, and it's killin' 'em. His grandfather, Rene, your great-grandfather, inherited this house, and French law protected it. When the Americans came, the law still couldn't touch us.

"Your mother was next in line to inherit, but after her falling out with Charles—"

"Grandfather did not approve of my father?"

"First of all, he was white, and that is frowned upon. And with all due respect, he was a piano player." Josie said. "Not like you, a classical player," she hastily added. "He played in bars and houses of ill repute. Charles didn't see much comin' from that. Your father had no stable future, and he was a dubious charmer. Your mother couldn't see through the spell your father cast over her. You know how love is."

Isabelle nodded; she knew how painful it could be.

"Your mother didn't contact Charles after she went to Canada," Josie continued, "so we didn't know about you. Believe me, it was hard to watch a family torn apart like that. Charles regretted the whole thing, but he and your mother were stubborn people. I told him many times to seek her out, but he said she would have to find him.

"And now he's gone," she sighed. "Twenty-seven years later I learn he has a granddaughter. I miss Charles terribly, but I know he is still with us in spirit, watching over us, particularly at such a difficult time as this."

"Difficult time? What do you mean?" Isabelle asked, confused.

"Isabelle," Josie began. The strange look from their first meeting at the door had returned. "I don't know how to explain it, but there is a dark history behind this house. Charles and I have lived here in peace for most of our lives, but there have been a few strange goings-on along the way. Charles was determined to keep this house, as it was his birthright. I was determined to stand by him. Marie ain't afraid of nothin', having been surviving on her own most of her life. But others have not felt that way, could not ignore their feelings that something was not right 'round here. That's why we never could keep staff. When you arrived, I had such an overwhelming feeling of dread."

"Dread?" Isabelle hated to be spooked. "What in heaven are you talking about?"

"I don't believe in coincidences," Josie said, repeatedly pressing her right forefinger to the table to emphasize her words. "Your arrival is no coincidence. You suddenly are discovered, the mirror-image of *her*," her tone was almost accusatory. "I've seen her face before, and now I understand the importance. I have the gift of seeing things, and what I saw when I first saw you was. . . ." she hesitated.

"Was what?" Isabelle demanded, her palms sweaty.

"Death," Josephine whispered. Isabelle turned to see Ben staring at her. They had forgotten about him. He should not be hearing this. Her imagination on fire, Isabelle felt as if he was coldly assessing her as a corpse in a casket.

"If you'll excuse me," Isabelle said tersely, rising from the table. She clamped down on her tongue before she said anything she might regret.

Josie looked hurt. "I know it sounds like madness, but—"

"You're right," Isabelle cut her off. "It does." She sighed, weary. "It's been a long day. I'll be turning in." She made for the hallway.

Furious, Isabelle climbed the stairs to her room. *Death, indeed! The old woman had lost her mind, been working here too long,* Isabelle reasoned. Sighing again, she realized she would be here for a while; she did not want to start off on the wrong foot with Josie, her only link to this new place.

As she readied herself for bed, Isabelle resolved to have another talk with Josie tomorrow to make her understand there was no time for nonsense. If only one credible thing was said tonight, it would be about the men who want the house—they will be coming now that they know her grandfather is dead. They've been waiting like vultures for a long time.

Dressed in a long gown and tying her hair with a ribbon, Isabelle sat in a Venetian chair at the window, which overlooked the front yard. *This day is indeed significant*, Isabelle thought, *but not for the reason Josie wants me to believe.* She had brought a stack of letters with her to the window. She opened several of them, spent an hour re-reading them for the hundredth time, the paper crackling at the worn creases. The last letter she received hurt the most.

June 20, 1833

Dearest Isabelle,

I hope you and your mother are well. I'm waiting at the dock. I have not eaten today, because I am so too excited to eat—but don't worry, I'll eat when we are all safely back in Canada. My new friends here tease me because they know I'm writing you yet again. They sing songs about the 'lovesick Canadian', but I don't care.

As always, my thoughts are on the day when I will hold you in my arms again. I cannot wait until this battle is over. I hear we will be securing Mr. Blackburn today, when he is released from the jail to be transported South. Do not fret—Daddy Walker and Sleepy Polly have a perfect plan. I know that you are upset that I involved myself in this battle, but I'm proud to be part of something so important.

Fear not, Love. I will be home very soon.

'Til then, Beloved,

Richard

Within that week, everything changed forever. The next letter Isabelle received was from one of their friends explaining how Richard had been shot helping Mr. Blackburn out of the city. When Mr. Blackburn was released from the jail, a crowd of Negroes rushed in on the sheriff, threw Blackburn in a cart and got him to the river, where he made it to Windsor. In the melee, Richard was shot.

Isabelle's tears fell freely. No one since had ever compared to Richard, to his kindness, his wit. Isabelle's mother had given up on steering eager suitors in her daughter's direction, only to be spurned. Isabelle had decided that the love she shared with Richard, though brief, only came around once in a lifetime.

She thought of poor Douglas, waiting for her back in Amherstburg.

With him, there might be a chance at a comfortable life, and she would not have to be alone. Her concerns about Douglas, however, would have to wait until she returned home.

Movement caught her eye out the window. A light rain fell. Wiping her eyes and drawing the curtains back further, Isabelle took another look. There was a man in the front yard. Though it was dark, Isabelle could make out he was wearing light-colored clothes, but unusual ones, a dated design. She guessed he was wearing a costume, but there was no masquerade ball here tonight. He was stood stone-like, intent. And he was staring at her. Swallowing hard, Isabelle leaned closer, her forehead pressed against the cold glass of the window. *What was he doing out there? Who was he?* she wondered. At this distance, she could not see his face clearly.

Without thinking, Isabelle ran downstairs and out the front door. She looked from side to side, but did not see anyone. She suddenly felt foolish. Who did she expect to see in her yard at this late hour?

"Isabelle, is that you?" Josephine called out softly from the porch. She sounded afraid.

"Yes, Josie, it's me." Isabelle said as she re-entered the house and passed a startled Josie, who took note of Isabelle's being inappropriately dressed without a robe. "Sorry to scare you. I thought I saw something." Isabelle gave Josie a hard look in response to the older woman's spark of interest in the mention of 'something' in the yard. "But it was nothing."

Once asleep in her bed, Isabelle had a fitful night. She dreamed of the man in the yard and heard the name "Celeste" over and over. The man held out his hand to her, and she found herself reaching for him.

CHAPTER TWO

White men and women in strange clothing surrounded Isabelle. They leered at her, mocked her, whispered about her behind their fans. It was October, but the air inside was sticky. The women wore full silk gowns covered in bows and lace with ribboned, powdered white wigs. The men, also in wigs, wore velvet jackets and knee length breeches. Isabelle seemed to know these antiquated people at this dance. Everything ended with a shriek, then she found herself drowning in the river. Again. And again.

~   ~   ~

Isabelle remembered bits and pieces of her dreams from the night before as she prepared for her first morning at the Fontaine. Absently, she put on a green day dress with a dark green lace-trimmed flounce. Her corset was already biting into her skin. Deciding to forgo the lace pelerine over her small shoulders, she tied green ribbons in her hair. As she pulled on her silk stockings, Isabelle remembered how everything from her dream seemed so real, right down to the light breezes coming from the fans. Her dreams were getting more detailed than ever.

Sudden hunger overtook any desire to ponder the situation any further. The smell of bacon frying brought Isabelle down to the kitchen. Josie was at the iron step-top cook stove, her white apron spotless despite the frying. Josie smiled at her, and Isabelle guessed she had been up for hours.

"Good morning, Isabelle. You hungry?"

Isabelle watched her warily, remembering their strange exchange the day before. She hoped that nonsense had been put to rest. "Yes, I am, thank you." Taking a seat at the table, Isabelle was awed by the size of the kitchen. There were two other rooms with closed doors; she knew one was Josie's room, partially beneath the staircase. A pantry was in the far corner, with wooden folding doors. There was also a water pump there.

"What would you like?" Josie asked. "We have eggs, hotcakes, sausage, biscuits, gravy."

Isabelle laughed despite herself. "I don't know if my stomach can hold all of that, but I'll try a little of everything, if you don't mind."

"Good," Josie said. "You need it. You too skinny."

As Josie prepared her plate, Isabelle sipped on strong coffee. Despite the bad start, Isabelle was glad for Josie's company. Her own mother was not the best cook. Watching Josie work magic in the kitchen, Isabelle could understand why the older lady wanted to scare her from the house. This was the only life she knew. Isabelle was a stranger who had come from nowhere to take over her home.

Isabelle felt guilty, for she planned to do that very thing, take over the house and sell it to the highest bidder as soon as possible. There was no reason to stay. Reliving her hurt over Richard last night only proved that her grief would follow her wherever she went. Running to the Fontaine to hide was a foolish idea.

While she ate, Isabelle noticed Josie stealing glances at her.

"Is something wrong?" she finally asked.

The woman averted her eyes, caught. "No. I apologize. It's just I know I may have upset you last night."

"It's alright, Josie," Isabelle said. "I'm sure you felt you should tell me these—er, things."

"I wanted you to know," Josie said earnestly, leaning forward. Isabelle hated to see such a smooth face wrinkled with worry over nothing. "It's only right that you be prepared. I'm just not sure for what just yet," she added.

Isabelle sighed. "Josie, there's nothing to worry about. I don't believe in spirits."

Josie went still. "You don't have to believe in 'em for 'em to exist," she said. "Do you sincerely believe the soul don't endure?" she whispered. "Think about those times when you sure you all alone, when you feel somethin', somethin' you can't see, but you know is there? How 'bout dreams where you talkin' to a loved one long lost?"

Isabelle thought about her strong unease the day Richard was killed, not yet knowing her fiancé was dead. She remembered her mother's claim of seeing Isabelle's father's face in dreams the day he died in the streets of Montreal. This gave her pause, but she would not admit it to Josie.

"Since there's no sure way to prove things like that," Isabelle said, "I honestly don't spend much time thinking about them," she said, tersely.

"You should, but I'll not trouble you with it," Josie said, clearly hurt.

"When you done eatin', I'll show you the rest of the grounds."

"The Fontaine is one of the oldest original ribbon farms left standing in this area," Josie said as they walked out the back door onto a large porch with two sets of steps. Isabelle couldn't believe how far the green grass stretched. Mr. du Roy mentioned at least 250 acres. There was a garden to the right with rows of corn, and a two-story carriage house to the right of a center stone path. "The house was built in 1703 for one of Cadillac's cronies. When Bennet Fontaine came upon this estate, Cadillac had been shipped off to Quebec, having wiped out more than a few folks in excessive taxes and corrupting the poor Indians with brandy," Josie explained.

"The very first owner lost this property to the King after Cadillac botched things up, but they eventually encouraged new settlers to come give the frontier a try. Bennet Fontaine was a fur trader, having come from France with his family. Bennet had the original house torn down, and built this one straightaway. The room I have now was the head slave's room.

"Mr. Ned tells me ole Bennett wanted to make a grand statement, let the other landowners know he was the wealthiest and the new leader in the community," Josie added. "He brought his slaves with him from France, then took on a handful more. The slave quarters have been torn down. In the North, the slaves usually stayed in the attic of the main house, but Bennet's wife didn't want 'em in the house overnight. One slave was allowed to stay in the garret upstairs, though."

"The garret?" Isabelle asked. "That padlocked room upstairs?"

Just then, Ben ran up and tugged Josie's apron. As before, he silently stared at Isabelle.

"What is it, Chile?" Josie asked, kindly. Isabelle wondered if Josie had any children. "It must be somethin' he wants sweet from the kitchen. Ain't much else to show you but the orchard over there," she pointed towards the northwest bank. "You can go on ahead. Also, the gravesite is out back, to the northeast."

As Josie and Ben went back to the house, Isabelle took the winding path towards the garden. Tall, neatly trimmed shrubbery enclosed and concealed the garden; they slumped over, one onto the next, as if they were struggling to hold each other up. She passed a large marble birdbath, which was empty. The shrubs cast long shadows on the pale grass in the late morning light. A chilly breeze rushed past her.

"*Celeste,*" a male voice whispered behind her.

Isabelle whirled around. She saw no one.

"Who's there?" she asked, wary.

"*You have come back.*"

Isabelle looked in all directions. No sign of anyone. "Who's there?" she repeated.

"*The baby, Celeste, the baby.*"

"A baby? What? Who are you?" she demanded. Certain it was another trick like with the stranger in the yard the night before, she dove into the bushes, shaking them. "Show yourself!" She felt a headache coming on. The voice suddenly came from another direction, right behind her. It sounded different this time, though.

"Yes, my lady, yes, my lady." Isabelle jumped. She turned, and this time, someone was there. He was upon her before she knew it. He gripped her shoulders very hard. He was poorly dressed, and his dark hair was fuzzy atop his head.

"Who are you? Why are you sneaking around like that?" she demanded, irritated. "You frightened me!"

"My lady," the man breathed again. There was something about him that seemed familiar, but Isabelle knew she had never met him before. Just then, Josie rushed up.

"Barry, no, get away from her!" Josie cackled. "Step back!" Chastened, the young man did as asked. Isabelle whirled upon Josie.

"What is this about?" Isabelle shouted.

"Miss Fontaine, I didn't know how to tell you about Barry. He is your cousin."

"Cousin?" Isabelle asked, as Josie put on a kettle for tea. Barry had run back inside the house, but Josie discouraged Isabelle from following him upstairs. She realized his room must be the one that had the dim light underneath the night before.

"Barry is your first cousin," Josie said. "I'm not surprised that your Mama didn't mention him. He's. . .different."

"In what way?" Isabelle inquired.

"He likes to draw, and that's all I knows 'bout him," she answered. "He keeps to himself, but comes out every now and again. I guess he heard you come in yesterday, and wanted to see. He's harmless, so you can just ignore him."

"How did he happen to come live here?" she asked.

"Your uncle Julius and his young wife died of influenza when Barry was about three. Your Mama helped take care of him, but when her war with your Granddaddy began, she busied herself with moving out. Barry cried for her to take him wit' her, but she didn't. I don't recall if she really said goodbye to him proper."

Isabelle fumed. *How selfish*, she thought. *But that sounds like Mother*.

"Barry's heart kind of turned hard so he kept to himself," Josie continued. Me and your granddaddy tried to work wit' him, but he got so involved with drawin', we couldn't hold his attention. He seems to be at peace at when he's drawin', so we lets him be most of the time. He comes down to eat, then goes back to his room. Sometimes, he might go out in the yard, or on the porch. Your granddaddy did love Barry in his own way, and he made sure in his will that Barry would be cared for the rest of his life.

"Hopefully, this won't make you leave," Josie said. Isabelle could tell Josie didn't want her to leave.

"Don't worry, Josie." Isabelle said. Feeling guilty over not disclosing plans about selling the house, Isabelle held herself back for some reason. Her mind returned to the disturbing voice in the garden. The voice had been clear—there was no doubt someone had said something to her out there, someone other than Barry.

"Josie, before Barry walked up, I heard the strangest thing out in the yard."

"Oh?" the older woman asked as she started to wash dishes. "That so? Well, all sorts of 'coons and squirrels run 'round here. Funny," she muttered, "haven't seen much of 'em lately, though."

"I heard a voice."

Josie's busy hands went still.

"A man's voice," Isabelle continued, "asking me about a baby."

"Dear Lord," was all Josie whispered.

Before Isabelle could ask Josie what she meant, there was a light rap on the wooden kitchen door, which had been left ajar.

"I'll get it, Josie." Irritated, Isabelle went for the door.

"Am I the only one who uses the front door?" she muttered to herself.

Isabelle was startled to see impossibly dark, velvety eyes staring down at her; the humor in them had returned. The man from the day's ferry ride tipped his hat to her again.

"Good day, Miss." His deep voice was hypnotic.

"Michael!" Josie rushed past Isabelle to yank the man through the door, locking him in a fierce embrace. She then planted a big kiss on his cheek. "You're back!"

She pointed at Isabelle.

"This the lovely Miss Isabelle come from Canada I was telling you 'bout!" Josie said with pride.

Michael stepped forward, his eyes trained on Isabelle. She felt smothered, as his presence engulfed her. He took her delicate hand into his large, strong one.

"A pleasure." He kissed her hand then, never taking his eyes away from hers. Isabelle felt a slight shock upon contact of his lips to her skin. She quickly pulled away. He did not let on to Josie that they had already met on the ferry. Isabelle was still too shocked to say anything herself.

"Isabelle, this is my nephew, Dr. Michael St. Vincent. He is a doctor," she added.

Michael looked embarrassed.

"Auntie, you told her I was a doctor twice just now." Around his aunt, Michael appeared to show a softer side, a contrast to the mysterious figure on the ferry.

Josie merely beamed at him, oblivious to his correction. "Tell me, how was the conference?"

Michael limped to the table, sat down heavily. He rested his shiny cane against the table. "It was. . .rejuvenating, to say the least," Michael said as he removed an expensive looking cutaway morning coat and his hat. He loosened the dark cravat at his neck as he accepted a cup of the tea, which was now ready. "I learned so much about Indian healing. They showed me many wondrous sites in Alberta." He turned to Isabelle, appraising her. His eyes flashed. "God has made many wonders."

Isabelle knew she was blushing, so she turned and walked back to her seat. "You say you're a doctor," she said foolishly, grasping for anything to say to curtail his assessment of her.

"Michael has a practice right here in the city," Josie chimed in. Michael put two teaspoons of sugar into his tea and stirred it slowly as she talked. "He's helping our people, those who can't get help otherwise."

"A very noble thing," Isabelle said. "No easy task."

"You can be sure of that," he said.

"Miss Isabelle, how do you like the Fontaine so far?" he asked.

Isabelle looked down, not wanting to show her disappointment at the empty feeling within. This place had been her last hope.

"It's a most unusual place," she began. "I like the garden and orchard, but I had the strangest incident out there earlier, though—"

"Michael, more tea?" Josie blurted out. Isabelle sensed it was deliberate.

"No, Auntie, I'm fine," he said. "You were saying?" His eyes had never left Isabelle's.

Tempted to continue, Isabelle then thought better of it. "The garden is just. . .lovely, that's all."

Michael nodded in agreement. "I like the garden. Wait until the spring. The lilacs smell so good."

Isabelle rose from the table, and Michael did the same out of courtesy. He looked surprised at her abrupt move. "I'm going to see Grandfather, now," she said to Josie.

Josie nodded her understanding, leaning against the sink. She told Isabelle where to find the grave, a hilly area a good walk out, at the far reaches north of the carriage house. "I'll be here if you want to talk, afterwards."

"Thank you, Josie." Reaching for her mantle, she acknowledged Michael.

"Nice meeting you," Michael said, his eyes seeming to say much more.

Isabelle nodded and quickly exited through the back door. She found Michael's presence overwhelming. Around him, she found it hard to breathe, let alone think, so this was as good a time as any to pay her respects.

Isabelle traversed a sea of rich, neatly cut green grass. The open sky was warm upon the top of her head. The land continued its strange reticence; no birds flapped their wings. Isabelle could not shake the feeling that everything was on hold for something that was coming.

The ground sloped upward. Grandfather's headstone stood at its crest. Isabelle knelt to read the inscription:

Charles Fontaine, 1774 to 1836
Devoted husband, good friend and guardian of the Fontaine.
May he rest in peace.

Isabelle smarted at the obvious omission of "devoted father" from the inscription. "You must have truly been hurt by Mother's leaving," Isabelle whispered. "I'm sorry things turned out this way. But I have come to see you, Grandfather." She wiped away sudden, fierce tears.

"It would have been nice to know you. My friends back home are so lucky to have their grandparents around for the special times. This will have to be our special time," she said as she plucked an errant dried out leaf away from the grave. Not a particularly religious person, Isabelle uttered a prayer for Grandfather Charles. As she did so, she felt an overpowering warmth flow through her body. She smiled and closed her eyes, sensing she'd been heard. Satisfied, Isabelle rose to her feet, dusting off her skirts. As she turned to leave the little hill, she saw a man standing not twenty feet from her.

"The man from the courtyard!" she whispered to herself. He was dressed in the same antiquated clothes, a tattered, high-collar white shirt. The warmth she'd felt upon visiting her grandfather was replaced with a frosty chill that crept up her body in snakelike fashion.

His eyes were rolled back in his head, revealing lifeless white; Isabelle recoiled at the horrible sight. He appeared to be moving his lips, but they produced no sound. Around his neck was a weathered rope, a noose, at which he constantly tugged.

Isabelle could only stare. Still tugging at his noose, the man raised his other arm slowly, pointing it at Isabelle. He then turned and pointed straight ahead of them both.

"The river?" Isabelle croaked. "Is that what you are pointing towards? There's nothing else in that direction."

The man simply stared that way, his silent lips no longer moving.

"Hello! Hello!" a voice could be heard in the distance, from behind them. She also heard a dog barking.

"Miss Isabelle, you out here?"

Slowly, the ragged man turned back to Isabelle. Pointing at her one last time, he disappeared, fading into the open air. Isabelle blinked several times and spun around in all directions, looking for where the man could have gone. She was in an open area; no one could have disappeared that quickly.

An old black man with whiskers and flat cap huffed his way up the hill. A brown collie ran ahead of him, barking in the direction where the strange man had been standing.

"There you are," he said. "Josie told me I'd find you up here." Smiling, he extended a wrinkled yet strong hand.

"Mr. Alders, groundskeeper. This is my dog, Scout." Isabelle took his smile to mean he'd not seen anything strange in the area. Or was he merely pretending?

She took his hand, her eyes still searching the area for her visitor. The iciness of the air had dissipated.

"I was out here working on the yard and thought I'd introduce myself," Alders said. His eyes seemed kindly enough. He waited patiently for a reply. Isabelle realized she'd not said a single word in response.

"It's a pleasure to meet you," Isabelle said, distracted.

He shrugged. "Same here." He turned to go. "If you need anything done, just holler."

Isabelle paused at first, then rushed to catch up to Alders.

Shaken, Isabelle decided against telling Josie a thing about what she'd just seen outside. Upon returning to the house, she went straight to her room. Josie and Michael had left the kitchen. On the way up the stairs, she heard their voices from Josie's room. Closing her own bedroom door, Isabelle busied herself first with unpacking. She then wrote a brief, vague letter to Bess, a flute player and occasional music partner. Isabelle was sure Bess was wondering where her friend had run off to, surprised at the sudden need for time away from musical engagements.

Isabelle would wait to write her mother, as she must first work through her anger over the new information regarding her family history. Besides, she dared not tell her mother about the strange incidents at the house; she would be accused of being outrageous yet again. She asked Marie to bring dinner to her room before leaving for the day. After an hour of pacing and absently reading a few chapters of a book in bed, Isabelle drifted off to sleep.

~   ~   ~

"Come here, Bright Eyes!" Celeste ran from her father's grasping, chalk-white hands, her ribboned pigtails bouncing. She squealed with glee.

"Can't catch me!" Daring, Celeste ran right between his tall legs. He laughed, out of breath.

"Child, you are too fast for old Bennet!"

A man with a leather satchel walked up seemingly from nowhere. He had a long, grim face. Celeste knew who he was. She stopped mid-stride.

"Hello, Sieur Fontaine."

"Sieur Duchene," her father sighed. "How have you been?"

The man shrugged. "I have seen better days. These Indians are trying my patience with their ambushes. Costing me money. Sorry to interrupt your, er, leisure," he said, eyeing Celeste. "You seem to favor this one." Celeste backed away in fear. This was the bad man. Every time he came to the house, someone had to go away with him, never to return. Who would it be this time?

Pere sighed again. Celeste knew he did not like this man. Why did he have to deal with him at all? Why couldn't he just send this man away for good?

"Celeste is an exceptional pianoforte player," Bennet said. Celeste could swear he sounded nervous. "She has a good ear. She picks up what I show her easily, can duplicate anything you give her. Her talent would be wasted picking crops. She is a good companion to my children."

"How sweet," Monsieur Duchene said. To Celeste, he did not sound as if he meant it. "Bennet, you have to understand that these are simple creatures God created to help us. Nothing more. You treat them too well, I'm afraid. If and when they go elsewhere, they will suffer because they've gotten used to being treated a certain way."

"To mistreat them is the difference between Heaven and Hell," Bennet said, angry." You know what happened to Sieur Beauchamps. Mean old man beat his slaves. Two killed him with a shotgun and escaped. Daimoiselle is a widow now."

"Have it your way," Duchene shrugged. "You know why I'm here," he said. "Let's go inside."

Bennet sighed. "Celeste, you run on along."

Reluctantly, Celeste did as she was told, running to the back of the house and opening the door to the scullery. Evangeline was humming as she chopped carrots with a large knife. Mean most of the time, Evangeline's eyes softened whenever she saw Celeste. Celeste watched Evangeline for a while, certain that the woman knew Monsieur Duchene was here.

"What is it, Child?" Evangeline asked, impatient. Her eyes never left the knife while she made quick, decisive chops.

"Do we belong to Pere?" Celeste asked.

Evangeline stopped chopping to look down at her. "First of all, you need to stop calling him 'Pere,'" she said. "He is not your father. He lets you amuse Louis and Suzette, something like a pet. It is dangerous to call him that."

Celeste was stung by the words. "He doesn't mind."

"Humph," was Evangeline's response. "Yes, we belong to Sieur Fontaine. You and your mother were sold to him when you were a little baby. After your mother died of the cholera, he put you in my care."

"I know all of that," Celeste said, petulant.

"I tell you this to remind you of your place," Evangeline said. "You have privileges the other slave children do not, 'cause he favors you." Evangeline's voice was angry, but she looked sad. "One day, when you grow up, you will not be allowed to play with Louis and Suzette. You will truly be one of us then." She went back to work.

Celeste, hurt by these words, ran from the kitchen to Suzette's room upstairs. She stopped in the doorway. Suzette was having her hair tied in ribbons by Damselle Amie, her late mother's sister, visiting for the summer.

"Celeste!" Suzette squealed her excitement at seeing Celeste. The pale girl was smacked on her bare arm by Damselle Amie.

"Never shout like that. It's not ladylike." She glared at Celeste. "What are you doing running through this house? You know better than that." Her tone was severe. "I've got to talk to that Bennet about letting you run all over the place." She shook her head. "Would not do any good, though. He loves his little Negress," she muttered.

"Well, don't stand there," Amie said. "Suzette's room is a mess! Make that bed and get some sweeping done in here!"

~   ~   ~

After tossing and turning for hours, Isabelle was awakened by a noise from downstairs. Remembering that she was at the Fontaine, she sat up in bed. Not sure if Josie was a night owl, Isabelle briefly considered Marie, but the girl only worked during the daytime.

Moonlight was Isabelle's only light. She heard a thump beneath her, downstairs. Rising, she tiptoed to the door. Slowly opening it and taking a few tentative steps into the dark hallway, Isabelle found her way to the stair railing. She held on tightly as she descended the stairs, counting as she went, a game from childhood.

No lamps were on downstairs, but moonlight filled the main hallway. She regretted not lighting a candle first. Something brushed past her in the dark. She cried out when she unexpectedly hit a wall. The wall cried out.

"Umpf!" It was a man's voice. Two strong arms grabbed her from behind in the dark. She struggled fiercely.

"Let me go!" She tried to wrench herself free.

"Isabelle," the voice breathed. It was Michael. She stopped fighting, and he quickly released her.

"Michael, what are you doing here?" Isabelle asked, irritated. She rubbed her sore upper arms. His grip was strong.

"I saw some flickering lights," he said. "I came out to look."

"Came out from where?" she asked.

"My room," he answered. "The other room opposite Auntie's. She didn't tell you I stay here sometimes? Did you hear something, too?" he asked.

"Yes," Isabelle answered, bothered. "A loud thump. I—"

They heard something again, from the front of the house.

They rushed up the hallway, Michael limping heavily; apparently, he'd left his cane behind. The closer they got to the door they tiptoed, Isabelle on Michael's heels. Instinctively, he reached behind him and found her hand in the dark. She did not resist.

The front door was gaping open, a cold breeze knocking it back and forth against the inside wall. Isabelle could barely make out Michael's silhouette as he went down a couple of porch steps ahead of her.

"Do you see anything?" she whispered. Her breath came in short, frosty puffs of air.

"No," he said, without looking back. "I. . .ouch!"

"Michael!" Isabelle whispered sharply, tugging at his hand. "Are you alright?"

They stumbled together, balancing each other at the last moment. They rushed down the remaining steps, then quickly turned to see what Michael had stumbled over. Isabelle noticed that Michael was hobbling from one foot to the other. She rushed to lean against him for balance. Before them lay a spiral of worn rope, tangled and frayed at the ends. It looked very much like a noose.

"What in God's name?" Isabelle gasped.

CHAPTER THREE

As morning fog clouded the windows of the house, Isabelle left her room. She decided against telling Josie about last night. There was no good way to explain what had happened. Michael came up with a logical explanation for the noose, assuring her it was just some old rope Alder's dog must have dragged and left there. Isabelle readily accepted this idea, not wanting to consider any other possibilities.

Michael had come close to twisting his ankle, but he'd told Isabelle he would be fine. He'd made Isabelle promise not to alarm Josie.

"Don't tell her anything about this, Isabelle," he'd said. "She would surely worry herself into a frenzy, and that would be bad for her heart."

Not finding Josie in the kitchen, Isabelle ate a little of the breakfast left for her on the stove. She then found Josie in her room, dressing for church in a brown dress and matching hat of brown feathers. She was on tiptoe, reaching for something off the top of her tallboy.

Suddenly, anger flashed through Isabelle as she wondered if Josie had anything to do with the bizarre events of the past two days. *Was she trying to scare me away from the house?* she wondered.

"Good morning, Josie," Isabelle said, rapping lightly on the door. Josie turned around quickly. She smiled.

"Good morning, Dear." She pulled a dusty book down, with a groan.

"Maybe your mother will come visit us?" Josie asked. "I would so like to see her."

Isabelle did not want to disappoint Josie, but she did not know what her mother would say about coming back home.

"I hope she will come. She's been away too long," Isabelle said. Josie handed Isabelle the book she'd pulled down.

"This is for you. Your Granddaddy wanted to give it to your Mama, but, well. . ." She shrugged. "It has a little of the family history."

Reverently, Isabelle took the book, turning it over in her hands. It was a journal, but very aged. "Thank you, I'll take a look at it later." Her thoughts turned to the night before. "Is Michael still here?" Isabelle remembered his strong hands, his voice in the dark. *Had he been as frightened as I was last night?* she wondered.

"No, Michael left early this morning," Josie answered. "He had some patients to see. He's so dedicated."

"Tell me," Isabelle said, "how did Michael's parents die?"

Josie looked down. "My sister married a good man, and they were very happy. But the Lord took 'em on home one rainy afternoon. Carriage accident. Michael was with them, a young man barely out of childhood. His father died right there, but his mother was still alive. She had severe injuries, though, and as Michael tell it, two kind people appeared out of nowhere, carried her as far as the nearest hospital a mile or so away. But she was denied treatment when she got there, 'cause she was a Negress. Michael said they slammed the door in his face. Ella died there on the hospital's doorstep. The hospital was kind enough to donate a wagon to take my sister to the undertaker, though." Isabelle noticed the bitter twist in Josie's mouth. "Anyhow," she continued, "you can see why Michael tries so hard, what path he chose."

Isabelle nodded. She envisioned the proud Michael she had met as the helpless boy out in the rain, begging for help. "I know you are very proud of him."

Josie smiled again. "He was always so smart as a child. He loves books an' learnin'. I had no children, till him. When he got the chance to study in Paris, I'd kinda' hoped he would make a life for himself over there. But he was determined to learn what he needed, then come back."

Josie pulled on her gloves. "I'd best be on to church," she said as she headed to the back door, Isabelle following. "Marie will be here shortly, and Alders will be within hollerin' distance after he comes back from droppin' me off at the church. I'll be back by lunchtime."

As Josie opened the door, they were surprised by a man walking up the porch steps. He was tall and dressed in a suit only the wealthiest of men could afford, a suit far finer than Michael's. His thick, dark hair was graying at the temples.

"Miss Fontaine?" Even though he smiled at Isabelle and Josie in a warm fashion, but his pale blue eyes were like tiny pebbles. "I'd like a word with you, if I could."

Isabelle stepped aside to let him in. "Certainly, Mister?"

"Beaufort," the man filled in. "Mr. Beaufort."

Isabelle led him to the front, wondering why he came to their back door. Leading him to the front of the house, she gestured for Beaufort to have a seat in the parlor. Before he sat, Beaufort handed Josie his card through his fingers, careful not to make any more hand contact than was necessary. He looked around the room, scrutinizing the seat of the needleworked chair before sitting down.

Josie, looking troubled, handed over the card to her new mistress.

"Beaufort Properties, Ltd.," Isabelle read aloud. "How may I help you today, Mr. Beaufort?" she asked.

The insincere smile returned again. "I do apologize for stopping in on a Sunday morning like this, but let me begin by saying I have had the pleasure of seeing you perform a few years ago. I know who you are, Miss Fontaine. When I heard that you were in town, I had to stop in for a visit."

"Who told you I was here?" Isabelle asked, curious.

"Why, Ned du Roy, of course. We belong to the same gentlemen's club. He seems quite taken with you. I told the other gents there that du Roy was not exaggerating about your talent, because I too had the pleasure of witnessing it firsthand."

Isabelle looked down, never growing accustomed to the compliments she received. "Thank you, sir."

"I did not answer your question," Beaufort continued, "perhaps because I need to approach this topic with care."

Isabelle leaned in from her seat opposite him. She was intrigued. "Do go on," she said. "You've piqued my curiosity."

Josie had left and returned with a glass of water for Mr. Beaufort. He politely declined, handing the glass back quickly. Josie slipped Isabelle a knowing look, displeased with the apparent snub.

"I run a profitable property holdings company," Beaufort began. "I have several holdings in this great city, several along the river. A couple of my friends and I are currently seeking new ventures in this very area, in fact."

"I see," Isabelle said, getting a sense of where Beaufort was heading.

"I have long been an admirer of the Fontaine Estate and its place in history, with it being the last standing ribbon farm estate and all," he said. "Your esteemed grandfather kept pretty much to himself except for his, er, relationship with Ned."

Isabelle noticed Beaufort could not bring himself to utter the word "friendship".

"I'll get right to the point," Beaufort said. "We, meaning, my partners and I, are interested in buying this estate."

"Buy the estate?" Isabelle echoed, bemused. She thought of how she callously planned to sell this house, and here is someone who wants to take it off her aching hands! Yet, Isabelle was surprised by her hesitation. "Well, I—"

"We are prepared to make you a very generous offer," Beaufort jumped in. "I know that with you being a woman and all, and one with no husband I might add, you may be a little overwhelmed with discussing business affairs," Beaufort said. "But let me put you at ease. I am an experienced businessman. I can guide you through this quickly and easily."

Isabelle was furious at Beaufort's offhand comment about women and business. She faced this male disregard everywhere she went. Her own fiancé tried in vain to convince her to quit her music career once they married. When would it end?

"Mr. Beaufort," I can assure you that I am well versed in business matters," she said.

Beaufort looked surprised, then angry. "I see. Then you understand where I am coming from when I say the potential for development of your land as commercial riverfront property is considerable. It's untouched land, and many businessmen are taking a serious look at it."

"That may well be," Isabelle said slowly, "but I am not sure if or when I'll be considering a sale."

Red in the face, Beaufort glared at her; it was obvious he was accustomed to having his own way. "Let me say this, Miss. There are others who also covet this property, and they will not be so polite in trying to acquire it as I was. Your grandfather is dead, and you're an outsider. You cannot stop progress."

"I'll take my chances," Isabelle said. "If the property is sold, it will be at the time of my choosing. Not before."

Beaufort stood abruptly. "Then I guess our little discussion is concluded. Good day, Miss Fontaine. I'll see myself out."

Isabelle jumped when Beaufort slammed the door behind him. Josie rushed to her side.

"The nerve of that man!" Josie huffed. "This is your place now, fair and square. All we have to do is call on Ned and he'll make sure those vultures are kept at bay."

"Josie, I'm afraid Ned will only be able to do so much," Isabelle said, worried. "Did you see the look of determination on that man's face? He'll stop at nothing. I'm sure he has illegal means at his disposal. You can't get that wealthy without having dirty hands."

"You are wise for so young an age," Josie observed. "I, too, saw the evil all 'round him when he first walked through the door."

"It's only a matter of time, I'm afraid," Isabelle said, worried. He'll be back, with friends."

"What are we going to do?" Josie asked.

Isabelle rubbed her aching hand. "I don't know."

Preferring to keep busy rather than worry over Beaufort's veiled threat, Isabelle decided to inspect the attic. When she got to the upper level, she thought of stopping by Barry's room to see if he would talk, but she decided to wait. Josie had gone on to church. Whether Isabelle sold the house or not, she needed to know all of the secrets that lay obscured within the house.

Walking to a door just opposite of Barry's with a lit lantern, Isabelle turned the knob. Behind the creaking white oak door was a stairwell. She climbed the creaky stairs, assailed by dusty, musty odors. Wiping away cobwebs as she went, Isabelle reached the attic. A small stained glass window of flowers was covered in dust, filtering the daylight into gray pools on the wooden floorboards. Rotting wooden beams supported the large attic's walls. Isabelle looked upward to the ceiling for more damage; the last thing she needed was a collapsing roof. Large black trunks lay around the attic like unearthed caskets. Isabelle rummaged through many to find old bed linens and tablecloths, hats and shoes. Returning these things to their resting places, Isabelle eyed a large trunk.

Kneeling in front of the chest, she reached inside to find dresses, fancy ones. Isabelle choked from the cloud of dust that rose to greet her. The dresses were intact, for the most part. Rummaging further, she found a heavy bundle of fabric that rustled when touched. Taking it out, Isabelle unraveled it with care.

It was a wedding dress, with an amazingly intricate design of lace and pearls throughout. It was old, though, for it seemed to fall apart as she held it. She stood and held what was left against her own body. Whoever wore it was tall. Isabelle tried to guess what type of woman would have owned this dress. Noting its finery, however, she was certain it did not belong to any of the slaves who lived there. More likely than not, the slaves would not have had any type of formal ceremonies, she thought bitterly. No honeymoon. No guarantee of being together until parted by death. Angry, she bent to shove the dress back into its trunk.

Opening another trunk, Isabelle found men's clothing. They were from the past, somewhat similar to what her mysterious visitor from the yard was wearing. She noticed a medium-sized scroll of heavy antique paper underneath. Unrolling it carefully, Isabelle gasped as the image unfurled before her.

An oil painting presented a shocking image: that of Isabelle's face. Or what looked so much like her. Isabelle took note of large, light eyes and long, fanlike lashes, the sculpted cheekbones, the oval face, high forehead, the thick dark hair. Suddenly light-headed, Isabelle sat down next to the chest and blinked furiously as her vision faded.

~ ~ ~

"You look so pretty!" Suzette beamed as she flitted about Celeste, brushing her hair and pinching her pale cheeks for rosy color. "Louis has such good ideas. You have the perfect face for a painting to hang on a wall." Celeste clenched her hands, uneasy. Louis had decided that he would have a painting done of her, to place on his own bedroom walls. Celeste did not want his attentions focused on her in such a way. Suzette, ever the young girl, was either not aware of what was going on or she chose to ignore the ugly truth.

There was a light rap on the bedroom door. A small man with a large mustache was shown in by a servant.

"Ah, Monsieur Bichet, come in," Suzette said excitedly. "Celeste is ready. Isn't she lovely?"

Bichet looked at Celeste in an appraising way, then his look of admiration turned to scorn, for he had the painter's eye; he realized she was a Negress. It would be considered beneath him to paint a woman of color. Suzette handed him an envelope that presumably contained a considerable amount of money.

"My brother appreciates your service, Monsieur," she said meaningfully.

Clearing his throat, Bichet took the envelope quickly. "Let us begin."

~   ~   ~

"Isabelle! You here?" Isabelle heard her name being called from a distance. Shaking her head, she realized she was still in the attic. Not knowing how much time had passed, she rose and dusted off her skirts. The rolled painting in hand, she went back downstairs and closed the attic door. She left the painting on her bed to study later, and went down to the kitchen. Josie had traded her Sunday dress for her house dress and apron.

"Lunchtime," she said. "What would you like?"

Isabelle sat down at the table, weary. "Anything will be fine, Josie."

As she watched Josie work at the stove, Isabelle heard a rap on the kitchen door. She found herself hoping it was Michael again. Instead, it was an older white man with gray hair and whiskers and spectacles. He had a kind face. He was carrying a black leather bag.

"Hello, hello!" he sang as he walked in.

"Hello, to you, Mr. du Roy," Josie smiled. "Just in time for lunch."

The man set his bag down, hung his coat over the back of the chair, and walked up to Isabelle. He took her hand and kissed it. "Miss Fontaine, so glad to have you home."

"Thank you," Isabelle said, smiling. She liked Mr. du Roy from the first time he approached her in her dressing room at a concert in Canada. He took a seat opposite her. After drinking from a glass of water offered to him, du Roy took off his spectacles to clean them with his handkerchief. "So, Miss Fontaine, how are you faring so far?" he asked.

Isabelle averted her eyes. "I am still getting used to being here," she said. "It's very different from Canada."

Ned nodded. "Detroit is an exciting city of promise, but it still has its demons to vanquish." He turned to Josie. "Tell me, Josie, what else can we do to make our guest's stay more enjoyable?" he asked.

Josie set down a bountiful lunch of leftover roast turkey, cheese, and grapes on the table.

"We can definitely work on gettin' her to eat. Nobody's happy when they are too skinny." All three laughed.

"All joking aside," du Roy went on, "we hope your brief stay here will be pleasant."

Isabelle took note of the use of the word "brief," but made no mention of it.

"Thank you."

"I'd be happy to take you into town one evening. There are some friends of mine who would love to meet the famous Miss Fontaine."

"That would be lovely," Isabelle answered. She noticed that despite Mr. du Roy's friendliness, he appeared to be uneasy about something.

"Later this week, I'd like to stop by to discuss the house with you," he said. "As executor of your grandfather's will, I need to make you aware of a few things."

Isabelle nodded. "Certainly."

Mr. du Roy stayed to finish his lunch, and chatted lightly with Isabelle about Detroit for a while longer, then he left. Josie fixed a lunch plate for Barry and took it upstairs. Isabelle was left to her own devices.

Deciding to avoid it no longer, she went to visit the music room. Once inside, she closed the door so as not to be disturbed. Or heard, for that matter. She eyed the black ebony instrument, circled it, sized it up like an enemy. Taking a seat on the velvet emerald green bench, she feared the worst about her left hand. Would she ever be free of this pain again? She could avoid seeing a doctor for only so long. Between the pain and her trances, Isabelle doubted her future as a concert pianist.

After running through a few scales and arpeggios, Isabelle took a deep breath and plunged into her song, an original composition in progress for the last several years. A passionate account of doomed lovers, Isabelle's song remained incomplete for some unknown reason. Never satisfied with the endings she had concocted, Isabelle wondered if she would ever complete the piece and perform it. Having come close to discarding it countless times, she found herself unable to do so, the melody so deeply embedded in her head she could not forget it if she tried.

The beginning of the song flowed from her fingers, as if she'd played only yesterday. The song opened with trills reminiscent of the birds in the trees, describing the delicacy of the first touch. Halfway through, her left hand pounded chords at the peak of the crescendo, releasing the tempest of passion at its full intensity. As she continued to play, Isabelle felt like she was floating above the keys, the music wrapping itself around memories of her own blissful first kiss with Richard. His gentle face quickly faded, however, transforming into that of the mysterious man in her dreams, his luminous eyes speaking to her.

"Jacques," she breathed as she closed her own eyes, embracing him. As their lips touched, however, a searing pain like liquid fire shot through her left hand, paralyzing her. In terror, Isabelle nearly fell from the bench to the floor. Shaking, she stood. *What was happening? Who was Jacques?* she wondered.

The door swung open with force then, slamming against the wall behind it. Ben raced through in silent glee, his eyes wild. Isabelle jumped.

"Ben! Stop that! I told you to stop running!" Marie rushed through the doorway after him, breathless. Grabbing hold of his too small hand, she yanked him hard to the floor. Ben, knocked back to his senses, calmed down.

She turned to Isabelle. "Miss Isabelle, forgive us," she said, her eyes downcast. "Ben has never acted like this before."

"I was told to hurry in to hear the song," Ben explained to Marie. Isabelle was startled to hear Ben talking.

"Hear the song?" Isabelle asked him. "Who told you to do that?"

Before he could answer, Marie jerked Ben to his feet and out the door. Isabelle shook her head, shivering as a chill went past her. Just then, Josie came to the doorway.

"That's a beautiful song, Isabelle. Sad one, though. Sorry to disturb you, but someone is at the door. He says he knows you."

Isabelle rose. "Thank you, Josie." She rushed to the front room, very curious. No one from back home would have come all of this way. No one, except. . .

She was greeted with a smothering embrace and kiss on the cheek.

"Surprise, My Dearest!"

"Douglas, how did you get here?" she asked, trying to feign delight at seeing the last person she wanted to see. Josie rushed up, then halted. The look she gave Isabelle demanded an explanation.

"Josie," Isabelle said as she broke free of his embrace, "This is Mr. Douglas Burns, my concert promoter from Canada. He has come to surprise me."

Douglas offered his hand to Josie, who remained wary. Isabelle was not surprised at Josie's distrust; after all, Douglas was white. Taking Isabelle by the hand, he guided her to the settee. He did not let go.

Just then, Scout ran up out of nowhere, and started barking viciously at Douglas. Douglas did not flinch, but his eyes were large. "Looks like my surprises don't work so well, huh?" he joked.

Alders rushed into the room to get Scout. "So sorry about this," he said, backing out of the room, dragging a still barking Scout with him.

Douglas turned back to the ladies, nonplussed. "Oh, Josie, I'd like to say I am more to Miss Isabelle than just her concert promoter," he continued. "We—"

Just then, Michael entered the room. He towered over everyone. His eyes went straight to Isabelle's and Douglas' interlocked fingers. Douglas rose to greet him.

"Michael St. Vincent, this is Mr. Douglas Burns, from Canada. He's here for Isabelle."

Isabelle could not read Michael's expression, but she could feel his anger.

Reluctantly, Michael eventually took Douglas' hand.

"St. Vincent? Are you the talented doctor I have been hearing so much about?" Douglas asked.

"The very same," Michael said. Isabelle was annoyed at his sudden lack of modesty.

"I am from Canada, but I am an entrepreneur with interests on both sides of the river," Douglas said, enthusiastically. I thought I would surprise Miss Fontaine and take her out on the town. I have been trying to get her to come with me to Detroit for quite some time. For some reason," his smile faded ever so slightly as he turned to look at Isabelle, "she decided to come here on her own."

Isabelle was outdone by the surprise visit, and uncomfortable in front of Michael. "Douglas, I don't know about going out. I look a mess. I'm sure there's dust on my dress."

Josie chimed in, "Not hardly a mess, please! Don't you say, Michael? Don't she look so pretty?" Josie went to fluff Isabelle's skirts like a mother preparing her daughter for her first social.

Isabelle's eyes riveted from Douglas only to rest upon Michael. His eyes held hers in a private exchange; Isabelle felt warmth steal through her.

"Yes, Auntie, she does," he answered, his eyes never leaving hers. "Like an angel."

Failing to find any words, Isabelle was relieved to hear Douglas's cough.

"Isabelle and I will be leaving now. Isabelle, I'll be outside." He went out the door.

Michael looked from Douglas to Isabelle, his previously seductive gaze turning cold.

"Just in town and already running the streets at night?" he asked her pointedly. "Not good for a young lady."

Isabelle was taken aback by the sudden hostility. All thoughts of canceling her evening flew out the window.

"This is a business appointment, nothing more. And it's no one's concern where or when I conduct business," she said smoothly.

"Ah," was all Michael said, as he stroked his smooth chin. This served to infuriate Isabelle, as she expected him to say more, not merely pass judgment. She curtly excused herself and went to her room to freshen up. After grabbing her mantle, bonnet, and gloves, she returned to a waiting Michael, brushing past him.

"We're leaving," she said over her shoulder as they walked to the door.

"Have a lovely evening," Michael said. Isabelle felt his eyes boring into her back as they left out the front door.

CHAPTER FOUR

Douglas chattered nonstop as his carriage glided up Fontaine to Jefferson Avenue, the main street. Heading east, they made their way to Grand Boulevard, an immensely wide street of large homes under the shadow of towering trees. They were in Douglas' new barouche, a four-wheeled, four-seat leisure carriage with a collapsible hood. The driver had the two horses slow their paces to a leisurely gait.

"Detroit has become the center of the world," Douglas told Isabelle. "They say two stagecoaches a week can make the round trip from Detroit to Chicago, and as many as two-thousand arrive in Detroit a day by way of the river. The population has nearly tripled," he added. "I predicted this a few years ago, before I met you. My business friends will tell you so. You have yet to meet them." Isabelle rolled her eyes, thinking that if Douglas' friends were anything like Mr. Beaufort, then she would never want to meet them.

Restless, Isabelle nodded or gave brief answers when Douglas pointed out the houses of certain well-to-do Detroit residents.

"You know, it's customary for Detroit's wealthiest to come out here on Grand Boulevard for a Sunday carriage drive," Douglas said. He was grinning like a little boy at the fair. "You never know who you might see out here."

Isabelle had only a passing interest in the homes of these wealthy people. As late as 1830, the census showed 32 slaves in the territory, and some of these very people were slave owners until 1833. She looked at Douglas then, appreciating that he honored her request that any known slave owner was not allowed into her exclusive concerts. She then felt bad for not having given him her full attention since he had come to see her.

"Douglas, I'm so very surprised to see you here in the city," she said. "But I thought we agreed that we would talk once I returned to Amherstburg," she said.

"I know, but I missed you, Isabelle," he said, turning to her, his gray eyes misty. His handsome face was broad, an open plain. "I wish you would hurry up and make up your mind about us," he said. "I know how I feel about you, and I think that you care for me, too."

Isabelle gave no reply. There were times when she thought she could feel something for Douglas. After all, they shared a love for music and he believed in her musical abilities. He had no problem with her success, Isabelle reasoned, and he was ambitious, striving to become a prominent entrepreneur. *But why do I keep hesitating?* she wondered.

Douglas sighed and turned back to the window. "I'm staying at the National Hotel, as always. Take your time, Isabelle," he said, softly.

After she returned home, Isabelle did not go immediately upstairs to her room. The house was dark and quiet, so she assumed that Josie had already turned in. She dared not contemplate what Barry was doing. Tired, she leaned her head against the back of the parlor settee. After the nice carriage ride, dinner at a well-known restaurant was a little more difficult. Isabelle and Douglas had run the risk of being thrown out, due to Isabelle's being a *coloured*. Douglas liked the idea of fooling everyone because of Isabelle's fair features, so he was not nervous at all. Over a five-course meal, Isabelle said very little, even afraid her voice would give her away.

Isabelle was intrigued, however, over how she was treated like everyone else; the others never suspected anything. Her home town, Amherstburg, was full of free and successful people of color, as well as kindly whites, so she went just about anywhere freely. Detroit was a different matter, so she had been prepared for ill treatment. But it did not happen at the restaurant. Douglas even joked that despite intermarriage between Negroes and whites being against the law, they could probably get away with it. He'd then said she should seriously consider it.

Drawing her legs up onto the settee, Isabelle pulled up a crocheted throw over herself. Having had some wine, she did not feel like moving at the moment. After she drifted off, she sensed that someone was in the room with her.

She imagined that the scary man from the yard and the cemetery was seated beside her. He was not disheveled, nor was the noose around his neck this time. His light eyes were glowing, and somehow, she could feel his love for her.

"Our love will last forever," he whispered. "You belong to me."

"Jacques," Isabelle moaned as she felt a light caress across her cheek.

Isabelle awoke to find Michael leaning over her. He was frowning.

"Michael!" she gasped and quickly sat up. Snatching the cover about herself in modesty, she forgot she was still wearing her dress. Early morning sunlight made rosy halos behind the drapes. "What are you doing in here?"

"I should be asking you the same thing," Michael replied tersely. He was in a white dress shirt and was freshly shaven. "I thought your bedroom was upstairs," he said. "Did you have such a lovely night with him that you continued it in here?" he demanded. Before Isabelle could respond to that barb, Michael added, "I'm assuming the 'him' is indeed Douglas?" his mouth twisted. "Or is it someone else, a Jacques?" He turned his back to her and crossed his arms, his white shirt stretching across his broad shoulders.

Isabelle was taken aback by the mention of Jacques' name. Michael must have heard her muttering in her sleep. She knew no more about the man than Michael; Jacques was a man who did not exist.

"Michael, I—"

"Michael? You out there?" Josie called from down the hall.

"Yes, Auntie, it's me," he called back in a sweet voice. "Thought I would take you to breakfast this morning in town."

"How nice," Josie said as she entered the room. "Would Isabelle like to join us?" Josie stopped short upon seeing Isabelle's disheveled form.

"I think you two should go ahead," Isabelle said. She gave Michael a sidelong glance. "I'm not hungry right now."

"If you sure, Chile," Josie said, looking worried.

Hearing the back door close, Isabelle climbed the stairs slowly, her limbs slow from last night's wine. Though she felt somewhat embarrassed over being found slumped in the parlor, she could not find enough words to express her anger at Michael's behavior. He had treated her as if she were a lady of the evening. She would not stand for that. *If he only knew what she had been going through!*

But he would never know, she thought. *After all, I don't owe him any kind of explanation.* She would be here for a couple of weeks, no longer, and the house would be sold. She would never see him again.

Still deep in thought, Isabelle did not see Barry in her room. He was holding the rolled-up painting in his hands. He looked afraid.

"Barry? What are you doing in here?" Isabelle demanded. Barry looked down at the floor.

"My lady, my lady," he started chanting again. Isabelle took him by the hand, sat him down on the bed. She would not scold him; he was family, and she wanted to get to know him.

"Barry, stop that," she said. "I'm not angry. I just did not expect to see you in here. You found the picture?" he nodded. "I do not know about you, but I think that picture looks something like me." Barry nodded again.

"But it cannot be me, Barry, because this is a very old painting. Look at the edges of the paper. My only guess is that she is some distant relative of mine. Of ours," she added. Barry smiled then.

"Ours?" he echoed.

"Yes," Isabelle said, taking his hand in hers. "Barry, I am so sorry about what my mother did so long ago. I'm sure that she feels badly for leaving you when you needed her. She left because she was making Grandfather unhappy. It had nothing to do with you," she added.

"That is what Josie told me back then," Barry whispered.

"You see? Believe me, that is what happened. I plan on writing Mother to tell her how handsome you are, and that you are doing well." Barry squeezed Isabelle's hand in gratitude. "Now, let me get dressed, and we will have breakfast together."

After returning downstairs in a simple day dress and no ribbons, Isabelle started frying eggs and bacon in a skillet in the kitchen. Barry came in then and took a seat at the table. He waited patiently, but still looked preoccupied.

"So, you like to draw?" Isabelle asked after fixing their plates and joining him at the table. He nodded as he ate. She realized that she would have to do most of the talking.

"What do you like to draw the most?" she continued.

He stopped chewing then, and stared deeply into her eyes, making Isabelle nervous.

"You," was his answer.

Isabelle finished the rest of her breakfast with Barry in silence. He ate his meal, then walked away from the table without a word. Isabelle made no attempt to detain him, having been shocked by his strange remark. *How could he have been spending all of these years painting me, considering he had not met me until a couple of days ago?* she wondered.

Ladling hot water into the sink from a copper pot on the stove, Isabelle started washing dishes. She looked out the window onto the side yard. She could see Scout running around the yard in wild abandon. The sun was bright, but she could feel the air growing cooler. Her hands down in the warm water, her vision faded again.

~   ~   ~

As she grew older, Celeste saw less of Pere, who had taken ill over the last few months. His full head of hair turned stringy and limp. Evangeline said his heart was going out. He was hit hard with failing crops and the fur supply was woefully short that year. A bateau of French-Canadian voyageurs Bennet relied upon to supplement his income had sunk on its way in from Montreal; it was carrying bales of deerskin, boxes of herbs, tea, sugar, and candles. To add to the misery, the newer habitants to the area were trying to remove the Indians by force. Pere found himself having to sell off some of his best "help".

Whenever she could, Celeste read the Bible to him in the evenings. He particularly liked the story of the Prodigal Son.

"That's me and Louis," Pere would say. "He comes back to me after a failure, and I always take him back. I'm trying to tell him the right way to go, but he won't listen, has his own ideas. I wish you could inherit," he'd said frankly.

"No, Pere," Celeste had said. "You don't mean that. He is your son. We all know he is wild right now, but surely, he will do what's right when the time comes."

"No, Dear One, the day is coming when Louis will inherit all of this—the good and the bad. What he does with it will seal your fates."

Celeste hated to see him so worried. She was startled when Bennett grabbed her arm. "Bright Eyes, I must tell you," he wheezed.

She leaned in so he would not have to strain himself. "Yes, Pere?"

"I am the only parent you have known, child. Your mother, she was so beautiful. When she was brought here, I knew there'd be trouble. My brother-in-law could not leave her alone." Celeste looked away, not able to hear it. "Amie could not divorce him without scandal. . .Your mother died bringing you into this world, and I took it upon myself to look after you. 'Till then, none of my help was ever mistreated in such a way. You are all in my care. What he did went against my biblical principles."

At fourteen, Celeste was not sure that Bennet's "biblical principles" were right—she was his property. Every time they attended Mass she wondered about it. But she still loved Sieur Fontaine as a father.

"What I'm trying to tell you," he continued, "is that some men have natures about themselves that can overwhelm them if they are not strong. Louis is such a person."

"Pere, what are you saying?" Celeste's stomach was in knots.

"Louis has always fancied you. I told him to mind his business, but he has always had his way, ever since he was a boy. That's my fault, spoiling him so. We were wealthy back in France, we should have stayed there. This frontier life. . ." he drifted off for a moment. Celeste shook him awake, but his eyes were heavy.

"Be mindful, Child," was the last he said that night.

~ ~ ~

The back door swung open, waking Isabelle from her reverie. Confused, it took her a moment to recognize Josie, who was hanging her coat on a nearby rack.

"Ah, Isabelle," she said when she noticed her at the sink. "Chile, you didn't have to do that," she said. "You are a guest here."

"I don't mind, Josie," Isabelle said. She found herself looking at the door, wondering if Michael was coming in as well.

"Michael went on back to his rounds," Josie said as she tied on her apron. "Did you get a good breakfast?" she inquired.

Isabelle assured that she had, and cooked for Barry. Josie's eyebrows shot up in interest. "You don't say. Barry is still full of surprises. It's nice he's taken to you. Maybe he'll talk more."

In some ways, Isabelle feared what her dear cousin would be saying next. "Josie, I'll be heading out this afternoon with Douglas. He's invited me to go horseback riding on Swan Island."

Josie busied herself with wiping down the kitchen table and said nothing for several minutes. "I see. Tell me, it's none of my affair, but how long you been knowin' Mr. Douglas?" she asked.

"A couple of years. He was at one of my performances," Isabelle said. "He came up afterwards with a bouquet of roses for me, said he had been admiring me for quite a while. I was just starting out, putting on soirees. He offered his services as an informal promoter, arranging bigger performances in concert halls and at the college. He has a way with people."

"Humpf," Josie said. "I think he is interested in being more than your promoter," she commented. Isabelle shrugged.

"I know. I have told him that I am very busy with my performing and that any personal decisions will have to wait," Isabelle explained.

"You don't say," Josie said. "How does your mama feel about him?

Isabelle sighed. "Mother adores him. He's got money, and the potential to make more. He's got connections both here and in Canada. "

"And he's white," Josie added. "You could 'pass' and no one would know the difference."

"This is true," Isabelle commented, "but I will not willfully deceive people. If I choose to marry Douglas," Isabelle said, "I will be the same person I was before. He'll have to understand that."

"Well, I hope you two have a nice time on the island," was all Josie said to that.

"Do you know why the island is also known as Rattlesnake Island and Hog Island?" Douglas asked as they disembarked after a short ride on a small ferry.

"No, why?" she asked.

"An Indian legend says it was named for a beautiful maiden protected by the Great Spirit who then surrounded the island with snakes to protect her and the island from intruders. The snakes began to worship her, and they made her a Goddess to rule over the island," he explained. "The other story is that the island was so overrun with snakes that the locals released hogs onto the island to rid it of the snakes. That story seems more like the real one to me," he added.

Isabelle fought the urge to retch. "Nice name for an island." As she looked about, however, Isabelle's turning stomach subsided. The island was truly beautiful; she imagined it looked like Eden, with rich green grasses, and swooping willow trees every few feet. Deer drank from the creeks, and swans floated down past them as they rode alongside the creek on a paved path to the wooden horse stables. Other couples were there as well, with ladies dressed in fashionable riding habits similar to her own brown one.

After picking two of the finest horses, Douglas tipped the stable clerk. Handing one set of reins to Isabelle, he assisted her into her side saddle on Daisy, the smaller of the two horses. He then deftly swung up onto his own horse, Striker. As they walked at a leisurely pace down the main road, Isabelle felt at peace, a feeling she had not had for months. Some of the last orange leaves on the trees clung for dear life, and bushes were turning flaming red.

"How are you doing?" Douglas asked. He was in front of her on the narrow trail.

"I'm off to a good start, I believe," she answered. She had only been on a horse a few times back home. She was in no way an expert.

"Don't be nervous. Remember to stay calm, that's paramount," Douglas said. You never want to scare a horse into doing what you want. Just follow me."

They rode for a long while in silence, and Isabelle was grateful for that. She wanted simply to enjoy the beauty of the scenery and not have to think so hard about her future. She noticed that the trail had virtually disappeared, and they were surrounded on all sides by drooping, thickly thatched branches. The deeper they went, the darker it became. The branches were long and wild then, and a few scraped her face like long, cold fingernails. Isabelle realized they were off the path, but Douglas went on ahead.

"Douglas?" she called ahead. "Perhaps we ought to turn back now. It's getting dark in here—"

"Heyah!" Douglas shouted, slapping his horse on the rump. Startled, the horse set off on a wild gallop.

"What!" was all Isabelle could shout before her own horse took off after them. She gripped the reigns tightly as Daisy ran to keep up with Striker; it was all she could do to stay in the saddle. She tried to slow the horse with the reins and her legs failed. If anything, Daisy gained speed. Isabelle called Douglas' name once to get his attention, but he seemed not to hear her.

They were then alongside the creek Douglas had mentioned before. Douglas swerved and took his horse on a flying leap over a narrow bend in the creek. Daisy pivoted and tried to do the same, but Isabelle was not prepared for it. Her head collided with a low-hanging branch and she was thrown off the horse and into the creek. She heard a big splash, then was plunged into darkness.

~   ~   ~

Celeste was caught by surprise while hanging freshly washed bedclothes on the clothesline. Before she knew it, Louis had snuck up on her from behind. Grabbing her by the waist, he spun her around to face him, her loose hair blowing in the wind.

"I've got you!" he laughed. Celeste started giggling.

"Louis, you lout! You see that I am busy," she said. They were both sixteen now, their birthdays just days apart. She wriggled to get free, but Louis would have none of it.

"You're mine," he whispered in her ear. Celeste felt an unfamiliar warm feeling stir within her as Louis held her close. She liked the feeling.

"Louis, what are you doing—" Before she could say anything else, Louis' lips softly brushed her own. Her knees instantly went weak. It was her first

kiss, and Celeste realized she wanted more. Tentatively, she reached up and touched the baby-fine hair on the nape of his neck, then allowed her hands to roam over his muscular arms.

"Mmm, Celeste, I've have wanted to kiss you for so very long," Louis said. His grip on her waist grew tighter. Celeste remembered the warning Pere had given her just last fall, deciding he had been wrong about his son. Louis would never hurt her. He loved her.

As Louis kissed her, Celeste wondered when things had changed between them. They had been raised together almost like brother and sister, Celeste being allowed to play with them at any time. Perhaps it was last fall, when she played for some of Pere's friends at the annual harvest dance. She noticed how handsome Louis had looked in his first grown man's suit, and noticed how all the girls circled around him waiting for a dance. Celeste was not allowed to dance, but Louis had turned all the other girls down that night, choosing to sit in a chair next to Celeste at the pianoforte for the night.

Celeste heard rustling on the side of the house. It was Eulalie, another slave. Reluctantly, Celeste broke away from Louis, who had not heard a thing.

"Right here, Eulalie," she called back. Smoothing her skirts, Celeste slowly backed away. Grinning, Louis reached to twirl a few strands of her hair, then took off the other way. Just then, Eulalie walked up. Recently bought from a plantation in the south, Eulalie had been brutalized by her master to the point he'd had her tongue cut out for laughing too loud. The master had recently died under suspicious circumstances, so the slaves had been sold off.

Mute since they'd known her, Eulalie pointed in the direction of the cookhouse, then gave Celeste a knowing look. Laughing, Celeste took her by the hand. She could not tell her what happened, at least not yet.

"Oh, don't be so silly. Let's go."

Celeste was happy that summer. Suzette and Louis spent their days free of their Jesuit tutors and lived carefree in the warmth of the sun, slurping on juicy pears from the trees the Jesuits planted. Whenever Celeste was done with her chores or with tending the King's Gardens at the fort with Father Levette, she would join brother and sister in their rooms or on the front porch.

This did not bode well with the other slaves, particularly Silas, an old stable hand, who gave Celeste mean glances whenever he passed her way. There were nine other slaves on the farm, Silas and his son, Caleb, two other women, three children, and of course, Eulalie. Eulalie was often angry as well, not understanding whenever Celeste left her to be with Suzette and Louis. Sometimes, Eulalie had to serve all three. With Pere bedridden these days, there was nothing to stop the three friends from doing whatever they wanted.

Celeste was no fool, however; she was reminded of her place every time that guests came to the house, particularly their aunt, who often threatened to beat her if she got too close to her niece and nephew. Little did she know about her precious nephew and me, Celeste thought. Whenever they had a chance, Louis and Celeste would sneak a breathless kiss when no one was around, which was not too often. These too-brief moments left Celeste wanting so much more.

Trouble came that fall. Celeste had a feeling that something had changed drastically. Her fears were confirmed when she overheard Louis in his father's room upstairs as she was cleaning Suzette's.

"No, Pere, I will not do it!" Louis shouted. Celeste wondered what was wrong.

"Listen to me, Louis, it is for the good of the farm. Her father is very well connected, and he believes you would be an excellent choice for a husband.

"You are a man now, and frankly, I don't have much time left," Bennet wheezed. "Don't worry if you do not feel anything for Briane upon first sight," he said. "Love comes with time."

"I will never love her," Louis said.

"Louis, we can both agree that you have been a rebellious child. I even had to send you away for a while after what happened to Madeleine." There was silence after that. Celeste wondered about Madeleine, who was metis, a child of one of the Hurons and a fort soldier. Louis had taken an interest in her, but she disappeared one night last year, and she had yet to be found. A group of Huron warriors camped out in front of the house for days, but Father Levette eventually convinced them she must have run away. Louis was placed under protection in the fort, and he always said he couldn't understand why Madeleine left. The Hurons left reluctantly, and war was averted.

"What I am trying to say is that it is time that you own up to your responsibilities to this family, after all you have put us through," Pere went on. "I know that you love your sister Suzette dearly. French law says you both inherit equally, but with the fur trade slowing, you both will be struggling for some time.

"I have a plan for your future, though." Pere coughed for a moment. "I've

been told by Captain Deschamps de Boisebert, our new fort's Commandant, that Governor Charles de Beauharnois de La Boische plans to contract the building of small sailing vessels. That's what's going to save our hides out here in the wilderness, boat building. I just need you to behave until I get this up and running. And that includes becoming Briane Hubert's husband."

"But, Pere, please!" Celeste was not used to hearing Louis, who was always so proud and self-confident, beg.

"Do this for me, Louis," Bennet said. "Forget Celeste, for that can never be. You know that."

Stung by these words, Celeste tiptoed past Pere's closed door and down the stairs, tears in her eyes.

~   ~   ~

CHAPTER FIVE

Isabelle heard voices from a distance. Opening her eyes, she saw Josie's moon-shaped face break into a smile. Michael's face replaced Josie's, his dark eyes concerned, his full lips pursed tightly. Slowly, Isabelle tried to raise her head, but it was difficult. A throbbing pulse echoed in her head like crashing ocean waves.

"Is—is she alright?" Isabelle recognized Douglas' voice in the background. He sounded shaky. Without saying a word, Michael gently lifted Isabelle to a sitting position and placed a large white pillow behind her back. She realized she was in her own room at the Fontaine. Looking past Michael, Josie, and Douglas in the corner, she saw Ned du Roy standing in the room as well.

"Young lady," he said, "this was not what I meant about having a good time in Detroit."

Isabelle wanted to smile, but it hurt to do so.

"Isabelle, you were thrown from a horse," Michael said bluntly. All eyes turned to Douglas, who was squirming. "Douglas here does not seem to know how he allowed that to happen," Michael said, his voice like steel.

Douglas rushed to Isabelle's side and took her hand. He looked worried, his usually impeccably groomed blonde hair ruffled atop his head.

"Isabelle, I'm so sorry. I never should have gone so far ahead without looking back. I thought that you had the horse under control—"

"How could she have things under control when she was racing to keep up with you?" Michael barked. "If not for that couple canoeing through there, who knows when you would have noticed Isabelle was down?" Josie gripped Michael's shoulder to quiet him. He stormed off to the window.

For the first time she could remember, Isabelle saw a flash of anger in Douglas' usually genial manner. But when he looked back at Isabelle, the look was gone.

"Isabelle, you must believe that I had no idea Daisy was such a restless horse, I swear," he said, caressing her shoulder. "The minute I realized what happened, I was terrified. The kindly people in the canoe pulled you in, and paddled you back to the front of the island. I put you in the carriage and we rushed back here as fast as the driver could take us." Isabelle was touched by his concern.

She had to clear her throat before she could speak. "It's alright, Douglas. It was an accident. I'm sure that if there was any serious injury, Dr. St. Vincent would have ordered me to the hospital," Isabelle said this to Michael's back; he would not turn around. Josie brought Isabelle a glass of water, and she took a few sips. "I thank you all for your concern, and I am truly sorry I worried you for nothing."

"Oh, don't be ridiculous," Ned said. "You've only been here for a short while, and now we don't know what we'd do without you around here. Isn't that right, Josie?" he asked. Josie nodded enthusiastically. Isabelle looked to see what Michael thought. Without a word, he grabbed his coat, nodded in her direction, then left the room. Douglas glared at the door Michael had just exited, then turned back to Isabelle.

He kissed her on the cheek. "My dear, I will let you get your rest now. I will be by to see how you are doing tomorrow, after my meeting." He turned to shake Ned's hand. "Nice to meet you, Mr. du Roy."

As he rose to put on his coat, something fell from one of the pockets, landing with a thud on the floor. Josie was the first to get it, then she looked funny when she realized it was a shiny pocketknife with an ebony hilt. Douglas gave her a quick smile and took the knife.

"I like to carve in my free time," he explained, then hastily left. Josie and Ned followed, with Ned closing the door behind himself. Isabelle reached for the lamp on her nightstand, and turned it down, her head feeling better in the cool darkness. She quickly fell into a deep sleep.

~   ~   ~

Celeste saw Briane for the first time that fall. Visiting the Fontaine with two of her friends, Briane Hubert suddenly appeared one afternoon in a fine carriage. Celeste learned from Evangeline that Briane's family was from Montreal, so she had come a long way. Her father and Bennet were friends. Celeste watched the visitors from a distance. Briane was taller than the other girls, not as pretty, and awkward, frequently stumbling over her own feet. All three young women were dressed in satin gowns with snug bodices and floor length bell shaped skirts. Their plunging necklines hid nothing. Celeste looked down at her own plain day dress, and decided to stay as far out of sight as possible. Suzette, so enamoured of the stylish older girls, never once sought out Celeste that weekend. Even worse, Evangeline showed Celeste no mercy, making her wait on the snickering guests at every meal.

"Might as well get used to what it's going to be like once Briane is mistress of this house," she said. Celeste was practically raised by Evangeline, but she could be merciless. Having suffered as a young girl under a cruel master before being sold to Bennet, Evangeline's resentment at Celeste's special treatment showed every now and again. Celeste believed this to be one of those times, for she did not want to believe that things would be that different.

But things were different from that day onward. Briane visited on a regular basis, and Louis was forced by Pere to visit her in Montreal. Louis was always in a foul mood now, and had started drinking heavily in the evenings.

On one of Briane's recent visits, Louis showed Celeste a side she had never seen before. After drinking with his friends, Louis publicly stated that he wanted Celeste to join him on a hayride with him, Briane, and some of their friends. Everyone went silent in embarrassment, and Celeste tried to run into the house. Louis chased her and swung her around fiercely.

"Louis, what are you doing?" Celeste whispered. "You know that I cannot go with you anywhere. You know how we must live now. I cannot be a part of your world any longer."

"To hell with them." Louis said it loud enough for the others to hear. At this, Briane made her way over to them, the rest of the group looking on.

"Louis, what is the delay?" she asked, too sweetly. Celeste avoided Briane's pale pasty glance by looking downward. She wished she could be elsewhere.

"I'm just talking with Celeste. I'll be with you shortly," Louis said. The tone in his voice was deadly, and Briane quickly stumbled backward, mumbling that she would be waiting with the others.

"You listen to me, Celeste," Louis said, gripping her chin in his hand and forcing her to look into his eyes. "Don't you ever disobey me. I'll see you when I wish." With that, Louis released her. Rubbing her jaw, Celeste watched him stroll back to the waiting group.

~   ~   ~

When Isabelle awoke late the next morning, she had a headache. Lately, she was awakening from those strange dreams feeling drained, as if a little more of her self was being taken each time. Throwing the covers back, she willed herself to get out of bed; she refused to spend another minute there.

Readying herself for the day at the washbowl of fresh water Marie had brought in, she dressed in a day dress of dark blue silk and tied one blue ribbon around a simple braided chignon. After pulling on her stockings and shoes, she went to the stairwell, taking the time to go near the garret. She tried the rusted padlock, but a deep vibration ran through her arm, and she felt dizzy. Pressing closer, Isabelle could not seem to be able to touch the door itself, feeling like there was an invisible wall between them. Attributing the strange sensation to her ordeal the day before, she went downstairs to the kitchen.

Josie was busy preparing breakfast and was surprised to see Isabelle fully dressed in the doorway. "Oh, Isabelle, I was just gettin' ready to bring your food to your room."

Isabelle took a seat. "No need. It's time I got up," she said.

Josie set a cup of coffee before her. "Glad you are up and around."

Isabelle took a few sips of the hot coffee, then asked, "Will Michael be around today?" She had decided that she wanted to find out why Michael was so mean to her and Douglas, who had done nothing wrong to him.

"Oh, I don't know, Dearie," Josie said as she sipped her own coffee. "When he left out yesterday, he had a few choice words with Douglas at the door. Michael can git pretty worked up," she laughed.

"I see," was all Isabelle said. Marie walked into the kitchen.

"Mr. Burns is here to see Miss Isabelle," she said, then left out just as quietly as she had come.

Isabelle rose and went to the front of the house to greet Douglas. Wearing a dress shirt, vest, dark tailcoat and trousers, he met her with a hug and kiss.

"You are looking so much better, Isabelle," he said, smiling.

"Thank you," she answered. "I was just about to eat a little breakfast. Won't you join me?"

Douglas followed Isabelle to the breakfast room, where Josie met them. "What would you like this mornin', Mr. Burns?" She had brought in Isabelle's breakfast plate.

"Just coffee for me, thank you. I ate at this morning's meeting." When Josie left the room again, Douglas turned to Isabelle. He looked excited. "I just had the most auspicious meeting today, my dear!"

"Do tell," she said, curious.

"Today, I made the acquaintance of some of the most powerful men in Detroit," he began. "This is the meeting that I have been trying to make happen for months. I have been going to several of the gatherings where these men meet in order to get noticed, and finally, I was invited. The group is called the Cass Farm Company. The company has already bought the farm of Governor Lewis Cass, which is more than five hundred acres and extends three miles from the Detroit River to the northern railroads."

"My goodness," Isabelle breathed. "That is extensive."

Douglas nodded. "The front, below Larned Street, was covered by the river until last year, when the company started filling it in to make it usable for a business and residential property. The plan now is to build a magnificent hotel on the site, with a beautiful view up and down the river. The Company is sure that with the multitudes of people coming to the city every day now, foreign capitalists will want to stay here also. Augustus Porter is the trustee, and he sells the lots. Many buildings have already been erected, as you saw when you arrived. Thus far, the Company has sold lots on contract and for cash totaling nearly one hundred ninety-two thousand."

"Where do you fit into all of this, Douglas?" Isabelle asked.

"That is the best part," he said. "I plan to invest in the hotel. That will be my first one, then I have plans to develop another part of the river for a second hotel."

"Grand plans," Isabelle commented. "I have read about the Cass Company. Its members are the wealthiest men in Detroit. I think Shubael Conant, Elon Farnsworth, Oliver Newberry, and Edmund Brush are members. Do you believe you have the means to participate?" she asked.

Douglas turned red. "Isabelle, do you think I would involve myself in something I could not handle?" he asked, incredulous. "No, I'm not as rich as those men, but I am young and clever. I have a plan to come up with the investment money. Don't worry."

Isabelle felt bad for embarrassing him. *I'm worried*, she thought, *but then again, had he not helped my own career immensely?* "I know if anyone can do it, you can, Douglas," she said, reaching out to hold his hand.

Douglas left shortly thereafter, as he had another meeting elsewhere in the city. Alone again, Isabelle decided to get some air on the back porch. The late October morning was rather warm, but she knew there would be fewer mornings like this. Taking a seat on a wooden chair, she wrapped a quilt about herself and sat back. Closing her eyes, she felt the sun on her face. . .

~   ~   ~

Celeste's future was as bleak as the gray January sky above their heads. With the activities leading up to Louis and Briane's engagement party, it was easier for Celeste to avoid Louis. With their time apart, Celeste realized how foolish she had been to allow their childhood friendship to turn into anything else. Perhaps she had wanted to forget for a while that she was owned not only by Pere, but by Louis as well. She was sure that she would never be set free, would never see anything other than the lonely rooms of Maison Fontaine. If she ran to Canada to be free, she knew Louis would hunt her down.

She was seeing more bateaux and French army boats with fresh soldiers for the fort these days. She wondered what adventures they had experienced coming from Montreal. She admired their freedom in the river, wished it could take her to some far away land.

At the river now, Celeste was busy filling buckets of water to take back to the house when she heard the wheels of a wagon grind to a halt from behind. Turning, she noticed that it was an open wagon with several Negro men seated inside. Seated side-by-side, they were chained together. She surmised that Pere had made a purchase, but wondered why. They had just sold off an entire family last week because things had gotten so bad. In addition, the wedding plans were surely putting a strain on Bennet's purse, so why buy another slave now?

Curious, Isabelle walked as close as she dared to the side of the house for a better view. It was dirty old Monsuieur Duchene, of course. He hobbled from the top of the wagon. In the old days, he had been wealthy enough to afford a driver. Not anymore. Sieur Bennet was rolled out onto front porch in his wooden chair on wheels. He was extremely pale and was wrapped in layers of blankets. Monsuieur Duchene went to the wagon and unshackled one of the men, then tied some rope around the man's hands. The man did not resist. Knowing that some of the other Fontaine slaves had stopped to see the new arrival, Monsuieur Duchene tried to make a show of yanking the slave out of the wagon and onto the ground.

This did not happen, however. Despite Duchene's yanking and tugging, the man smoothly stepped from the wagon, and stood firmly. Weak Duchene could not make him budge; the man held his head high. Finally, Duchene had to ask the man in a lowered voice to come along, and then the man complied. Celeste noticed little grins of triumph on the faces of the other men in the wagon. The slave, who towered over everyone else, was brought over to Pere. His skin was a sun-kissed warm brown, and his brown hair had sandy-red streaks throughout. His eyes were slanted, almost almond-shaped. Despite his clothes looking worn and dusty from the trip, the man had a regal stance. This was not lost upon Pere.

"Monsuieur Duchene, please release him," Pere said. "He will do us no harm."

Annoyed, Duchene did as he was asked. "Certainly, Sieur Fontaine." Duchene was obviously perturbed by having to release the man, but he did so. Freed, the man rubbed his wrists. Pere gestured for Millie, another Fontaine slave, to fetch a bucket of water and ladle. The man, who most certainly had to be thirsty, drank slowly and evenly, never giving in to the urge to gulp his water. When he had his fill, he offered the bucket back and quietly thanked the woman, who seemed mesmerized by his deep, resonant voice.

Celeste knew that on the rare day a new slave was purchased, the other slaves often came out to see the person briefly, then went back to work to gossip about it. In this case, however, every single person had come outside to witness today's event. No one left, and no one moved from their spot. The new man was intriguing, for he dared to look Pere, a slaveowner, in the eye. Pere had Silas hand Duchene a drawstring leather sack of coins, the payment. Duchene's mustache was twitching as he looked back one last time. He returned to his wagon and rode off.

"Silas, this is our new boat builder," Sieur Bennet wheezed. "Get him acquainted with us." Silas signaled for the man to follow him. As she was in the path towards the back of the house, Celeste was in their way; she had been so entranced with the scene that she did not think to move. As the new slave passed her, their eyes met, and Celeste stopped breathing. Time seemed to stop as he strode slowly past her. With one glance, his light eyes bore deeply into hers, filling her entire being with a glow that spread from her heart into the tips of her fingers and toes. He seemed entranced by her as well, a look of wonder brightening his face for a moment. Right then, Celeste knew she had been changed, somehow.

~   ~   ~

Isabelle's vision came into focus when she felt a hand upon her bare arm. She turned to her right and found little Ben sitting next to her. He did not say a word, but his eyes seem to say that he understood what had just happened to her. Isabelle immediately brushed that thought away as nonsense.

"Ben, how are you this morning?" she asked.

"Fine, Miss. Isabelle," he said. As she looked as his chubby cheeks and hands, she was reminded she did not have any children yet. As a musician, she was always busy with concert dates. At twenty-seven, however, her time had just about run out. Ben was probably bored from not having any playmates. Isabelle scooped him into her arms and wrapped her shawl around them both. They stared out into the yard together.

A young white messenger on a bicycle rode up. On his back was a sack. He came to a stop at the foot of the porch steps. Reaching into the sack, he pulled out a couple of sealed envelopes. As he climbed the steps, Ben leapt out of Isabelle's lap and ran into the house. The messenger handed Isabelle the mail. Josie came out the door onto the porch and handed the boy some coins. The boy tipped his hat, left the porch, and rode off on his bike back up the road.

"Anything interesting?" Josie asked. Isabelle got up to hand Josie the letters, then noticed that one was addressed to herself. "Just one, Josie." Josie took the envelope and went into the house. Isabelle sat back down in her porch chair and began to read the letter. It was from her mother.

It read:

October 1, 1836

My Dear Daughter,

I am writing this letter in the hope that you have successfully made your way to the Fontaine Estate. I know that going there was of great importance to you, but I still feel that you should not have gone. Your prominence in our community has risen to such heights that it is causing me great embarrassment to have to explain your whereabouts. This was not a good time for you to leave, with this being the beginning of the concert season.

I know that you have amassed a considerable income from your musical engagements, along with your trust from your dearly departed father-in-law, but you should take heed that any extended diversions from your profession will have dire consequences. I am also concerned that you will become too entranced by that environment, considering your recent "condition."

The letter went on to say that her friend Bess was to be married and wanted Isabelle to return right away to help her with planning, and added that Isabelle should have some good news to share as well regarding marriage. The letter closed with no mention of Josie or her father.

Isabelle was surprised by the news about Bess. She had just seen her before leaving for the trip, and Bess had not said a word. *Or had she?* she wondered. When Isabelle thought about it, she realized that Bess had made some mention of her beau surprising her soon. Isabelle had been so preoccupied with her nightmares and completing the song that she had been ignoring everyone around her, not really listening to anything they had to say.

As far as Douglas went, wouldn't Mother be shocked to hear that he was already down here with her? Isabelle grinned at the impropriety, with her and Douglas out of Mother's sight, free to do whatever they wished.

"Something funny?" Isabelle was startled by Michael's voice. He had walked up from the road and was standing in the yard.

Quickly, Isabelle refolded the letter. Remembering how he had acted the day before, Isabelle's smile faded. "No," she answered his question, "absolutely nothing at all."

Michael shook his head. Without the shelter of the covered porch, the sun seemed to give Michael a hazy glow, making him look like an angel, maybe somewhat like his namesake. Isabelle smirked, then, thinking that this particular man was no angel.

Michael climbed the stairs slowly, his eyes never leaving her face. "May I join you?" he asked. Upon his approach, Isabelle's mouth went dry.

"No," was her quick answer. Chuckling, Michael put up his hands in mock surrender. "You have every right to be miffed, Isabelle. I behaved badly yesterday."

"I was not 'miffed', Michael, I was angry," Isabelle said. "Just who do you think you are, talking to Douglas like that? He has been nothing but cordial to you."

Just then, Michael's seductive grin was gone. "He may be cordial, but he is careless. You could have died out there, and all he could say was that you must have had a problem keeping up. If it had been me—" he began.

"Tell me when that would have happened?" Isabelle cut him off. "You and I together, frolicking on horseback?" she taunted. She took a perverse pleasure in this. "You, sir, don't look like you know how to have that kind of fun."

Isabelle could tell that she had gone too far. Michael looked furious.

"Oh, you'd be surprised at what kind of fun I know how to have." His voice low and seductive, Michael did not bother to hide his approval as his eyes trailed from Isabelle's lips to slowly traverse the entire length of her body.

Isabelle had thrown off the quilt in her anger, and from where she sat, her figure was quite visible in the simple sheath without layered petticoats. Outraged, she wrapped the quilt around herself again.

Josie came to the door. "Michael?" she called. "I thought I heard your voice. Come on in. You too, Isabelle," she added. "You been in the air long enough."

Michael opened the door for Isabelle. Brushing past him quickly, she caught a whiff of his morning shave cream, which smelled so fresh. It was a heady experience for her. In the kitchen, Michael pulled out a chair for Isabelle, then sat directly across from her. She did her best to ignore him. He took the cup of coffee offered to him by Josie.

"Thank you, Auntie," he said.

Isabelle mentioned that she'd been in the attic.

"All kinds of stuff up there," Josie said, as she peeled apples for a pie. "Your granddaddy said there were a lot of family mementos up there, some things probably quite valuable. Bein' a man and all, he didn't know what to do wit' half of it after your grandmama died. She liked to pretty things up, he said, but he had no idea what to do with 'em, so he stored a lot of it in the attic. He knew the china was valuable though, so he locked a lot of that away in the ballroom, thinking his descendants, er—" she abruptly stopped.

"I'm sorry, Isabelle, this might be too sensitive a topic just now."

"It's alright, Josie, this discussion doesn't bother me in the least," Isabelle said. Josie looked relieved.

Michael's eye lingered on her a while longer, then fell upon Josie and her bowl of sliced apples.

"You know I love your pies, Auntie," he said. "I'm looking forward to a taste." He then turned to wink at Isabelle in a flirtatious way.

Josie, oblivious to Michael's risque comment, beamed. Isabelle realized that if Michael was found out to be the Devil himself, Josie would never believe it. But Isabelle would.

CHAPTER SIX

Seated at the writing table in the front hallway, Isabelle spent the rest of the day writing back to her mother and Bess. Before leaving for the day with Ben, Marie did her work tidying the bedrooms and was quiet as usual. Isabelle wondered where mother and son lived when Marie was not working at the Fontaine.

Writing slowly, Isabelle avoided Michael, who stayed in the kitchen with Josie. Setting the pen down, she heard the back door open and close some time later. She sighed in relief, but then was annoyed that Michael had not come to wish her good night.

While sealing the envelopes, Isabelle thought about how the letters were not worth sending, considering their vagueness. She was deliberately keeping Mother and Bess in the dark about when she would be return to Canada and about how she was really doing at the Fontaine. Something was making Isabelle reluctant to leave, a feeling that something was unfinished.

She took dinner in her room, leaving the emptied wooden tray on a hallway table for Josie. As she set the tray out the door, Isabelle saw the same wavering candlelight coming from under Barry's doorway. Closing her door and dressing for bed, Isabelle wondered when she would speak with him again. She thought about discussing Barry with Michael, to seek his medical opinion, then thought better of it; she would hate to give Michael the satisfaction of her asking for his help with anything. His mockery would chase her for the rest of her life.

Determined to get something accomplished, Isabelle spent hours on her concerto with pencil and eraser. She scratched out the beginnings of the third movement yet again, which was supposed to be a triumphant *presto agitato*, signaling the reunion of two lovers for eternity. Frowning, she quickly erased two hours' worth of notation. The "triumph" did not ring true. *But why not?* she wondered. Isabelle had been hopeful that Detroit's change of scenery would give her some new ideas, but she appeared to be in the same rut as before.

Frustrated, Isabelle tossed the pencil and tablet aside. Throwing herself backward onto plump down-filled pillows, she drifted off into a fretful sleep. She willed herself not to dream.

She was awakened by the sound of her bedroom door creaking open. Only half awake, Isabelle could tell that the door was open, because of the moonlight lighting the hallway. Deciding to get up and close the door, Isabelle was stopped cold when she felt a tug on her right heel. Jolted awake, she tried again to leave the bed. A hand gripped her ankle this time, and held on tightly. Isabelle had never felt such cold before, and it made her whole leg ache.

"Let go of me!" she whispered. Isabelle was too afraid to shout, as this would mean that she believed what was happening to her. "Please," she said, "I don't know what you want, but you must let me go. Barry, if this is you, I am so angry with you!" she said this with a twinge of hope, for at least Barry was a real person. "Barry?" she repeated, weakly. There was no response.

Finally, Isabelle closed her eyes, allowing an inner darkness to consume her. Deep inside, she knew the hand did not belong to Barry, or to anyone else living in this house. Or to anyone living.

Slowly, she mouthed Jacques' name, as if in prayer. The hand released her immediately, and Isabelle scrambled out of the bed and to the door. Rushing down the stairs while holding the railing, she managed to get downstairs quickly in the dark. Finding her way up the hall to the writing table, she felt for matches and the heavy brass candleholder there. Lighting the candle, she took a seat in the parlor closest to the stairs. Taking a seat, Isabelle let herself exhale as she recalled what happened. The moment she'd said his name, she knew that Jacques had taken leave of her, and the house. She no longer felt his presence. At least for now.

Despite her fear, Isabelle could feel herself drifting off again. She hadn't slept a full night in weeks, and she was at her wit's end. Rising, she walked quietly over to a wooden cabinet against the far wall. As this room was originally the men's parlor, there was a cabinet full of spirits. Setting down the candle on a card table, she slowly pulled on the brass handles of the cabinet; it opened from its center to reveal two doors holding bottles of brandy and whiskey on either side.

Reaching for the brandy and a short glass from another cabinet, Isabelle poured herself a small taste. Reaching the sofa, Isabelle leaned back and took a sip. The brandy was warm, and it soothed her as it slowly went down. After several more sips, Isabelle felt that she could return to her room, convincing herself that her nerves had gotten the better of her yet again.

Climbing the stairs quietly and entering her room again, Isabelle promptly climbed into bed. The spirits quelled the warnings in her head about not going back to her room. Sleep was the only thought on her mind. She welcomed the darkness.

Isabelle did not wake until late morning. She only stirred then because Marie had surprised her, leaning over so close Isabelle could smell whatever soap she'd washed her hair with that day.

"I didn't mean to wake you, Miss Fontaine," Marie said. "I can come back—"

"No, Marie, come in. I was just getting up." Isabelle rose from her bed and wrapped herself in a dressing gown. She smiled at Marie, who was a little taken aback at the sudden good humor.

Isabelle could not help but smile; it had been so long since she had a full night's sleep. Waking up rested, she did not feel as anxious, and she even began doubting that her visions had any significance whatsoever. She knew that lack of sleep could make a person unbalanced.

Deciding that today would be a new start here at the Fontaine, Isabelle dressed quickly after Marie left, and fairly glided down the stairs. Entering the kitchen, Isabelle snuck up on an unsuspecting Josie and gave her a quick hug.

"Good morning, Josie!" she said. Startled, Josie blinked at Isabelle's upbeat mood, but, as was her nature, she readily joined in on the fun.

"Well, howdy-do, Miss Isabelle!" she grinned. "What got into you?"

Isabelle shrugged. "Nothing in particular. Just realized that I have been too grim for far too long."

"I sure would say so," Josie added. "No good for a pretty young woman to be frownin' all the time. That's for after marriage." They laughed.

Josie reheated the breakfast she had waiting for Isabelle earlier, and gave Isabelle a note from Ned before taking up Barry's breakfast. The note was an invitation for lunch at Ned's office in the city. He would be sending a carriage at 11:30.

A few hours later, Isabelle found herself in a carriage bound for Detroit's financial district. The air was cool, and she was dressed in a high collared tawny afternoon dress with starched petticoats, brown mantle, and a ribboned bonnet. She kept the curtains of the carriage closed to block the harsh sunlight, a reminder of her brandy the night before. Despite that feeling, she was still glad she had not dreamed of anyone or anything.

The carriage came to a stop, and she was helped out by the driver. Isabelle found that she was on Jefferson and Griswold. Everywhere she looked, she saw bricklayers, young and old men. New buildings seemed to be going up every day. Ned came to the doorway of the building she was facing. He was smiling as he held the door open for her.

"Do come in, Isabelle," he said. "Glad you could join me."

Isabelle entered the doorway, and followed Ned through his first floor offices, where a young clerk was busy writing at a desk. He did not bother to look up. They reached Ned's large office, where he took her cloak, hat, and gloves and offered her a seat in a leather chair. He sat opposite her, behind his mahogany desk. He leaned back in his chair.

"Our lunch is on the way," he said.

"Thank you," Isabelle said as she looked around the office. There were certificates and diplomas on every wall.

Ned pushed his glasses up on his nose. "I wish to speak with you about your grandfather's will."

Isabelle nodded for him to continue; she was anxious to know where this discussion was headed.

"Your grandfather was a friend of mine, a caring, funny gentleman who had only one purpose in life," Ned said, "that being keeping the Fontaine in the family."

"I can imagine that this was very hard for him," Isabelle said.

"You are correct," Ned replied. "The hounds were always at the door. But Charles hung on, and I was always over there with the deed and the will whenever someone came by to challenge his right. When the Americans took over Detroit, many of the original ribbon farm deeds were not recognized. But our family always finds a way to protect your rights. After the great fire in 1805, we were able to get the house qualified as one of the donation lots that Negroes were allowed to have. Then as recently as 1815, your deed was re-recorded, along with all others as required that year by the probate court."

"I guess adding my thanks to my grandfather's is still not enough," Isabelle said, in admiration, "but I'll do it all the same."

"My family owes a lifelong debt, from when Bennet Fontaine bailed out my great-grandfather—he kept him from being killed in an Indian raid on Ste. Anne's in 1712. The Bishop there was killed, but Bennet was able to get my ancestor out in time, as they witnessed the worst atrocities. The Foxes were shooting arrows with balls of fire, burning everything down."

"I see," Isabelle said.

"Oaths like that were taken seriously back then. These days, huh?" he shrugged. Just then, another assistant walked into the office with a tray of petite sandwiches and hot tea. He set it down on a nearby table, placed napkins in Isabelle's and Ned's laps, and offered them their plates, which Ned said was fine to place right on his desk.

"No formalities here, young lady," he said. "Get to eating. Josie insists."

"Yes, sir," Isabelle said. "Tell me," she asked between bites, "Do you have the deed now?"

He nodded. "Yes, locked in my desk, until I return it. I want to tell you, however," he continued, "that despite the oath, things have changed drastically since Charles' death."

"Changed?" Isabelle asked.

"Until I found out about you a few weeks ago, plans were set into motion to deed the house over to some investors interested in the land."

"Oh," Isabelle said. "But what about Josie? What about Barry?" She felt guilty for her near relief over the prospect of the house being taken off her hands, without her having to do anything about it herself. But then there was sweet Josie, who was so loyal to Grandfather, and Barry, who would have no one to take care of him.

"Josie has not been told anything yet," Ned answered. "In many ways, we must realize, Josie's job at the house is over anyway. Your beloved grandfather is gone now, and you will be returning to Canada. Your mother has made it clear that she never intends to return," he added matter-of-factly. Isabelle was a little surprised at his bluntness. "As for Barry," he sighed, "there was never much any of us has been able to do. He should have been institutionalized a long time ago, but your grandfather objected, and even Michael did not like the idea."

Isabelle was secretly pleased that Michael perhaps saw Barry in the same light as herself, that Barry was not beyond help. *But was it too late for that?* she wondered, then realized that it all depended on what she decided about the house. *The time had come for me to sign off on the house and head home*, Isabelle thought. *Maybe I could accept Douglas' proposal and plan a wedding for next summer.*

She was startled from her thoughts when Ned slid some papers, pen and an inkwell across the desk. It was the deed to the house, written in calligraphy. The edges of the papers were brown with age. A new sheet of paper was under the stack. Isabelle could see her name in rich black ink, with a blank left for her signature.

"I drew up the new signature page for you," Ned said. Despite it being a chilly morning, he was wiping perspiration from his low forehead. "I'll be returning this to the Register of Deeds after you sign it. They trust it in my care."

Isabelle took up the pen, flipped to the last page, then dipped the pen in the inkwell. She started to sign her name, then suddenly stopped. She could not be sure that she was stopping herself, for it felt as if her hand was being held in an icy grip just inches above the paper.

Ned noticed her abrupt pause, hand mid-air. "Something wrong?" he asked.

Isabelle shook her head slowly. Something was not right. "Ned, I think I need more time," she said, and before she knew it, the pen was out of her hand and back on the desk.

"Now, Isabelle," Ned's words were fast. "I know this is all so much for you, first finding out about your family, then your grandfather dying before you met him, then coming here to a strange city—"

"It's not that, Ned," Isabelle said, as a comforting clarity set in. "This is my family's legacy. My grandfather struggled to keep this house not out of duty to an oath, but out of hope, hope for his own family's future, that they would always have something that is truly theirs. At the very least, I owe him to truly get to know the house he preserved, then make the best decision."

Ned looked pale. "I, well, certainly can respect that, Isabelle. But I must tell you," he added, "do not tarry too long on this. The particular investors that are interested have exciting plans for the house, and even promised to include some sort of historical marker on the property—that can be your gift to your grandfather, ensuring that all who visit that site in the years and generations to come will know what he did. Investors are an impatient lot, though. Remember that you will be leaving soon, and I'm advancing in years. Then, to whom could we entrust everything?" he asked.

Isabelle rose and retrieved her cloak, bonnet and gloves. "I'll remember that, Ned," she said. "Thank you for the nice lunch. I'll be in touch very soon. I'll see my way out."

On the ride back to the Fontaine, Isabelle could not shake the feeling that Ned was pressing her to sell the house quickly. It was true that she would be returning to Canada soon, but why the rush? At the very worst, the deed could be signed over after she returned home, and it could be sent back to Ned. Or he could come and retrieve it from her himself. There was something he was not telling her, and that was worrisome.

When the carriage reached the Fontaine, Isabelle tipped the driver. Noticing Ben in the backyard, she decided to go over and speak to him. He was dressed in a little wool coat and he wore a knitted hat and mittens. He had a stick in his hand and was bent over in the garden path. Marie was nowhere to be seen.

"Hello, Ben," Isabelle said, as she walked up. "Having fun?"

Ben looked at her and did not say a word. He had gone back to being silent with her. He scribbled in the dust. The drawing looked like three wavy lines, one on top of the other.

"What are you drawing?" she asked. "Do you like to draw like Barry?"

Ben looked up at her at that comment, seemed to think about it, then shook his head vigorously.

"All he draws is the same picture of that lady," he said, finally. "He's not supposed to remember her. You are," he said, pointing at Isabelle's chest.

Isabelle shuddered. "What do you mean, Ben?" she asked.

Ben went silent again. Determined to not let those strange, frightening feelings return, Isabelle decided to take leave of Ben for now. As she entered the back door, Isabelle heard what sounded like shouting from the front of the house. It was no voice she recognized.

"Where is she?" he demanded. He had what Isabelle believed was an Irish accent. "You better tell me, Girlie, or that pretty face won't be pretty for long!" Isabelle closed the door behind her quietly, praying that Ben would not come rushing through. Tiptoeing to the kitchen doorway, then up the hall, Isabelle spied a big burly man in a short wool coat standing over Marie. Marie was calm as always, not making a sound as the man barked at her.

"I'll make ya talk." He took Marie's arm and twisted it behind her back. Her long, dark hair swung with the movement, but her facial expression never changed. Outraged at this abuse, Isabelle rushed back to the kitchen, where a shotgun was mounted on a wall in the corner. Taking it down, she opened a few lower cabinets until she found a tin of bullets. Loading the shotgun, she ran down the hallway in a mad rush. When she reached them, the man looked surprised.

"Take your hands off her right now!" Isabelle growled, as she took aim. The man quickly released Marie, who quickly moved behind Isabelle. "Who are you? What business do you have here?" she demanded.

"Oh, a *coloured* with fire," the man grinned. He had reddish hair, a fat neck, and big hands. "They didn't tell me that."

"Either state your business, or I start shooting," she said.

The man was angry again. "It's very simple, Miss," he said. "You are on some prime land, ya know, and it's been high time for all of you Negroes to get out!"

"This is our house by right," Isabelle said. "There is no question of that. We have the deed."

"You think you have the deed," he said. "I've been sent to tell you that is no longer the case. A claim has been made on the house, and I am here to make sure you all get movin', now."

"That can't be true," Isabelle countered. "I just saw the deed today. It is in our possession." She noticed that the man looked bewildered. Just then, she heard Michael and Josie behind her. Never losing focus, she curled her finger tighter on the trigger. "I think you'd better get moving," she told the stranger. "If I see you here again, you'll be feeling a bullet right in your *arse*."

The man's face went white, and Josie stifled a shriek.

As he backed out of the open front door, the man's eyes stayed trained on the shotgun, and had not yet registered Michael's massive size. Michael was trying to push past her to get at the man, but Isabelle stood in his way, shaking her head.

"It's fine, now, Michael," she said, "He's leaving." From the doorway, they could see the man quickly run down the walk and hop on a single horse. He rode away, and did not look back.

Relieved, Isabelle lowered the shotgun slowly. As the anger drained away, Isabelle felt a vague feeling of satisfaction of having almost shot someone, allowing her to vent some anger. But she quickly felt ashamed. She turned to find Michael waiting for her. He offered her his arm. He had a look of astonishment on his face.

"With you, there are surprises upon surprises," he said, admiringly. "Remind me to call upon you whenever I am in trouble."

They gathered in the kitchen. Josie boiled water for tea. Marie ran out the back door to get Ben. They returned with Mr. Alders, who had been working in the orchard.

"Marie just told me what happened," he said, looking worried. "What was this about?"

"The man was trying to throw us all out of the Fontaine," Isabelle said. "Immediately. He said that we no longer had the deed, but I assured him that we had, for I had just seen it."

Josie looked surprised. "You saw it? Today?"

Isabelle nodded. "Yes, Mr. du Roy wanted me to sign it over to some group of investors, but I told him that I wanted more time." The room went silent after she spoke, and Isabelle saw different emotions on every person's face, from sadness on Alder's grizzled face, to anger on Josie's. As usual, Marie was blank, but Michael looked disappointed, and that seemed to bother Isabelle the most.

"I never dreamed Ned would try to sell the house out from under us," Josie said. "But you told him absolutely not, right, Isabelle?" she asked. All eyes were on Isabelle. "Not exactly, Josie," she said. "I told him I would think about it."

Josie was clearly hurt at this comment, for she turned her back on Isabelle to resume making the tea. "What about Barry? What about Michael's plans?" she asked, softly.

"What plans?" Isabelle asked, turning to Michael. It was his turn to look away. "Auntie, don't," he said.

For once, Josie honored Michael's request, and did not force the issue. Alders politely excused himself, saying he wanted to return to his work.

"Well, I didn't say that a final decision had been made yet," Isabelle said, trying to cheer everyone up. "Ned was the one who mentioned it to me. I know the house means so much to you, Josie, but you know that Grandfather's will provides for you for the rest of your life, no matter where you are."

Josie turned back to her. "That is true, Chile, but I promised your granddaddy I would take care of this house. But I also want to finally bring peace to this house. You know what I'm talkin' 'bout. I believe you have a lot to do with that. When you got here, I knew the time had come."

Isabelle held in a groan. She knew what Josie was talking about—the "spirits" in the house. Apparently, Josie did not want to discuss that part in front of Michael, and Isabelle found that interesting. Michael appeared to not have heard them, for he looked lost in thought.

"As I said before," Isabelle said, "No decision has been made, so let's not talk about it right now. We have more immediate concerns. These men are serious about doing us harm. We will have to be on guard around here until—"

"Until when?" Josie asked.

"I don't know." Isabelle sighed.

Isabelle left Michael and Josie in the kitchen to talk, presumably about her. She was being blamed for trying to sell the house, but Ned was the one who'd brought it up. She chided herself for hiding behind what Ned did, knowing that she had been thinking about selling the house long before he'd said a word. Then she'd surprised herself by not jumping on the offer he made. A perfect way out, and she'd turned it down. *Why?* she wondered. And how long would she have to stay here to find out?

A note from Douglas arrived by messenger, advising Isabelle that they would be visiting his friend's farm. They would take a ride on the friend's boat, then picnic on the shore of Lake St. Clair. Isabelle was not in the mood for this, but she did not want to disappoint him. Finding the music room, Isabelle decided to play a couple of Chopin etudes, just to keep her skills up. She dared not attempt to work on her piece, noting that she'd had enough stress for one day. It was growing dark, so she decided to light a couple of the table lamps. As she began to play, she felt better, and as she continued to play some familiar drills, she felt more relaxed. . . .

~   ~   ~

Celeste was so glad to be able to play again. Sitting before the ivory and ebony keys, she felt restored to where she rightly belonged. Guests were always stunned upon first exposure to Celeste's talent; she'd hear whispers while she played, comments like, "I never would have guessed a negress could learn something like this—I don't even think they have trained chimpanzees this well!" or, "Sieur Fontaine had better watch letting his slaves have too much leeway—she is beautiful and all, but too much training and she'll be, well, discontent." Ignoring those comments, Celeste was grateful to play whenever she could. Hosting soirees, Pere enjoyed unsettling his friends, casually strolling over to the most shocked guests with his arms clasped behind his back, a little hop in his step, asking, "So, what do you think? I taught her myself."

Her playing often brought tears to the eyes of many, and glares from others. She knew they all resented her ease in pulling their emotions to the surface. This power over others fascinated Celeste and she wielded it as her aegis, shielding her soul from the degradation of being owned by her own "family." As Celeste played she thought of Pere, close to death in his room upstairs. Celeste wondered if he could hear her playing in his deep sleep. He was clinging to life long enough to ensure that Louis was married, and Celeste was certain it was his last effort to protect her.

It had been weeks since Celeste was allowed to come near the music room. Briane was at the house more frequently now, and if Louis was not around, Celeste was ordered away from the piano, and sometimes, out of the house. On those nights, Celeste had to stay in the shack with the other slaves. They loved to see her in the gloomy darkness, so they could taunt her mercilessly.

"Ah, so the Queen has come to visit her subjects." Silas would always begin first. The other slaves would laugh. A couple of the other young women always cornered Celeste and shoved her around. They took rusted shears to rip her silk dresses. Eulalie would gesture wildly in her friend's defense, but Celeste did not bother to fight for herself. Saying little on those cold nights, Celeste hid her proper speech. The slaves usually left Celeste alone after a while, however, probably tiring of taunting a fellow captive, no matter her elevated status on the farm.

Lately, however, Celeste's burden was lighter, because she could watch the new slave, Jacques. From the day he arrived, Jacques was admired by the other slaves; Celeste even heard Evangeline speaking his praises, for he was handsome and courteous. Even the white habitants buying the new, swift boats were impressed with Jacques, and word went around that he built beautiful, strong boats. A few times, he was coaxed into telling tales of his worldly adventures as the captain of his own ship, The Therese. He was also an expert card player, so the men enjoyed that.

"Tell us again about the Seychelles, your homeland, Jacques," Caleb would beg as Jacques passed thin cards around on the floor. Unlike the main house, the slave quarters were drafty. In the place of wood floors, there was beaten earth; instead of glass windows from Montreal, there were animal skins scraped thin enough to see through.

"My island is one of a chain of islands, and each one has white sand beaches kissing sparkling blue waters," Jacques always began, as if he was telling a fairy tale to small children. When he talked, Celeste could hear a faint singsong accent. "We have tall coconut trees and juicy mangos. My people are fisherman and boat builders by trade. In the sea are fish of every color in the rainbow, and giant tortoises walk the shore. Our people feel blessed by the sun."

"Wow," Caleb said every time he heard this, and Celeste was sad that the young man would never get to see this for himself.

Celeste heard from Evangeline that while on a fishing expedition near home, Jacques' ship had been taken by a massive French slave ship. Many of his crew lost their lives fighting to stay free, but Jacques backed down when his beloved younger sister, Therese, had been taken hostage. The French wanted the ship more than they wanted slaves that time, but they realized the profit of making a strong man with skills their slave.

Eulalie had snuggled close to Celeste. She darted her eyes from Caleb to Jacques, then blinked hard; to Celeste, this meant, "Tell me more about him."

"After returning to France with Jacques and Therese in tow," Celeste whispered while Jacques told Caleb his story again, "they'd set off for Montreal a year later. The only way to keep Jacques cooperative was to barter on the safety of Therese. He then fell into the hands of Duchene. No one at Maison knows of Therese's whereabouts, Evangeline says, but she has a feeling Louis knows quite a bit."

Jacques nudged Celeste with his hip as he talked to Caleb, letting her know he could hear her whispers to Eulalie. He was seated next to Celeste in the slave quarters, as always. The women hated Celeste even more for that reason; they could not get the captivating Jacques' attention if they tried. All taunts and mockery of Celeste stopped immediately, however, with one look from Jacques.

Every time she could be near him, Celeste enjoyed Jacques' attention. She always looked forward to watching him work on the boats at the river's edge. As the mornings grew warmer, she spied him shirtless, his back muscles rippling as he sanded down birch bark with even, masterful strokes. If Evangeline was in a good mood, she allowed Celeste to take him water. Whenever he took the ladle from her, Jacques took slow, purposeful draughts, his hungry eyes telling Celeste that he'd like to take her in the same manner.

The only person who did not adore Jacques was Louis, which was no surprise. There was nothing he could do about it, for Pere had paid a high purchase price. Always challenging Jacques, Louis' darkest nature showed itself. Celeste watched him push Jacques as far as he could, but Louis lost every battle. When he tried to supervise the building of Jacques' new boat the other morning, Jacques shamed him with a quick comment about Louis' getting his "pale ass" burned by the sun. Celeste had never before seen Louis that red in the face before, even at his angriest.

To her relief today, Louis was gone to the fort. He had taken Briane along, as well as Suzette, who had made the acquaintance of a handsome young soldier. Evangeline had given Celeste permission to play for only a little while, as the house would not be empty for long. Celeste had her eyes closed while she played, so she did not notice someone standing in the doorway. When she stopped playing, she heard soft clapping. It was Jacques. He gave a slight smile.

"That was beautiful," he said. His voice was velvety smooth. Celeste was sure that he was probably a good singer, if he ever sang.

She nodded her greeting. "Thank you."

"Evangeline was kind enough to offer me some lemonade." His eyes captured and held Celeste's own.

She felt short of breath. "I know that it is difficult to come to a new farm, not knowing anyone here—"

"I have already met the only person I want to know," Jacques cut in. "And she is in this room. I do not wish to speak of sad times, Cherie, just play some more. For me."

As she resumed playing, Celeste felt such an overwhelming feeling of closeness to this stranger in the doorway. She felt that they already knew everything about each other, that words were so unnecessary between them. As she played, she heard his soft humming, the vibrations surrounding them both, protecting them from their shared circumstance. She could still feel his warmth around her when she looked up again, but he was gone.

~   ~   ~

"They would adore you in Paris." Michael was in the music room's doorway. Isabelle felt dismay, realizing that her mind had wandered off again to some far away place and people. Michael was watching her closely, for she had not said anything in return.

Finally, Isabelle found her voice. "Thank you." Her vision clearing, she noticed it was now completely dark outside. She rose to close all of the pairs of drapes around the room. Michael came in and assisted her. For once, he did not appear to be irritated.

"I must also compliment you on how you handled that man earlier today," he added. Again, Isabelle was surprised at his friendliness. "Where did you learn to handle guns?" he asked.

"My stepfather taught me," she answered. "He would take me out in the yard, and show me how to shoot. My mother was absolutely horrified at the thought of her delicate daughter doing such a manly thing, so I really took an interest in it then." She smiled, and Michael sounded as if he was trying to chuckle. "But I'm glad he taught me. Though I never thought I would need that teaching down here. It's come in handy before, though." Isabelle stopped herself, thinking she was telling too much.

Michael was patient. "Do go on. I take it you've had to shoot before," he said.

Isabelle nodded slowly. "Yes. Richard and I. . .well, Richard was my fiance. We both met through our association with an abolitionist group. We made a good pair, you see, young and idealistic. We had our fair share of shootouts trying to help slaves escaping to Canada. Richard forbade me to come to the South with him, so I always helped on the last part of the stretch, on the Canadian side. There are always slave catchers in the northern states, but many people do not know that there are slave catchers waiting in Canada as well," she added.

"No, I did not know," Michael said, looking intrigued.

They took two facing chairs. In the evening lamplight, the room had a hushed quality about it. Isabelle felt very comfortable about talking then, because Michael seemed to be a good listener.

"I was involved in the anti-slavery movement in Niagara," she began. "We saved many former slaves from being returned to slavery. Niagara is now one of the sanctuaries in Upper Canada for runaway slaves from America. Canada was moving to abolish slavery long before the British government did away with it. But there was one poor woman a few years ago, though," Isabelle said, her voice trailing off.

"Do go on," Michael urged. "This is fascinating."

"What I am about to say is not fascinating," Isabelle said, "for it was a great travesty. Even though the Coloured Corps had been put in place there in Queenston Heights and Stoney Creek, a young woman was lost. A Negress had escaped to Queenston and was living there in peace when she was kidnapped by a slavecatcher, but that time, the people stood by and did nothing. Richard and I had just gotten wind of the situation, and were trying to get there as fast as we could. But we were too late. She was put onto a ferry boat and that was the last time anyone saw her."

"I don't understand, Isabelle," Michael said, leaning in. "You were not there when it happened. There was nothing you could have done for her."

Isabelle sighed. "That is my point. I was not there."

Michael reached over to take her right hand. Isabelle allowed him, feeling as if it was the most natural thing in the world. Through his hand, she drew strength.

"You are too hard on yourself," he said.

"I thank you, Michael," Isabelle said. "It feels good to talk about this with someone. Bess is my friend, but she is always afraid for me, and, of course, Mother feels that my revolutionary activities could hurt the precious family reputation."

Michael grimaced. "I, too, tried to do what I could for the cause."

Isabelle nodded in earnest. "I remember Josie telling me that you were involved with the Blackburn incident. "

At this statement, Michael's humor died away, and his eyes took on the hardness she had witnessed on the ferry.

"That day, I'm afraid, is one I am not able to discuss," he said, his voice distant.

Isabelle could feel the loss immediately. She did not want to lose the connection they had made, and felt betrayed by his refusal to share his story.

"Michael, tell me what happened," Isabelle pleaded. "I know it was probably awful, but it would be good to discuss it. Even a strong man like yourself should not have to hold everything back all the time."

Michael's hardness turned to sadness.

"Sweet Isabelle," was all he said before he rose to walk out of the room, leaving her behind.

CHAPTER SEVEN

Morning found Isabelle sitting on the side of her bed, gloomy again. She had been wrong to think she would have one night free of the strange dreams. At least, she thought, without a drink. Rising and dressing slowly, Isabelle was not looking forward to Douglas' cheerfulness. Not wanting to worry him with her problems, however, she would force herself to be cheerful for his sake.

Donning a tan silk carriage dress, Isabelle wrapped herself in a short brown velvet mantle and matching bonnet. After reaching the first floor, Isabelle found Josie in the kitchen, packing a wicker picnic basket with bread, a hunk of cheese, some freshly fried chicken, and rich, red apples.

"Is this for the picnic?" Isabelle asked, surprised.

Josie gave her a quick smile. "You modern young women of today don't know how to pack a nice picnic," she said. "I thought I would help you out." Isabelle noticed Josie's wistful look, and thought that maybe Josie was remembering some picnic from her youth, or the idea that she did not have a daughter of her own. Thinking of her own mother, Isabelle knew that Rosalie would not have bothered. Overcome with emotion, Isabelle rushed over and kissed Josie on one smooth cheek.

"Douglas is already waiting for you in the front," Josie said. "Remember to mind your manners," she added, as she handed Isabelle the packed basket.

Grateful, Isabelle took the basket. "Thank you, and I will," she said, smiling.

Feeling better about her adventure, Isabelle made her way up the hall to the front parlor, where she heard Douglas' voice. She was surprised to see Marie there. The two of them appeared to have been in a serious conversation. Marie quickly walked out of the room, feather duster in hand.

"Are you ready to leave, my angel?" Douglas asked, smiling.

Isabelle wondered what the two of them could have been discussing, but decided it was not important. She took his arm, and they were out of the front door.

During the carriage ride, Douglas explained to Isabelle that the friend they were visiting had newly acquired a farm along Lake St. Clair.

"Almost 500 acres!" he exclaimed.

Sometimes, Isabelle found it annoying how much Douglas seemed to admire other people's prosperity, but she could understand why. Douglas' family did not have much, with his father working in the factories and dying at an early age. His mother died soon after, and Douglas was left to make his way as a young man in Detroit. A good student, he worked as a clerk, where he'd learned how business deals were made.

Douglas had told Isabelle with pride how he talked himself into his first deal, management of a rooming house that he would later buy off his partner's hands. Several acquisitions later, Douglas found himself becoming a well-known entrepreneur. When he added entertainment as a venture, he'd crossed paths with Isabelle.

Douglas' carriage pulled in front of an expansive farm property, complete with cows, horses, and pigs in a trough. Soft grasses reached a sandy shoreline. In the distance was a waiting sailboat. As they stepped from the carriage, two people rushed up to meet them, a young man and woman. It was breezy off the shore, and both women had to hang onto their bonnets. The sky was darkening by the minute.

Douglas made the introductions. Francis and Gamelin Bridgeforth were newly married and given the farm as a wedding gift from his parents. Pretty with upswept dark hair and a sprinkle of freckles across her nose and curiously dark eyes, Gamelin gently chastised Isabelle.

"Now, what did you go to all of that trouble for? I have an entire feast laid out for us," she said. "But that's okay. Your food will probably taste better than mine!"

Douglas and Isabelle followed them to the shoreline, although she did not feel good about how the sky was changing.

"I hate to say this, Douglas," Isabelle whispered as they followed Francis and Gamelin, "but the weather looks a little threatening."

Douglas looked up at the sky briefly as he walked, never losing step. "It's nothing, Isabelle," he said, dismissively. "Things will lighten up once we get in the boat." Isabelle had worn tall boots, and was glad, because her feet were sinking into the sand. The men helped her and Gamelin into a small paddle boat. Gamelin had Isabelle sit next to her on one side. Francis and Douglas untied the mooring, shoved the boat into the water, then climbed in. They paddled on either side out into the deep water, then anchored it. A young man appeared on the deck of the sailboat, where he tossed over a rope ladder.

The men helped the women climb aboard, and the young man, Pete, pulled each the rest of the way. Pete spoke with Francis briefly. Isabelle could see him pointing at the sky; Douglas rushed over, pressed a coin in the lad's hand, and sent him on his way. Pete waved one last time to everyone before climbing down into the paddleboat to return to shore.

"This is our last excursion for the year," Francis began, as he took the helm. "The weather is changing, and winter will be here soon. Gamelin and I love to go boating, so it's sad to not be able to do so," he added.

"But, darling, do we not find other ways to enjoy ourselves?" Gamelin asked, playfully. Francis blushed at his young wife's tart remark, then grinned.

"We certainly do, My Dear," he laughed.

For Isabelle, it was nice to see such a happy young couple, a couple free of worries and frightful happenings. Isabelle looked at Douglas then. His eyes were off on the endless water, and he looked deep in thought as he paddled. She wondered what he could be thinking about. Was he thinking about their own future together? Isabelle had a feeling that was not the case. She reached across to touch his arm. He stirred, then smiled at her.

"What are you thinking about?" she asked.

He smiled at her then. "Just our own future, Isabelle. I am sure that I could make you happy."

Isabelle was touched by his certainty. She smiled back, nodding. "I am starting to think that you can," she said. Being out on the water, away from trouble, and with friends, Isabelle found herself getting caught up in the moment. She gave Douglas a seductive look. He looked pleasantly surprised for a moment, eyebrows raised. He grinned, promising an interesting carriage ride home.

The sailing was smooth at first, but once they were several miles out, the change in the weather was drastic. The overcast sky turned nearly black, and the water's waves became choppy. Isabelle found herself holding the side of the boat. Gamelin had begun handing out the lunch of ham sandwiches to everyone, but each time she stood, she lost her footing. Francis held the wheel more tightly, and was entirely focused on the steering now.

"I think we should start thinking about heading back, I'm afraid," he said. "I am so sorry."

"Is it that bad?" Douglas asked. "I've seen skies like this before, it could blow over."

Francis looked uncertain. "Well, it's true you have more sailing experience than myself, so do you think we could press on?" he asked.

Douglas nodded. "I think we will be fine."

Isabelle turned to Douglas. "You never mentioned knowing how to sail," she said, admiringly.

Douglas shrugged it off. "Any entrepreneur has to keep himself abreast of the activities of the wealthy," Douglas said. "I just do not own my own vessel, is all," he added, tersely.

Looking at the sky again, Isabelle surmised that even the wealthy would not allow themselves to be caught out in a storm like this. Despite Douglas' assurances, things had turned far worse. The rain was coming down heavily now, and everyone was soaked. The boat was creaking from side to side. They were several miles out; the land was barely visible. Francis fought with the white sail. When Douglas took the wheel from Francis, Isabelle was sure they would be quickly returned to shore, but that did not happen. A large wave rolled underneath the boat and practically turned it over.

"Francis!" Gamelin screamed, as the bottom of her dress was submerged on the low side of the boat that had been dipped. Francis rushed to pull her closer towards the center of the boat. Isabelle was near Douglas at the helm, her back to him, where he'd told her to stand, for balance. She tried to clutch the rail as the boat dipped again, this time at the front, where she was standing. The hard rain made her hands slick, and to her dismay, the pain in her left hand flared up, keeping her from getting a better grip.

"Douglas!" she shouted over the waves. "Can you get us back to shore?" she asked, looking down into the dark water. "Is there anything else we can do?"

She had planned to turn around so that she could hear Douglas better, but Isabelle never had the chance. As the front of the boat was still leaning forward, Isabelle felt a great, sudden pressure against her back. Before she knew it, she tumbled headfirst into the water. The last thing she heard was frantic voices screaming her name.

~   ~   ~

"Celeste, tell me something," Suzette said as the two young women shared a seat on a stone bench in the garden. Celeste was scribbling in the journal

Pere had given her before he fell ill.

"Yes, Suzette?" Celeste asked. It had been unreasonably cool this spring day, a light breeze with a chilly edge.

"What is it like to be in love?" Suzette asked.

Celeste turned to look into Suzette's rosy, questioning face. She hesitated before answering. Thinking about her early feelings for Louis, Celeste cringed inwardly in embarrassment over how infantile her feelings had been for him. Her feelings for Jacques, on the other hand, were so powerful she had no words to describe them. She just knew that she loved him, and he loved her.

"How would I know anything about love, Suzette?" Celeste asked, cryptically. Celeste was taken by surprise when Suzette punched her in the arm. Given the sudden dark turn in Louis' behavior towards her, Celeste wondered if Suzette held the same kind of violence within herself.

"Don't play games with me, Celeste," Suzette said, laughing. "Everyone around her knows you and Jacques love each other."

"Everyone?" Celeste repeated weakly.

Suzette nodded, and her eyes told Celeste that she shared the same worry that Louis knew as well. She took Celeste's hand in sympathy. "I can't imagine what it is like for you and Jacques. If things were in my hands. . . ." her voice trailed away. "I can't set you free, and odds are Jacques will never be set free. Pere needs you both. He loves you as a daughter, and he feels he needs Jacques to save the farm with his skills.

"Believe me, I have tried to get Louis to concentrate on his alliance with Damselle Briane," she continued. "I try my hardest to remind him that you, he and I are all friends, and nothing more."

Celeste was touched by Suzette's words, but she knew that the young girl could not help her. Louis made it clear to her the other night that his mind was on one thing, claiming Celeste as his own, even in the face of scorn and ridicule by polite French society. She had even heard the parish priest, Father Levette, reminding Louis about his obligations to the family and not to scandalize them. As much as she hated Briane, Celeste had come to dread whenever the curly-haired witch was not around, because that meant Louis would be on her trail.

Louis grew more brutish by the day, groping her and pinning her against walls in the hallways. He told her that he always got what he wanted, and denying him only made it worse for herself. She was powerless.

"Suzette, you have not let me answer you about what love is," Celeste said, trying to change the subject. Suzette's face lit up, Celeste's plight easily forgotten.

"I've met a wonderful man!" Suzette gushed. "I saw him at my friend Genevieve's dance last fall, and he has been asking about me. He is a soldier at the fort, and at first Pere was not so sure it would be a good match, but he has recently reconsidered, since he has a chance for promotion to Commandant at a new fort that will be built soon. You haven't been to the fort in a while, but Pierre's one of the soldiers responsible for walking the palisades around the fort, fiftenn feet high, so they can see over the walls."

Suzette rambled on about her beau, and about what dress she would wear when he came calling tomorrow night. Celeste was genuinely happy for Suzette. At least someone would get to be happy.

Suzette's happiness was overshadowed by Pere's impending death a couple of days later. He had taken a turn for the worst the night before, and the doctor, who had been summoned from Montreal, could do nothing else for him. Pere had gone into a deep sleep from which the doctor doubted he would awaken. That night, Briane was there, so Celeste spent the night outdoors.

The other slaves talked about Pere in hushed whispers, and a few tears. They belonged to him as property, but he had never beaten them, and he let them share in the best of the crops for food. With Louis in control, the future was uncertain for them all.

Celeste leaned on Jacques shoulder in the growing darkness of the slave quarters. He stroked her hair and hummed to her to ease her sadness. Eulalie was still in the house with Evangeline, on the deathwatch. Pere had asked for Celeste the day before, but Louis forbade it; Celeste knew it was because one of Pere's dying wishes would be that Louis leave her alone. By keeping Pere and Celeste apart, Louis would not have to honor any so-called wishes.

"I know that Sieur Fontaine was like a father to you," Jacques said. "The only father you ever knew."

Celeste nodded, wiping away tears. "Yes, I will miss him. He taught me how to make music."

"That he did," Jacques agreed.

"Yeah, and Louis is going to teach you some other things," came a voice from the dark, followed by snickers. It was the two women, Sally and Millie, the ones who always tormented her.

"What did you say?" Jacques roared, and the entire house went silent. The cackling women whimpered their apologies and turned in for the night. Silas and Jonas busied themselves with their carving by the fireplace. Jacques *took a blanket and pulled it around himself and Celeste.*

"Cherie, I can't tell you what the future will bring," he began. "I only know that whatever happens, I will be with you. Always. Even if I have to kill Louis."

Later that night, after everyone had fallen asleep, Celeste was awakened when the front door swung open. Moonlight burst in, temporarily blinding her. When she could see again, Louis was standing in the doorway, drunk. He looked haggard, with his thick hair standing on end, and his shirt half open. In his hands was his favorite pistol. He surveyed her like a wolf about to devour his prey. She smoothed back her unbound hair and looked down at where she lay, on Jacques' chest. The minute she'd moved, Jacques had sleepily grasped her arm tightly, as if to never let her go.

"Celeste," Louis said from the doorway, "come here." It was something about the way he said it that made Celeste shiver. Jacques, now awake, seemed to sense where this was going as well, for he jumped to his feet and stood in front of Celeste, blocking her from Louis' sight.

Celeste hesitated, not wanting to leave Jacques' side, but she knew if she did not comply, it would be trouble for Jacques, who was speaking his own death just then.

"What do you want, young Master Louis?" he growled. Celeste felt her insides freeze. Mon Dieu, she thought. Jacques wouldn't dare challenge Louis right there!

The redness of Louis' face was richer and deeper than the night.

"Jacques, this does not concern you," Louis said, slowly. "I've come to take Celeste to Pere's bedside to say goodbye. He has passed on."

Celeste let out a sigh. "So, he is gone," she whispered. She felt sadness, of course, but she was more concerned with what Louis was up to.

"Celeste, I will not ask again," Louis said. Just then, some of the other slaves had awakened and were watching them silently. Louis called out to two of his drinking friends, Desmond and William, who had been staying at the farm the past few days. Larger than Jacques, Desmond stumbled over to join Louis in the doorway. Louis reached in to grab Celeste's arm.

"Do it, and you die," Jacques whispered; this gave Louis pause, but Desmond was undaunted.

"C'm ere, girl, he wants ya!" he laughed, and pulled Celeste through the doorway with one quick jerk.

Jacques was right behind her, but Louis had swiftly taken hold of Celeste.

When Jacques stormed towards them, Desmond had swung around behind Jacques, locking his arm around Jacques' throat. Quickly, Jacques stepped back into Desmond, swung him around and slammed him to the ground like a rag doll. Desmond lay stunned, and William went to help him up. Jacques resumed his advance on Louis.

"Louis, no!" Celeste begged, for she knew how quickly Louis liked to reach for his pistol.

"Don't worry, dear Celeste," Louis whispered in her ear, "I will not kill this man. My father has left too much in his gifted brown hands. We need his miraculous skills, for now, at least," he added. "But he will be trained before it's over."

"We'll see who shall be trained, young Louis," Jacques shouted. Celeste could hear the other slaves begging Jacques from the doorway to stop and come back inside.

Just as Jacques took another step forward, Louis raised the pistol. Celeste tried to pry it from him, but William, who was not as drunk, was able to skirt around quickly enough to tackle her to the ground. As Celeste struggled to get back to her feet, she heard a single gunshot, then two more in succession. She rushed to Jacques on the ground, bleeding, his glaring eye strained on Louis. Louis simply stood over him, the pistol smoking.

Someone in the slave house screamed. Desmond reached down and scooped up a screaming and kicking Celeste. As she was ripped away from Jacques' side, she felt like a part of her was being ripped away. Louis turned and walked off with William, Desmond carrying Celeste over his shoulder, following.

~   ~   ~

Isabelle took gulps of air when she reached the surface of the lake. The rain was still pouring heavily, so she could not see anything. She tried to call out, but her calls were swallowed by the howling winds. She was not a good swimmer, but Isabelle used everything she could remember to try and stay afloat. After a short time, however, her legs grew tired, and she started to feel that this might be the end. Surprisingly, she thought about Mother first, about how she'd wished they could have been closer. She then thought about Michael, who would have scolded her for coming out here in the first place. She envisioned Maison Fontaine then, with its sparse beauty, strange lineage, and its unfinished business. Choking, Isabelle realized she would regret not having put that part of her past to rest.

Then she saw Jacques. He was in the water with her, his hands outstretched to her.

"Cherie, come with me," he mouthed. "It is time." At first, Isabelle reached for him, his handsome face very serene and loving. This would be a good way to die, she thought deliriously, with the love of my life. Isabelle then shook her head in confusion, for she did not feel it down in her bones; no, what she imagined she felt for Jacques was more of a shadow of love, a powerful, but empty feeling, like a half-remembered dream.

Briefly, Michael's image came into view, an image of him standing in the front yard in the sunlight, and Isabelle's heart seemed to stop at that moment, as a different, soul-stirring longing overtook her. She realized she would miss Michael. Isabelle quickly backed away from the waiting Jacques, whose face was unchanged.

"No," she coughed. "You are not real. Let me be!"

Turning in the direction she hoped was the shore, Isabelle swam dazedly towards what she hoped was the shore, and to Michael. It was not her time. *At least*, she thought, *not yet*.

~   ~   ~

Celeste was thrown onto the floor of the carriage house. William had gone back up to the house, muttering that he did not want to know anything. Desmond, with a wicked grin, reached down to caress Celeste's cheek. She turned away in disgust. Louis pulled on Desmond's shoulder, but she could see that he had a sudden look of uncertainty on his face, realizing that if Desmond wanted to do something, he would be powerless to stop him. Slowly, Desmond got to his feet and patted Louis on the shoulder.

"Lucky man," he said, and walked out, closing the door behind him.

Louis turned to Celeste, then helped her from the floor. She made a move for the door, but he stopped her.

"Now, now," he cooed. He spun her around, then began planting hard kisses on her neck. "Finally, we can be together," he breathed in her hair.

Celeste shivered, thinking about how Pere's body was not yet cold, but she was out there with the true corpse.

"Louis, please," she pled. "Pere would not approve of this."

"Pere is gone, and he knew that we were meant for each other!" Louis shouted. "You used to believe that, too, Celeste."

"No, Louis, we were so young then. We did not know what we were doing!

I know what true love is now, and I do not feel that way for you." The minute she said it, Celeste realized she'd sealed her fate.

Louis' face hardened into a mask, a youthful boy's disappointment turning into a man's cold rage.

"Oh, when I'm through with you, Bright Eyes, you will know what true love feels like, a mixture of pleasure and pain," Louis said, knocking Celeste to the floor with one hard back-handed slap across her jaw. Within two deft moves, Louis pounced on her, ripping a stunned Celeste's undergarments to shreds.

He forced his way inside her. As he tore into her, each thrust more savage than the last, Celeste shed silent tears for the loss of a pitiful young life. She was the pet of the family all through her childhood, and now she was Louis' whore. She wept for her lost dream of a tender wedding night with Jacques.

When Louis moaned and fell off of her in a sweat-soaked stupor, Celeste felt hot blood pooling in the folds of her petticoat. In some ways, she thought absently, being treated special in her early years made this inevitable moment far worse. As a child under Pere's love and protection, she had known what it was like to be a real person, a person with a name, and dreams and desires. Now, she was nothing. No one.

~   ~   ~

When Isabelle awakened again, she was lying face down in sand, its soggy grittiness rubbing her cheek raw. Sitting up, she looked around, then screamed when she remembered the horror of her last vision as she swam for her life. Looking back out on the water, she could not believe she had made her way back to the shore. The water was dark, as black as night, but she could hear the waves, the same waves that tried to swallow her alive. Looking from side to side, Isabelle found no one around, just the moon and the light rain tapping her face.

Her vision blurry, Isabelle tried to stand, but could not. Shivering, she wrapped her arms around herself and lay back on the sand in a soggy ball. The wind was still howling, and her teeth chattered. She thought about how Douglas must think she was dead, and how all their plans were ruined. She then thought about Michael being disgusted with her, having died on the shore like some beached seal. She was too tired to get up and press on.

Jacques' face came to her again, floating before her eyes.

"My precious Celeste," he whispered. She felt a cold caress across her forehead. Isabelle wanted to tell him that her name was not Celeste, but she could only manage to mumble. Just then, a warm feeling seemed to cover her from head to foot, filling her with a pleasing sense of comfort that shielded her from her dark spot on the sand. She could see large rocks in the dark beyond, but within her cocoon there was light. Isabelle felt safe then. She felt loved, loved beyond words.

Isabelle heard buzzing as if from a distance, then the buzzing became louder. Opening her eyes, she saw Gamelin smiling at her in relief.

"Francis," she called out, "she's awake."

In rushed Francis, who was ashen, with Douglas on his heels.

Douglas looked afraid. Isabelle realized that she must be inside of Gamelin and Francis' house. Sunlight was beaming through the windows, and robust, large leafy plants surrounded her. Another woman, much older than them all, stood in a corner. She was wearing a shawl, and her hair was jet black. Somehow, Isabelle sensed she was up in age, but the woman's face showed no wrinkles.

"What happened?" Isabelle asked.

"We thought you were lost, for sure," Francis began. "We looked and looked for you," he said, sadly. Isabelle could tell that Francis probably felt guilty for having made it back without her. "Gamelin went back out one more time at first light. She found you, not too far from here, but none of us could believe it, for we had searched there before and found nothing. You appear this morning, like a mermaid from the sea." Isabelle reached out to take his hand and squeezed it, letting him know that she understood.

Douglas dove to his knees at her side, tears in his eyes.

"You just don't know, Isabelle, how we called for you. You went over so fast, I could not believe my eyes. It was my fault I had everyone in such terrible danger." Francis put one hand on Douglas' shoulder. "There was no way any of us could have known a storm like that was coming," he said.

Gamelin ushered the two men from the room. Douglas eyed the old woman as he left, and she watched him very hard. Gamelin returned to Isabelle's side.

"You need your rest. Is there anything I can get for you? I hope you do not mind wearing one of my dresses, though it's probably a little too long for you," she smiled. She turned back to look at the old woman, who had remained silent all this time. "How does she look to you, Nanette?"

The woman said softly, "She just needs some rest. And some hot tea. What ails her does not come from the storm."

Isabelle was perplexed by what the woman had just uttered, but she wanted to let Gamelin know how she appreciated finding her. "Thank you, Gamelin," Isabelle said, "for everything."

"Think nothing of it," Gamelin said, "for we have to look out for each other."

Isabelle raised one eyebrow at the mention of 'we'. What did Gamelin mean?

"I, too, share your secret, Isabelle," Gamelin said.

Isabelle panicked, wondering if she had been babbling in her sleep about Jacques, or about this Celeste woman. Gamlin must be horrified to have a madwoman in her house.

"I am also of a mixed heritage," Gamelin continued. "I walk carefully among the other, say, 'ladies of distinction' in our fair town. But Nanette here knows my real story, because she is my grandmother."

Nanette huffed at that comment, then walked out of the room. It was not lost on Isabelle that the woman had deliberately kept her distance. Isabelle asked Gamelin about this.

Gamelin looked troubled. "We are of Fox and Sauk descent. The Fox were chased her after the massacre at the fort a century ago. The Jesuits hated our people, but there are always two sides to every story," she said. "Grandmother is considered an elder in our tribe. She raised me and my sister after the cholera killed our parents back in '32. Others in our tribe around these parts still listen to her wisdom. When I found you, I sent for her to bring her herbs, in case you needed medicine.

"When she first saw you," Gamelin hesitated, "she said there was something very wrong with you. I pressed her to explain, but she could not quite express it herself, which was odd."

"Odd?" Isabelle asked. "In what way?"

"She said she could only say that you had died a long time ago, and that you should not be here. Now."

CHAPTER EIGHT

What is it about old ladies and scary stories? Isabelle wondered as she snuggled under a blanket to warm up. Gamelin had left to check on the teakettle. *First, Josie, now Nanette. They think the absolute worst about me, but they don't even know me.* But the more Isabelle considered this latest warning, the more she worried. It was no mere coincidence that all of these odd happenings always seemed to have something to do with her. To make things worse, she still felt that time was short.

The parlor door opened, and in walked Nanette. She was carrying a tray with a teapot and two delicate white porcelain cups. Setting the tray down, she pulled up a chair opposite Isabelle.

The woman never said a word, so several minutes went by until Isabelle could not stand it any longer.

"Is there something you wish to say to me, Nanette?" Isabelle said not too kindly. She was tired.

The old woman's expression was still statue-like. "How long have you been dreaming?" she asked.

Isabelle froze. How would this woman know about that? "I beg your pardon?" Isabelle asked.

"Don't play with me," the old woman warned.

Startled, Isabelle heeded the warning. "I...I have been dreaming things for about a couple of months, before I came to Detroit. But since I have been here, I see things all the time, whether I am awake, or asleep. People that I think I know, but I have never met."

The old woman nodded. "I see." She pulled her shawl tighter again. "I am sorry for what you have been going through, and I wish you the best with it. You see, you are being shown these things for a reason. Some terrible thing happened to you and two others long ago, and your souls are not at rest. He is very angry," she said.

"'He?'" Isabelle bolted upright. "How do you know about Jacques?" she asked, breathless.

"So, that is his name," Nanette nodded. "I have seen this Jacques, on the shore, from time to time, for all of my life. He walks up and down, up and down, but never makes a sound. Now that you have come back from the river, he is trying to claim you again as his own."

"His own?" Isabelle echoed. "From what I can tell, he lived a long time ago. His clothes are ancient."

"He did live long ago," Nanette agreed. "But so did you." Before Isabelle could open her mouth in obvious protest, Nanette put a hand up to silence her. "I know that you are Isabelle, born into this place in time, but your ancestor walked this land before you, a young woman who looks so much like you. Her agony is so strong, and Jacques' rage is so great that it has outlived them both. They are looking for each other."

"And I'm in the middle of it," Isabelle filled in. Saying those words aloud made Isabelle shiver, for they had such finality to them. Being caught in the middle meant there was no sure way out.

For the first time, Nanette's harsh expression turned sympathetic. "You are not her, but as you are one of her line, you have been chosen to remember.

"I also know that cycles repeat themselves," Nanette continued, "but a bad cycle like this must end. When I see you, Isabelle, I see death all around you, and that you do not have much time left on this earth. There's something else that I can't put my finger on regarding someone close to you, some other, more immediate danger," she added.

"So, you believe that this Jacques means me harm?" Isabelle asked.

Nanette frowned, looking uncertain. "I'm not sure. I do know that Jacques believes you are the woman he seeks, and he is determined to take you back with him. You cannot let this happen. You must remember in order to survive."

After a hasty goodbye early the next morning, Isabelle and Douglas were on their way back to Maison Fontaine. Gamelin and Francis gave tearful hugs at the door, but Nanette would not say goodbye. The old woman looked stricken when Isabelle thanked her for the entertaining "ghost" story, and that she would be sure to tell it around a campfire one day. Her arms folded over her slight chest, Nanette mouthed one word to Isabelle from the door:

"Remember."

As their carriage took off, Isabelle mulled over Nanette's outrageous tale. She'd had a dreamless sleep last night that distanced her from her worries, making the visions more like a long-forgotten nightmare. Isabelle was not willing to believe those dream-people were real. *Perhaps I read some book long ago, and was suddenly remembering parts of it*, she reasoned. *Maybe I am simply exhausted from touring and need a good year off to rest fully.* "Maybe," she muttered, discouraged.

Douglas held her hand the entire way. He watched her intently, as if he was going to be watching her every move from now on. Isabelle found the attention too much to take at the moment.

"Douglas, everything will be fine," she said. "You are worrying too much. Accidents happen."

"I know," he said, "but it just makes me realize I do not know what I would do if you were taken from me. Which brings me to ask for your hand, right now. In this carriage, before you get home," he blurted out. "I love you, Isabelle, and I want you with me, for all time." Cupping her face in both of his hands, he looked deeply into her eyes.

Panicked, Isabelle suddenly saw Michael's face again, but she shook her head in denial. Michael had no place in her thoughts, particularly now. Michael had never expressed any interest in her in any other way than as someone he liked to taunt.

The only time Michael had come close to showing Isabelle his real self was the other night in the parlor. But when she tried to get him to share some of his feelings, however, he walked away. Isabelle knew that there were hidden secrets eating away at Michael's soul, and she wanted to help him, despite his pushing her away. *But that has nothing to do with love*, she reminded herself. *Besides, if Michael had some sort of special feeling for me, he would die before admitting it.*

Isabelle looked one last time into Douglas' pleading gray eyes, then made her decision. She had been grieving long enough for Richard, and she should let him go. She had been outrunning one disaster after another since she'd been at the Fontaine. It was not lost on her that things got far worse after Douglas followed her there, but Isabelle took this as a sign that she did not belong in Detroit. With Douglas, she could start a new life. Back in Canada.

Isabelle caressed Douglas' smooth face and smiled. She ignored a nagging feeling that she was being too hasty.

"Yes, Douglas, I will marry you."

Josie was the first to greet the carriage when they pulled up. Isabelle could see from the carriage window that Josie looked worried, the grayness of her hair suddenly more noticeable in the dim morning light. Ben was on Josie's heels; he, too, appeared to be anxiously waiting for her. As she disembarked, Michael came out and stood on the porch.

Josie ran up to hug Isabelle. "Chile, where you been? We didn't know what happened to y'all. You s'pposed to been back last night. I thought them Indians got ya."

Isabelle smiled, to show Josie that they were fine. "Josie, I am so sorry to have worried you, but there was no way to send word ahead. There was an accident. The boat we had capsized out in the lake. There was this sudden storm, and—"

"Let me guess," Michael jumped in. The minute Isabelle had uttered the word "accident," Michael had come from the porch to Isabelle's side. "You were in another accident, Isabelle? And just where was Mr. Burns at that moment?" he demanded.

"I, Mr. Burns, was steering the boat, and I never let Isabelle out of my sight," Douglas said over his shoulder as he unloaded their bags.

Michael glared at Douglas' back. "Then just how did an accident happen?" he asked. He looked down at Isabelle's ruined dress and soggy boots that were still leaking water.

"I fell out of the boat," Isabelle said, sheepish. Michael threw his head back in frustration.

"Now, how did 'Captain' Burns allow that to happen?" Michael asked, angrily. Just then, Douglas rushed up on him. Josie stepped in between the two men, using her arms to hold each man back.

"I've had enough of you, *Mr.* St. Vincent," Douglas said, deliberately not addressing Michael by his professional title. "Isabelle has had some bad run-ins since she's been in town, but she is still in one piece. We all have mishaps, but her luck is about to turn around," he added. "I'll take it as a courtesy that from now on, you refrain from badgering my bride-to-be."

At those words, Michael blinked twice, slowly, as if in disbelief. Isabelle immediately regretted that he found out so abruptly. She had planned to tell him and Josie later that day. Michael looked at Isabelle then, and try as she might, she could not look away. Finding it hard to breathe, Isabelle felt faint, seeming to feel the impact the news had on Michael within herself. She felt as if she had done a dark, gruesome thing, that the universe had suddenly been turned upside down. Isabelle thought this should be a happy time, but instead, she felt that she had made the worst mistake of her life.

Isabelle had to pull her eyes away from Michael's before she could concentrate on what Douglas was asking her.

"What, what did you say?" she asked, dazed.

"I said, go in and get your things," Douglas repeated. "I will put you up in the National Hotel until you are ready to leave town."

Isabelle was stunned, not having contemplated actually leaving the house before her planned couple of weeks were up. There were still some things she wanted to try and find out before she left, and she was worried about Barry. And Ben. The little boy had overheard the adults' heated discussion, and for the first time, Isabelle could see a little emotion on his face. She realized that even though he did not say so, Ben did not want her to leave.

"No, no, Douglas. I will stay here," Isabelle said. "I have some things to look into before we. . .before we. . ." she could not bring herself to say the word "leave." But Michael finished her sentence for her.

"Before she leaves," he filled in. She could hear the pain in his voice, but his face had frozen back into its usual mask. He turned and walked back into the house, and out of Isabelle's heart.

Isabelle put all thoughts of marriage and packing and leaving out of her mind as she sank into a tub of warm water that evening. She'd wanted to go straight to bed, but Josie insisted she eat something, because she did not believe Isabelle had eaten anything decent for two days. Marie had drawn her a bath, and lit a few candles for her. Isabelle sighed as she allowed the water to cover her to just under her chin. Her shoulders ached horribly from swimming for her life.

Absently, Isabelle wondered how she had been able to swim that long, and that far, to actually make it back to shore. She assumed her fear drove her inland. How she wished she could relate her champion swimming experience to everyone, but it would only serve to make the capsizing sound that much worse. *Besides, Michael would not want to hear a word of it*, she thought. Reminding herself to stop thinking about Michael, Isabelle concentrated instead on the soothing heat of the bath. Closing her eyes, she could not fight the urge to fall asleep.

~ ~ ~

Louis had Eulalie draw a bath for him and Celeste, in his room. He had her sit with her back to him, where he nibbled on her right ear as he slowly bathed her. Celeste cringed at every caress. When Eulalie came back through with their towels, she dropped her eyes to the floor; this pained Celeste greatly, for they had once been close. Now, there was a wall between them, Celeste's wall of shame.

When Evangeline got wind of what happened, she'd knocked Celeste to the floor in her own rage. Celeste did not bother to get up from the scullery floor, but Evangeline had helped her up immediately.

"Forgive, me, Child," she'd said. "I just hate to see this happen. I told you to stay out of his sight," Evangeline said this through tears, "but I know it is not your fault. You cannot help your beauty, and you cannot help Louis' selfish madness."

It had been a few weeks since that fateful night in the carriage house. Pere had been buried in the yard out back, and whenever she could, Celeste went to pay a tearful visit. Briane was none the wiser about what had transpired, nor Suzette, who was now so preoccupied with her soldier suitor that Celeste rarely saw her. Besides, if Celeste told her the truth, Suzette's heart would be broken.

Louis bought Suzette out of her half of their inheritance and promised her a lavish wedding, since the soldier had proposed just last week. The young woman immediately set off with Tante Amie for the Isle Sur la Sarge, in France, the silk capital, for her bridal wardrobe. Louis sent a pouting Briane back to her parents in Montreal for a while. With Briane and Suzette out of the way, Louis made sure that he had Celeste at any time or place. There was nothing she could do.

Celeste was successful in avoiding Jacques, however. She'd gotten word through Evangeline that Jacques survived being shot, but was in a bad way for several days. He could not heal because he kept trying to go into the house to kill Louis. The other slaves had to watch him day and night. Evangeline also told Celeste that they were sorry for her and Jacques, the strongest of them all.

Sweating in the bath, Celeste envisioned Jacques at that moment, not needing Evangeline to tell her that he was alive. Celeste felt his presence with her, everywhere she went. If he were dead, she would know it immediately. In her dreams at night, Jacques was always standing just out of reach, arms outstretched. Celeste always ran faster and faster, but could never reach him. But he was always waiting there for her.

"What are you thinking about, love?" Louis asked as he gently massaged

a tea rose scented soap through her water-silkened hair. Celeste tensed, for she knew how Louis acted every time he sensed her thoughts were on Jacques.

"Nothing, Sieur Fontaine." Ever since Louis had attacked her, Celeste no longer saw him as Louis, but as her master only, and Louis hated it. He sighed at her response.

"I really do not like you calling me by my title," Louis said. Celeste said nothing in response. Louis stepped out, dried off, then kneeled next to the porcelain tub. "Lean back so I can rinse your hair."

Celeste complied, then was taken by surprise when Louis rammed her head under the water. Celeste twisted in shock and fear, as she'd had no chance to hold her breath. Louis' grip was unbreakable, and Celeste could not raise her head. Finally, after what seemed like hours, Louis yanked her up by her hair. Celeste coughed and sputtered. Soap burned her nostrils and throat.

"Now, again," Louis said, evenly, "how should I be addressed?"

Slowly, Celeste smoothed her hair back with one hand. She focused where she thought Louis was kneeling, but still could not see. No matter what he did to her, he was as good as dead to her.

"As I said before," she said, her voice deadly, "you are Sieur Fontaine." She tensed, expecting more of the same from Louis. Instead, there was an angry silence, then the sound of the door opening and closing.

～   ～   ～

Isabelle felt a tug on her left heel. Half asleep, she kicked away at the tugging hand, but bolted awake when the cold hand gripped her ankle, then slowly caressed its way up her calf. She sat up on her knees in bed, looking frantically from side to side. She did not remember getting into bed, but there she was, wearing her bedclothes, complete with an extra hand around her ankle.

The hand was a frosty reminder that her visions were too real to dismiss as fatigue. She couldn't even remember how she got into bed, but she knew what Celeste's bath soap smelled like. Isabelle had to admit that something was really happening to her, and it was time to face it. Like before, there was no one else to be seen in the room. Abruptly, all of her covers were thrown back off the bed, then her pillows were tossed into the air, one by one. Stifling a scream, Isabelle thrashed about, trying to shake off her unseen enemy.

Reminding herself that she wanted to find out the truth about the house before she left, Isabelle calmed down, took a deep breath, and waited. Finally, she whispered.

"Jacques, I understand that you are trying to speak to me," she began. "What is it you want me to know?" she asked. The tossing of blankets stopped, and to Isabelle's horror, she could feel someone sitting down next to her on the bed. The mattress sank in wherever who or it was sitting down. Isabelle's teeth were chattering, as she was suddenly freezing. She looked at the window, which was closed. The chill was coming from whomever was sitting with her now.

A long time passed, and Isabelle decided to close her eyes to allow the darkness to encircle her, as she had done before. It was not long before she could *see.*

~   ~   ~

The night of Briane and Louis' engagement party a month later, Celeste found great relief in not being at Louis' mercy. Briane's parents, the Huberts, were quiet, watchful people, and Celeste could tell they were pinning their hopes on the success of this impending marriage. With Briane on his heels like a pitiful puppy, Louis was too busy avoiding her to bother Celeste.

Eulalie spent time with Celeste, listening intently to some of the indignities the young woman was facing at the hands of their master. Celeste was glad to be able to tell someone. Evangeline was still so upset over everything, she only spoke to Celeste when giving household orders.

Eulalie and Celeste set vases of fresh flowers around the ballroom. Other slaves were busy with setting up tables and chairs. "I do not believe that he will ever leave me be," Celeste whispered, hopeless. "This will go on forever. Unless I end it."

Eulalie looked alarmed.

"It's exactly as it sounds," Celeste said, forcefully. "I will be putting an end to all of this very soon."

Briane entered the room. The nervous looking young woman was not yet ready for her special night, and without her rouge, her paleness made her look like a tall, lanky corpse.

"Celeste, come here," Briane called from the doorway. Sighing and taking one last look at Eulalie, Celeste complied. Briane's curly hair fanned out in all directions on her small head, like some petrified peacock's crown. As Celeste drew ever nearer to Briane, their eyes locked. The white woman's blue eyes seemed to bulge in her head as she watched her silently. As Celeste approached

her, Briane spun unsteadily on her heels and walked down the hall.

"Follow me," she said. Not sure what was going on, Celeste gave Eulalie a quizzical look as she left the room. They reached the cellar door. Briane paused before its doorway and pulled out a ring of large keys. Unlocking the cellar door, she turned, grabbed Celeste by the arm, and shoved her down the stairs.

Stunned, Celeste fought to stop her headlong tumble down the stairs, managing to grip a railing as her legs skidded down three steps. Finally catching her balance, she looked up at Briane at the top of the stairs, the waning daylight surrounding her like a red halo. She had a cruel grin.

"This is my night, whore," was all Briane said, as she backed out of the doorway and slammed the cellar door shut. Celeste did not bother to call out as Briane locked the door, leaving Celeste in complete darkness. Celeste sat down on the steps and put her head in her hands.

In the dark, Celeste could not tell if minutes or hours had passed. She could hear laughter and fiddling above her, so she assumed the party had begun. Staying put on the stairs, Celeste wondered in the smothering darkness if this was how it would feel to be dead.

After what she was sure was hours, Celeste leaned her head against the railing. She assumed Briane told a drunk Louis some lie about where she was. She was also sure some of the party guests would wonder where the celebrated slave piano player was tonight.

Sitting in the darkness, Celeste wished she were up there, playing. In music, there was no loneliness, no fear. In music, there was no slave, no master.

Just then, Celeste heard a creak behind her. It was the cellar door. Quickly, she got to her feet, her knees stiff from sitting so long. Celeste steeled herself, wondering what Briane was up to next. To her surprise, it was Jacques. He was holding a single lit candle.

"Cherie, I am here," Jacques whispered as he closed the door behind him and descended a few steps. Celeste ran into his arms, sobbing into his chest. She could feel his silent tears wetting the top of her head.

"Jacques, what are you doing here? You'll get into trouble," she hiccupped.

Jacques laughed softly, and she could feel the rumble in his chest. "Has that stopped me before?"

Celeste allowed herself a small smile. Clasping each other, the two lovers sat down on the steps together. Jacques rubbed Celeste's arms to warm her.

"Evangeline gave me her own set of keys," Jacques began. "She had no

idea what Briane planned to do with you tonight, and she is sorry. She says it's best to wait this one out, let Briane have her pitiful night and keep Louis from trouncing her in public."

"Sorry?" Celeste echoed. "There is nothing she can do. Nothing anyone can do."

"Don't say that," Jacques said. "I will find a way for us to be free of this life."

Celeste did not say a word, for she knew that would never happen. Instead, she reveled in the fanciful dream of being with Jacques, free and happy. The dream was all she would ever have.

"Louis has threatened to sell my sister, Therese, to the highest bidder."

"What?" Celeste asked, shocked. She put her hands over her face. "Jacques, what can I say?"

Jacques squeezed her hand. "Louis has told me she's safe for now, under watch. She's been put to work in the town bakery. Duchene has strict orders not to sell her, but no one trusts him. It's my fault. She begged to sail with me that week. Our parents are now missing two children. My poor mother!" His voice caught in his throat.

"Perhaps I could talk to Louis," Celeste said. "He would listen to me—" Jacques stilled her by placing one hand on her knee.

"No, Celeste, he's holding Therese because of you. Because of us."

Celeste frowned, not understanding.

"The day you were. . .taken. . . from me," Jacques continued, his voice raw, "Louis came to me a couple of days later. He was smug because I could barely move. He told me that if I lunged on him again, he'd have Therese sold immediately. Delirious, I laughed and told him that would never happen. He told me to consider what he'd said when I was walking again, then left.

"But I'll never stand down," Jacques continued. "I'm just biding my time. I've smuggled notes through an Indian trader here to some of the farms where my old crew were dropped off on the way here. There will be an uprising soon. I'll deal with Louis, break Duchene's neck, then get my sister safely back home. They can't stop us all. They won't stop you and me."

As Jacques uttered that vow, his eyes took on a burning brightness of their own, mirrors of the candle's fierce flickering glow.

"Why me, Jacques?" Celeste asked, looking into his eyes. "You want me, but I am chained to a monster."

"Why not you, Celeste?" Jacques countered, turning her to face him. "As *if any man could resist your beauty, your music! I consider myself the luckiest man alive to have your love."*

They kissed then, all troubles forgotten for the moment. Celeste let all worries about their lives fade away with each kiss. She was with her beloved at this moment, and she was grateful for that, for somehow, she knew time was running out for them all.

~   ~   ~

CHAPTER NINE

Isabelle was startled by something scratching her legs. Opening her eyes, she only saw darkness around her, but she was gripping a cold railing. Her legs were stretched out over wooden stairs, their sharp edges scouring the backs of her calves. The wood smelled rotten from the dampness in the air. She heard the steady *drip-drop* of water as well as something scurrying that she would not wait around to identify.

Angry and cold, Isabelle realized she must have "dreamed" again and wound up in the cellar. Pulling her legs in, up to the step where she was seated, she stood slowly. Turning around and looking up, she saw faint dawn light from the kitchen. Walking towards that light, Isabelle clung to the iron railing as she ascended.

Isabelle rushed upstairs to her room, avoiding the kitchen so she wouldn't wake Josie or Michael. By a lone candle's light, she wiped tiny pricks of blood off the back of her legs from where she'd been scraped at her washbowl. Not knowing whether the sudden coldness in the room was from just having been in the cellar or from a "visitor," Isabelle rushed from her room, but not before taking the journal from atop her tallboy at the door; the library would be a good place to wait for the morning.

Lighting a lamp in the library, Isabelle took a seat in one of the antique high back armchairs near the doorway. Amber light from the coming dawn burned behind the draperies. Bookcases standing ceiling high surrounded the room, all filled with medical tomes and dusty, loose papers on shelves. From looking at the layers of dust, Isabelle sensed that the room had gone untouched since Grandfather's death; Josie could probably not bring herself to come in there to dust.

The book opened with a crackle. The front pages were the most delicate. Pressed flowers dried nearly to dust rested between some pages. An early page contained the faint remnants of a flowing handwriting in French. Leaning forward, Isabelle squinted to read the date in the upper left corner, then gasped—the date was April 30, 1736. Shaking, but determined, Isabelle read the entry:

> Today, my darkest fears have been realized—I am with child, and Louis is the father. Evangeline attested to it after I fainted in the scullery. We dare not let anyone on the farm know. Louis has been away on his honeymoon with Briane this past month, but will be returning this Saturday. He had Jacques tied up and leased him to work on another farm for a month as well, to keep him from me. Eulalie has silently wept the tears I should be shedding now, but somehow, I cannot bring myself to cry. I feel nothing inside, neither fear nor sadness, just a nothingness that will be my companion until the end. I desperately miss Jacques, but because of this child, our time together has come to an end.

Sitting back, Isabelle sighed, understanding that what she read belonged to a real person—the Celeste of her dreams, the Celeste of some man's whispered yearnings.

The book threatened to fall from her lap. After catching it, Isabelle leaned forward to flip several pages ahead. Celeste's last entry was October 5, 1736. It was only one line long. Flipping further, she found several blank pages, then a new set of entries in a different handwriting.

After several hours of reading, Isabelle learned that the book had been retrieved by her grandfather, who made entries of his own. Glancing at these pages quickly, Isabelle saw the world through Grandfather's eyes as a young doctor saddled with a house he could barely maintain, the courtship of the young and pretty girl he would marry, then the birth of their first child, Rosalie.

One entry, written when Charles was a young man, tells of how he'd seen "her" once in his dreams, a beautiful but sad face. Subsequent entries, however, contained no discussion of Celeste at all, as if she was forgotten. Disappointed, Isabelle flipped back to Celeste's last entry and read it again:

> October 5, 1736
>
> They stopped her once before, but they'll all fail the next time.

Isabelle jumped when the library room's door creaked. The book did hit the floor that time, nearly splitting in two. In walked Michael. He appeared half-awake, and he was uncharacteristically unkempt, the shadow of a beard on his strong jaw. His thick hair was raised in mossy black tufts. He was in yesterday's day shirt and pants. In his hand was an amber colored drink.

"What are you doing up?" he asked, groggily. He kneeled before Isabelle to pick up the two halves of the shattered book. He would not look at her directly.

"I—I could not sleep," Isabelle answered. She hated to admit this to him, but she was tired of lying to everyone.

"That does not surprise me," Michael said, pausing, still bent over before her. "You always look tired. Luckily, your beauty masks this fact from most people."

Isabelle scrambled for a retort, but instead made a counter attack. "What are you doing up at this ungodly hour? And undressed, at that? Medicating thyself?" she mocked. Michael looked at her with a slight, rueful smile, with no smarting remark; this worried Isabelle.

He sighed. "I haven't been in here since Charles passed away," Michael said, looking around the room. "He spent much of his time in here, always reading."

"Were you and Grandfather close?" Isabelle asked.

Michael nodded. "He was like a father to me in many ways. From the first time I came here, I was treated so well. Charles gave me a room here, food. He was the one who decided I would go to Paris to learn from the best doctors, and paid my way. I owe everything I am to your grandfather."

Isabelle smiled. She was proud to hear this, but then a question came to mind. "Michael, I assumed that since Grandfather took a strong interest grooming you as a physician, you two would be partners of some sort when you returned from Paris. But I get the feeling that it did not turn out that way."

Michael nodded. "You were right to assume. I was the one who destroyed everything." He paused for a long moment, then continued. "When I came back from Paris, I was angry, angry enough to kill," he said. "In Paris, I was treated like a man, not as something less. But when I returned to this damned country, I'm spit upon by a white man the minute I'm back in town. I'd heard about the abolitionist meetings that were taking place in secret, and starting attending. Then came the Blackburn incident." He paused again. "That changed everything," he said, mysteriously.

"Since then, I questioned why I even bothered to learn a profession I would have fight every day to practice. Your grandfather was ready to get started, but I kept stalling. We had discussed opening a clinic, right in the old ballroom, which used to be a fur-trading storehouse in the old days. But then his health started to fade, and I was so busy dwelling in my anger that I was gone much of the time, gone out of the country. I didn't know he was that ill, and then he was dead by the time I returned home. All the kindness he showed me, and I failed him."

Isabelle felt sorry for him. "Michael, I'm sure that Grandfather is still very proud of you, and understands that you were going through some things at the time. He would not have held it against you if your plans didn't happen."

"There's no way we'll ever know that, Isabelle," Michael said, slowly. "It doesn't really matter, with things being different now."

"Michael, what can I say to make you feel better? What can I do?" Isabelle asked, sad. She leaned forward and rubbed his shoulder lightly. Michael froze, exhaled sharply, then pulled away. He rose and set the book on a little table to her left.

"Nothing you can help me with," he replied. He went over to another chair on the opposite side of the doorway and sank into it.

Determined, Isabelle forged ahead, because it mattered to her what Michael was upset about.

"Are you so sure that I cannot help you?" she asked, softly. "I want to help you." Isabelle was irritated at Michael's disbelieving *psh* sound at her comment.

"You can't help me," he said, surly. "Save your concern for Douglas."

Isabelle was angry. "Michael, I do not know why you are so upset about the engagement, but I did not intend for you to hear it before I could tell you myself. I thought that you and I had developed somewhat of a, well, special connection—"

"A 'connection,' you say?" Michael repeated sarcastically. "Just what kind?"

"Well, considering our relationship to this house, to our mutual losses."

"You mean, your loss," Michael cut in.

"Michael, you have suffered in the past as well, but you won't talk about it," Isabelle countered. "But just because you refuse to talk about it does not mean it never happened." She rose and went to stand over him. For once, he would hear her, without his walking off. "You are caged, Michael, trapped by your bitterness about your past, and you are afraid to reach for what you really want," Isabelle said, overcome. "You cannot go on like this. You'll be unhappy the rest of your life."

Michael looked deeply into Isabelle's eyes, and she felt whoozy. His eyes had a pleading in their depths that pulled on her like a magnet, drawing her into his soul. He took her hands.

"If I say what I really want, Isabelle," he whispered, "I do not think you would be ready to truly hear it."

Isabelle removed her hands from Michael's and walked out of the room, chiding herself for doing exactly what she was trying to prevent Michael from doing. But she could not do anything else.

After a fitful nap, where she refused to allow herself to fall completely fall asleep, Isabelle arose and dressed for Saturday Mass. It was overcast outside, again. Not a strongly religious person, Isabelle reluctantly agreed to attend with Mr. Alders, who had invited her the other day.

"The nice things about Catholic Mass," Alders said, eyes twinkling, "is that it ain't long at all. Can get right back to what you were doin' before." When Alders put it that way, Isabelle could not resist his offer. He'd invited Josie as well, but only in jest—Josie was a fiery Baptist, and was hard at work with other Negro members of First Baptist to found a church of their own on Monroe Street.

As Isabelle and Alders rocked along together in the open wagon, Isabelle took the opportunity for a chat with Alders. He was wearing his everyday cap to church. To Isabelle, it seemed Alders was always cheerful and seemingly unaffected by being around the house.

"Tell me, Mr. Alders," Isabelle began. "You have been at Maison Fontaine for nearly as long as my grandfather, but you do not seem bothered by it all."

"Bothered?" the old man asked. He shook his head. "I wouldn't say bothered. But, believe me, there have been a coupla things I thought I heard didn't turn out to be real, ya know. Can't say I ever seen anything odd. Have you?" he asked, turning to face her. Isabelle kept her eyes on the road.

"There have been some things I've seen that I can't explain, some things I have questions about," Isabelle hedged. "Some things that don't make sense."

"Oh," was all Alders said at first, then he nodded to himself, as if reaching a decision. "Since you been honest wit' me, I can now be honest wit' you.

"I don't go around howling 'bout spooks or anything like that," Alders began, "but over the years, there been some funny business goin' on. No Negro would come here to work, telling others about the restless house. I'm here 'cause your granddaddy did right by me, long ago. I was real sick from drinkin' all the time. My wife left me, my kids hated me, for drinkin' up the household money. I was wandering in the streets for months when I made it all the way down here. Your granddaddy took me in, got me sober, and kept me that way." For the first time, Alders looked sad, but just for a moment, then his face brightened again. "Gave me a job, but he told me this was an unusual house. I didn't care at the time, just glad to be myself again after so many years."

"So, you stayed," Isabelle said, "despite the warning."

Alders nodded again. "It was the only decision I could make. I owed him. Plus, I really ain't all that scared," Alders said. "I think I understand why the house is occupied. Lost souls trapped, poor devils wantin' somethin' been long gone, but they don't realize it," he explained, making it sound so elementary. "As a former lost soul, I can understand. Josie gets worked up, had me steal some holy water from my church a coupla times," he laughed, "and she's had a deacon or two come through to cast out demons and all, but they just do it to humor her, 'cause they never see or hear nothin'. She swears she hears stuff sometime, and I believe her.

"Like I say," Alders added, "I feel sorry for the poor devils, but I don't know how to send 'em on to the Lord. So I try to live in peace wit' 'em. 'Til the right one come along to set 'em free."

Isabelle's eyes widened when Alders made that last comment. *Surely, he doesn't mean I'm the right one?* she wondered. Nothing else was said the rest of the ride.

The spires of Ste. Anne's Catholic Church were in view long before their wagon reached the church. They were at the corner of Larned and Bates. Isabelle marveled when Alders told her the church spires were 110 feet high.

When her boots touched the cold, hard church grounds, Isabelle felt a disorientating thrumming sensation throughout her entire body.

"Ladies and gentlemen!" Isabelle whirled around after she heard a booming voice behind her. "Mr. Joseph Campau would like to present to you, Crow!" Isabelle followed the growing crowd to the end of the road. To her shock, Isabelle spotted a man climbing one of the church's spires. She tugged on Alder's coat sleeve. He patted her hand.

"Don't fret, young lady. This is the early Mass entertainment. Mr. Campau is one of the wealthiest men in town. Ya know, he lives on Jefferson with his wife, Adeleide. Their house is the one with the yellow façade. The Indians call Campau 'Chemokamun,' Big Shot. He gets one of the local

Indians, Crow, to do stunts from the church rooftop." Alders sighed, "Why, I don't know. I guess just because he can."

A muscular man with his hair in a ponytail, Crow continued to climb the shingled rooftop with his bare hands. He then stood, waved to the cheering crowd, then turned a sudden backflip, landing on his feet with ease. The crowd roared. Crow then ran at full speed to the other spire along the narrow roof's point. Turning, he leapt to his hands, and did a walking handstand all the way back to the other spire, one hand on either side. The crowd was breathless during this feat, as they watched Crow in suspense. He paused, then gracefully curled his legs forward to deftly regain his feet. Smiling, he waved to the clapping and whistling crowd. Like magic, he was gone. Isabelle marveled at Crow's prowess, but felt sorry for him, forced to perform for his owner.

The crowd then filed into the church. The sanctuary was lit with candles surrounding the room. All excitement from the acrobat was forgotten as the people entered a solemn service. The altar was identical, Alders had whispered, even after the great fire in 1805. Isabelle and Alders sat in the back. She could not help but notice all the people in the back were Negroes, with the wealthy whites up front.

Each time the priest read from the Gospel, everyone but Isabelle crossed themselves from forehead, to lips, then chest. All through the French homily, the priest was drowned out by the thrumming feeling in Isabelle's body. It was almost more than she could take, and she tapped her foot in anticipation of getting out of there. Mercifully, the homily was over, and Alders joined the others up front to receive communion. As she was not Catholic, Isabelle could not partake, and it was just fine with her.

Slipping out, Isabelle paused to take in some fresh air. The thrumming feeling did not subside, however, and actually intensified. Turning from side to side, Isabelle clenched her teeth against the bizarre feeling. Feeling a pulling sensation, she walked quickly around the side of the church, to the back. The feeling grew stronger as walked along the building's side, then neared what she found was the church graveyard. Isabelle trampled over headstones, her mantle brushing over their tops.

Suddenly sure of what she was looking for. Isabelle paused before an old headstone. Kneeling, she brushed away weeds and dirt. The minute she touched the cold stone, the thrumming finally left her, but her left hand started aching wickedly. When the etching on the stone became clear, Isabelle sat back on her heels. The headstone read:

Negresse Inconnue. 1736 Octobre.

"Unknown Negress," Isabelle breathed. Refusing to ponder the ownership of that body, Isabelle rushed from the site, and to the wagon. Alders was waiting there, but he did not ask her where she'd been. They rode back home without a word.

Cutting across the back of Maison Fontaine down a path Alders made years ago, the wagon came to a stop outside the carriage house. Isabelle did not go through the back door, but felt compelled to walk around the outside of the house to the front porch. She faintly heard Alders saying he'd see her later.

She found Barry on the porch. He was seated at the top of the steps, sketchbook in his lap. He appeared to be staring off into the distance when Isabelle walked up. Isabelle had to call his name a couple of times to get his attention, even though she was standing in front of him. It seemed to take a moment for Barry's eyes to focus on hers.

"Good evening, Barry," Isabelle said. "It's nice to see you out getting some air."

Barry laid his sketchbook back onto his lap and resumed sketching. Isabelle took a seat beside Barry.

"What are you working on this time?" she asked, softly, so as not to frighten him away.

"The same thing," Barry said. "Always the same thing. She won't let me draw anything else."

Isabelle tensed up. "Who won't let you draw anything else?" she asked, already knowing the answer. Barry pursed his lips and pointed one finger in Isabelle's face, which startled her.

"You know who I'm talking about," Barry bristled. "I wish you would stop pretending that you don't!" He sounded like a pouty child.

Isabelle sighed, not wanting to make him angry. "Okay, Barry, you are drawing *her*, aren't you?"

Barry nodded, then started sketching again. "This is as far as I've gotten, in all of these years," he muttered. His pencil was aflutter across the page. "Things are different now," he added.

Isabelle cocked her head at that comment, remembering Michael saying the same thing just that morning. "Different now, how, Barry?" she asked, leaning closer to him. "Tell me."

Barry turned the sketch so that Isabelle could see. She saw what looked like her own face, except with longer hair. Her shoulders were bare, and in the background was a body of dark water leading to some distant point, with turbulent waves. The waves had black outlines. On either of the woman's shoulders was a different man's hand, one dark, one white, one larger than the other; from the arc of the woman's neck, the hands appeared to be pushing her downward. Eerily, Celeste's eyes seemed to be looking directly into Isabelle's. Isabelle leaned to one side, then the other, and the eyes followed. Isabelle jumped to her feet, and stood on the top of the stairs behind Barry; the eyes followed. She gulped.

"Barry, put that away for now," she said. "Do it!"

Quickly, Barry flipped down the top of the sketchbook. Rising, he stood before Isabelle on the lower step. She was surprised to see such clarity in his dark eyes, which suddenly lost their usual cloudiness. Isabelle wondered what kind of man Barry could have become if he hadn't been so tormented. He reached up to caress Isabelle's face, then took a loose tendril of hair, and twirled it lightly. He looked sad.

"I'm so sorry that we have come to this," he whispered. Isabelle was entranced by Barry's sudden focus and his tenderness. "Things will be ending soon—for both of us, you know that."

Isabelle said nothing, not able to respond to what felt so much like the truth. Instead, she pulled away, and went into the house.

Pulling the door behind her quickly, Isabelle thought she heard music, strings, coming from her left. She entered the parlor, but found no one there. Walking through to the men's parlor, she still found nothing. She went up to the next connecting room, which was the ballroom. Pausing outside the closed beveled glass double doors, she pressed one ear against the glass. Isabelle could distinctly hear up-tempo fiddling and clapping. Turning the knob, she ventured inside to see what was going in. No one had mentioned to her that there were guests here this evening.

The moment Isabelle stepped inside the dark room, the doors swung closed behind her. She gasped, and frantically tried to open the doors from the inside. They were sealed tight. A cold breeze blew past her, chilling her entire body in an instant. Isabelle felt as if she was outside in the dead of winter. Her breathing became labored as the cold air froze her lungs, and she could not cry out. She sat down in front of the doors, no longer able to move forward. Huddling into a ball, Isabelle hugged herself to stay warm. In the mist, a form in the shape of a man walked slowly towards her.

~   ~   ~

Celeste wrung soapy water out of a mop and into a wooden bucket, which she dragged behind her around the ballroom. It was the morning after the engagement party, and all the guests were gone. Louis was upstairs in his room, passed out, and even Evangeline was still asleep in her room. The house was dead, empty of all life, not even Celeste's own. Fighting nausea as she swabbed the floor, memories of her dark night in the cellar came back to her. Jacques had been kind enough to sneak back upstairs and bring her some smuggled food and water from Evangeline, then left for good before dawn. If not for Jacques having snuck down there, she would have gone insane.

She did not tell him about the baby, for she knew he would have stormed into the party and gotten killed on the spot; there were many soldiers there from the fort, including Suzette's fiancé, Pierre. Celeste agonized over the day she would tell him because she knew it would be their last day together. There was no way that Jacques would still want her after this.

Celeste heard hard footsteps on the still-wet floor. Before she turned around, she knew who it was.

"Oh, so somebody let you out," Briane said with a smug grin. Celeste looked at her stonily, then resumed mopping.

"Don't you turn your back to me, slave," Briane said.

Celeste continued to ignore her, not caring what happened today. Briane reached for Celeste's shoulder and whirled her around. Celeste took the soaking wet mop and splashed Briane across the face with the filthy water. Briane shrieked, wiping water from her eyes. Her high hairstyle from last night was soggy and limp. Briane raised a hand to slap Celeste, but was stopped by Louis' voice.

"Don't you dare!" he bellowed. Surprised, Briane turned around to face Louis.

"But, Louis, she—"

"I don't want to hear a word of it," he said, rubbing his forehead, tired. He walked off, and Evangeline rushed in past him, still in her sleeping clothes. She gave Briane a foul look, then winked at Celeste.

"I don't know what your master sees in you," Briane said, "but I will be rid of you soon, one way or the other." With that, Briane rushed from the room,

slipping all the way. Eulalie rushed in, almost knocked over by Briane, who shoved her into a wall.

Evangeline did not enter the room, and her wink was gone. "Finish the ballroom, then get started on the dishes." She left, and the two young women were left to finish clearing the room. Eulalie chuckled, her crushed throat making her sound like a braying donkey. But for Celeste, Eulalie's laugh was like music.

A month later, it was hard for Celeste to hide the fact that she was at least four months pregnant; none of her small-waisted dresses fit anymore, and she had been gravely ill for weeks. Louis had ordered that Celeste not be forced to work, despite Evangeline's objections, which were really disguised to hide the pregnancy. Finally, the sickness abated, and she was able to resume much of her work around the house. She did not see Jacques once during this time, and was glad that she could stay in her room. Eulalie was her only help at this time, keeping Briane from barging in to threaten Celeste.

On that day, however, Celeste ran into Jacques in the yard. Evangeline had told her to go out to hang the wash, knowing that he would be waiting for her out there.

"I know you don't want to see him, Child, but he has been driving me insane every day, asking for you. He has a right to know."

Sighing, Celeste swung open the door and went out back. The early morning was very bright, with the sunlight reflecting off the golden leaves in the yard. She felt Jacques' presence before he spoke.

"This is my favorite time of year in this part of the world, when the leaves change," he said from behind her. "The world gets quiet." He kissed Celeste's cheek, wrapping his arms around her waist. She leaned back into him, throwing all thoughts of who might see them to the wind. She whirled around to face him, then kissed him deeply, as if she might absorb his entire essence just by kissing him. Jacques returned her kisses with even more urgency. Everything around them vanished for a while, then Celeste came back to awareness. She was the first to break away.

"Jacques, I must tell you something," she began. Jacques pressed a finger to her lips.

"Shh, Celeste, I already know," he said, softly. Celeste burst into tears, and Jacques held her in his arms for a long time. "Evangeline told me."

"Aren't you angry with me?" Celeste sniffled against his chest.

"Why would I be angry with you?" Jacques asked. "Darling, what that

animal did was not your fault. Louis will be going to hell for this. Of course I was sad, but not for myself. You don't know hard I worried over you dealing with this atrocity. Knowing that I could not be with you is what's been tearing me down."

He pushed her back so that she could face him. "Don't ever hide your light from me again, you hear?" He asked, lips trembling. "I could not bear that again. Ever. As soon as I can find a way to make sure Therese is safe, I will be ripping Louis apart with my bare hands, then we will leave for Canada. I promise."

Celeste shook her head, defeated. "Jacques, you'd better try to escape without me. You were a free man before. I'll be a fugitive. I've already brought you so much agony."

Jacques crushed Celeste to his chest. "Never say that again. Without you, there is no life for me out there. I will always be with you."

Celeste clung to Jacques, their tears nourishing the earth like a gentle rain.

~   ~   ~

Isabelle felt the doors behind her open quickly. She almost fell backwards, as she found that she was leaning against them. Spinning around on the floor, she looked up and up to see Michael standing before her, looking bewildered.

"What are you doing?" he asked. He helped Isabelle to her feet. She smoothed her skirts, and knocked away any dust off her backside. Smirking, she looked behind him.

"Where is he?" she asked, perturbed.

"Who?"

"Barry," she replied. "He must have locked me in here, throwing a tantrum," she said. "We had some words out on the porch, and I guess he thought he would scare me."

"Well, it looks like he did," Michael said. He reached out and wiped away the tears that were still glistening on Isabelle's delicate cheek. She turned away, surprised that her face was so wet.

"It. . .it wasn't him," Isabelle said, after a while.

Michael took a hold of her shoulders, determined. "Isabelle, it's time you tell me the truth. There has been something bothering you since you got here. I just can't figure out what."

Isabelle put one hand on his arm. For some reason, probably exhaustion, she decided to confide in him. She reasoned that at least he was a doctor, so maybe he could find her a nice insane asylum.

"I've been seeing and hearing things," she whispered. "People I don't know, but people living in this very house. It's like I'm watching them, but they think I'm someone else." Michael listened intently, so Isabelle felt the courage to continue. "It's frightening, because I feel like I know them, and I also feel like something terrible is going to happen to me."

"Something terrible?" was the only question Michael asked. "Like what?"

"Like I'm going to die," she said, slowly.

He sighed, dropping his arms. He took her by the hand, and led her back out of the ballroom. She looked back once, wondering about what she had seen in there, but relieved that Michael was leading her away from it.

They took a seat in the men's parlor. There, Michael sat a long time before saying a word.

"So, tell me, Doctor," Isabelle began. "Just how insane am I?" she asked half-jesting.

Michael turned to face her, and she was surprised at how suddenly open his face was.

"Isabelle, you're not insane," he said. "Not in the least. I've been a part of this household for years, but I've been in and out. The times I have been here, though, there has been nothing amiss. Except for two occasions."

Isabelle leaned in, intrigued. "Tell me," she urged.

Michael ran a hand through his hair, and Isabelle found herself wondering what that felt like. She refocused her attention on what he was saying.

"When I was a young boy here," Michael said, "there were a couple of friends who didn't mind coming to the house to visit me. I was aware that people were leery about coming here, with the tales and all, but I paid that no mind. I was a young boy, full of adventure, so I felt a certain pride in being known to live in a 'spirited' house," he grinned. "I dismissed Auntie's claims as just part of her eccentric nature.

"One stormy afternoon," Michael went on, "we were bored and decided to play a game of hide-and-seek. Your grandfather and Auntie were out of the house for some reason, but Alders was on the grounds somewhere. It was my turn to hide, so I chose the closet in the ballroom. Jonas and Nelson looked and looked for me all through the house, but they knew not to scare Barry, so they didn't go into his room; we tried to get him to play, but well, you know." He shrugged.

"At any rate," Michael continued, "I was so proud of my hiding place, I was giggling to myself. When I stopped giggling, however, I could swear I heard other voices in the room. Thinking that my friends had found me, I leapt from the closet only to be surprised by no one being there. Thinking I'd imagined hearing anyone else, I decided to go find Jonas and Nelson, since I'd won that round. When I tried to turn the ballroom doorknobs, however, I could not get the doors to budge. After a few failed tries, I slammed my body into the doors, hurting my shoulder."

"Like what just happened to me," Isabelle breathed.

Michael nodded. "It felt like I was trapped in there for hours. The room grew icy cold, and I was shivering. The room was black, but it looked like I could see fuzzy shapes all around me. I heard laughter, and I swear, a woman's voice saying 'the King's gardens are dreadful'. That's all I heard, but I'll never forget it."

Isabelle was stunned, and a little relieved, for at least she was not the first person to have heard something strange. Both Michael and Alders may have heard something, but Isabelle was the only one to see anything out of the ordinary; that still worried her, so she decided to keep that information to herself. Wringing her hands, she was breathless to hear the next part of the story.

"You mentioned that there were two occasions that you felt something was amiss," Isabelle said. "When was the other?"

"Today," Michael said, bluntly. "Over the years, I told myself that the darkness of the closet and the ballroom had wreaked havoc with my imagination. I quickly dismissed the entire thing and went on with my life. Until today. Until you tell me that you thought Barry locked you in the ballroom."

"That's right," Isabelle said. "He was upset with me."

"Barry may be upset with you, but he didn't lock you in that room."

"How do you know?" Isabelle asked.

"Because Barry has been in his room all day," Michael said. "I've been here all afternoon, since before you left for church. I've been up here in the front parlor reading the newspaper. No one passed this way, until you came through the front door."

Isabelle gulped. "Surely, you missed seeing him—"

Michael shook his head vehemently. "No, Isabelle. But that's not even the point. What I was getting to is that, like you, I thought I had been locked in the ballroom as a child." For the first time, Isabelle thought, Michael looked unsure of himself.

"Isabelle, there is no lock on the ballroom doors," he said flatly. "There never has been."

CHAPTER TEN

Before Isabelle could react to Michael's shocking news, they both heard a loud bang on the front door, then heavy footsteps.

"Hello? Anyone home?" To Isabelle's dismay, it was Douglas.

Michael stood quickly, and walked out of the room, not once looking back. He paused long enough in the hallway to turn his back on Douglas as the younger man gave a terse hello. By the time she reached the doorway, Michael was nowhere to be seen.

Douglas rushed to greet her with a deep kiss and a hug. "How are you, today, Dearest?" he asked.

"Just fine," she lied. *When will I tell Douglas the truth?* She wondered. *I've practically told Michael everything, but he's not my fiancé.*

"So much to tell, so much to tell," Douglas chimed. "After over a year of filling in the river's shoreline just below Larned Street, a good-sized wharf has been built up. The Company can now start building those storefronts," Douglas said breathlessly as he led the way back out onto the porch. Isabelle was hesitant to follow him, but she certainly could not tell him why, so she went ahead. Douglas led the way to the side of the house, near the orchard. The dark purple grapes looked ready to be picked. They took a seat on the stone bench nearby.

They were starting to get a little worried," Douglas continued.

"Worried?" Isabelle asked. "About what?"

"Some of the store owners sold out their leases for the year at an advance of one hundred percent of what they are potentially worth. They have to start yielding a profit, and soon. At today's meeting, the Trustee reported that the Company has not yet made enough profit to pay Governor Cass anything on the mortgage, nor to the stakeholders."

"That doesn't sound good," Isabelle said, concerned. "How is this affecting you?" she asked. Douglas shook his head slowly. "I'm not affected because I am not a junior investor. Not yet, that is. They are patiently awaiting my investment."

"How much of an investment?" Isabelle asked, uneasy.

"At least $5,000, about half of what the senior investors initially put up together."

Isabelle was incredulous. "Just where are you supposed to get that kind of money?"

Douglas gave her a dark look. "Isabelle, I know what I'm doing. I told you that I have a plan. It's just a matter of all the right puzzle pieces being put in place. You are a piece of the puzzle, too, Isabelle," he said mysteriously, "a bigger piece than you would ever realize. Let's change the subject, shall we? I just wanted you to know that the Company is making progress. Come on, I want to see the water."

Isabelle did not want to change the subject as they traversed up and down the water's edge, but she let the matter drop because she was still outdone by what Michael had said. If what he claimed was true about the ballroom not having any locks, despite her being locked in, she thought, then she had to take heed of the other part of this mystery—the overwhelming sense that she was going to die very soon.

Isabelle was pulled out of her thoughts by a scream in the distance. Looking at Douglas, she broke into a run, Douglas on her heels. The scream came from the house. Racing up the porch steps, Isabelle swung open the door to find Josie crumpled in a heap on the floor, and Marie wailing; seeing that usually emotionless young woman distraught like that frightened Isabelle even more.

"What's happened?" she panted. Douglas reached down to help Josie into the hallway chair.

"It's Ben," Marie said between wails. "He barged in and took him."

"Who has taken him?" Isabelle asked, alarmed. Marie handed her a crumpled note, which explained everything. It was them. The men who wanted the house. The note read:

Come and sign the deed. Gouin Street. Now.

Outraged, Isabelle went to the kitchen for the shotgun, then headed for the wagon out back. Douglas caught up with her.

"Isabelle, what do you intend to do?" he asked. "These are obviously some very dangerous men. I could go see what this is about."

Isabelle shook her head, then climbed to the top of the wagon and grabbed hold of the reins. Alders had already left for the day, and Josie said Michael had gone back to his clinic.

There's no time for that. He's a little boy. I know that Ben is counting on me to come get him myself. Go in and tell Marie I'm handling this. Tell Josie I'm going to get Michael, too. I'll meet you in the front."

As the wagon hugged the corner of Fontaine and Franklin, Douglas gripped its sides to keep his seat. His hat threatened to blow away several times. Isabelle kept her eyes on the road, of which some parts were still unpaved. She felt bad for the horse's hooves, but she was in a hurry. Michael's clinic was on Iron Street, and it was easy to find because it was the only solid structure standing.

On both sides of the one-floor building, open, weed-filled fields lay under an overcast sky. In the distance, Isabelle could see the outlines of tiny shacks with faint wisps of smoke from their chimneys. She knew this area was where some of the poorest people lived. There was a very fine carriage waiting in front of the building, with a white coachman in formal driving attire. Stepping from the wagon before Douglas could give her a hand, Isabelle rushed to the wooden door of the building and knocked hard.

Within moments, the door swung open, and a surprised Michael was standing there. He had put on his suit and combed his hair back, looking much like the doctor she'd met on the ferry. Isabelle was disoriented seeing Michael in this environment, away from the house. He looked even taller. His eyes went over her shoulders to grimace at Douglas; without looking back, Isabelle was sure Douglas was doing the same.

"What's wrong, Isabelle?" Michael asked. He still had not opened the door, so Isabelle pushed her way past him. Douglas reluctantly followed, deliberately brushing past Michael. Lamps lit the large front room, which looked as if it had once been part of someone's house. The room was cheery, with plants standing in tall Chinese vases; Isabelle found that curious, considering Michael's dark disposition. She could see the end of what looked like the post of a hospital bed in a lit room down the hall. Once inside, Isabelle spun around and pulled Michael by the sleeves deeper into the room. Douglas remained at the doorway, arms crossed. He looked displeased.

"Michael," Isabelle began, "something terrible has happened."

Michael looked ashen. "Is it Auntie?" he asked, and made a move for his medical bag, which sat on a desk nearby.

"Yes—no," Isabelle amended. "She did have a fright, but she seems to be alright. It's Ben."

She was surprised when another person entered the room. It was a tall, slender, honey colored woman, a few years older than Isabelle. She was dressed in a bright red silk dress covered with crewel-embroidered cranes. Her upswept dark hair was held in place with jade combs. Isabelle sensed the woman had been there before. The woman stared her down, and Isabelle angrily wondered why no introductions were being made, nor why the woman had not politely excused herself from the room. Michael looked sheepish. Too worried about Ben to absorb the sight, Isabelle went on with her story.

"Someone has taken Ben," she said. "It's the men who are after the house. They are demanding I sign the deed over to them, then they'll set him free."

"Those bastards," Michael said. "They would stoop so low as to abduct a child?" he looked incredulous. "I take it you have an address?" he asked, limping over to grab his cane from beside the desk. He gave Isabelle a long look, a look that said he would do everything in his power to get Ben back.

Michael looked back at the woman, and the look had an air of finality to it. She lowered her eyes. Michael went for the door, and did not look back.

"Let's go."

Michael said he was familiar with the street in question, so they arrived there within moments. Pulling up in front of a rundown shack that threatened to topple over, he pulled his coach to a stop. Having left her wagon at Michael's, Isabelle had anxiously jumped up top with Michael, leaving a pouting Douglas to ride alone below. When they'd stopped, Douglas leaped out to help Isabelle down before Michael could do so.

The three bounded the steps, then Michael turned to Isabelle.

"You wait here," he whispered. Isabelle was about to protest, then Douglas took her arm.

"No, Isabelle, he's right. We don't know what's waiting inside. These men might be armed."

Flustered, Isabelle acquiesced and stepped to the side, only because there was no time to argue. Looking at each other, the two men backed away from the door. Then, with one swift kick of his healthy leg, Michael flattened the front door. Douglas was the first to race in.

"Unhand the child!" he bellowed. Isabelle peered into the room. It was dim, save for one candle in a corner. Ben was seated in a chair, bound and gagged. He looked unharmed, but there were dried tears on his cheeks. To his right was the big Irish man from before. In his hand was a blade.

"Tell the gal to git in here," he rasped. He looked surprised, obviously not expecting that Isabelle would not have come alone. "The papers are a'waitin' over there."

"She'll be signing no such thing," Michael said, "and when I get through with you, you won't be signing anything either." He lunged for the man, who tossed the long blade from one hand to the other in preparation for battle.

"C'mon," he beckoned with one meaty paw, then lunged for Michael. Isabelle screamed.

Michael expertly dodged the initial blow, simply by stepping to one side at the last moment. Bewildered at Michael's swiftness, the man made another attempt, only to have the blade knocked from his hand by the silver dragon handle of Michael's cane across his wrist. He yelped and dropped the blade, cursing. Michael went for Ben, stepping over the man, who suddenly turned and jabbed Michael in his weak leg. Michael swore and stumbled.

A shot rang out, and the man yelped. All eyes turned to see Douglas holding a pistol, the smoke still rising from the barrel. He had shot the man in the foot where he lay on the floor.

"Enough," Douglas said.

"But—" the man began, looking stunned.

"Quiet!" Douglas barked.

Michael regained his feet and went to help Ben. Scooping him up into his arms, he made for the door. He then placed the little boy into Isabelle's grateful arms.

Douglas followed, but did not turn his back on the man. "You tell your bosses that even the Devil himself would be ashamed of what they tried to do. And if they try something like this again," he added, "I'll be the one sending them to meet him!"

All three quickly returned to the carriage and were on their way.

Isabelle was too shaken to eat any dinner. Josie had recovered enough to harass her about eating something, and cooked some chicken stew. When Michael also insisted she take in something, Isabelle agreed to a cup of tea. Everyone was seated in the kitchen. Michael had listened to his aunt's heart, and reassured everyone that she'd fainted, and it was nothing more serious. It grew dark outside, and Josie insisted that Marie and Ben stay the night, after their ordeal.

Marie was mute again, but not before giving Isabelle and Michael a tearful thank you. Douglas had left abruptly, pausing only long enough to kiss Isabelle goodnight. He wanted to get back to town to see if a patrolman could come look for the bad man and put him in jail.

Ben chose to remain in Isabelle's arms, not having let go from the moment he'd been rescued. The look of love that Ben gave her upon seeing her there was still warming Isabelle's heart. He slept now, his breathing slow and regular.

Josie smiled at her. "Babies can sleep through anything, can't they?" Isabelle smiled back, then caught Michael looking at her as well. His eyes had a brief soft look again, which touched her as well.

"Careful, Isabelle," he joked softly. "You might want to give up touring for a season or two."

Isabelle blushed. Abruptly, Marie jumped up from her seat, and grabbed Ben from Isabelle's arms and left the room. Isabelle felt cold and empty for a while afterward, then quietly sipped her tea. Michael said nothing else.

After a while, Isabelle, Michael and Josie joined Marie and Ben in the front parlor. Ben was still sleeping in Marie's lap. She hummed softly to him as she stroked his dark hair. Exhausted, Isabelle and Michael absently sat right together on one couch, across from a grinning Josie. As time went on, Josie was snoring.

Isabelle took this quiet time to ask Michael about the mysterious woman.

"So, who is she?" Isabelle asked softly. "The exotic woman." She knew that question made her look jealous, but she had to know.

Michael looked at the floor. "Diedre is an old acquaintance of mine, Isabelle, nothing more."

"Um-hum," was all she said, realizing that she was quite bothered by the prospect of Michael with someone else.

"She is looking into something for me," was all he said.

"You two are involved, then," Isabelle said, matter-of-factly. Michael looked as if he wanted to say more, but did not.

Isabelle stopped her questioning; she surprised herself, wanting to know so much about Michael's private affairs. He did not owe her anything, she reasoned. Sighing, she leaned back into Michael's sudden embrace. He held her tightly, and she liked it.

Some time later, Isabelle drifted off, dimly realizing at the last moment that the kidnapper must have somehow gotten the deed from Ned. If that was true, then Ned had some connection to all of this. Too tired to tackle that mystery until the morning, she nodded off.

~ ~ ~

When the weather turned cool and the leaves turned dark red five months later, Briane and Louis' wedding day hung over everyone like a soggy shawl. During the endless days of preparation, Briane was too busy to torment Celeste every single day, but she did her best, whenever possible. Celeste would find herself shoved into walls, or forced to scrub floors that had already been scrubbed spotless. Once her pregnancy was hard to ignore, Briane resorted to giving Celeste quick, sharp jabs when no one was looking. Despite her not wanting the baby, Celeste could not help but feel something for it, particularly for its future here . Or, if Briane has her way, she thought, no future at all.

Secretly, Celeste did not mind the jabs at her stomach, hoping that one would be hard enough to make her lose this unwanted baby. Who knew what was going to happen once this child is born? she wondered, anxious. She had planned to swallow enough laudanum to kill them both, then Jacques would be forced to go on without her, but Celeste's Catholic upbringing dogged her.

Some of Briane's hateful attentions abated when she learned that, two months after the dullest, plainest wedding in French history, she, too, was pregnant by Louis. The day of the wedding, Briane marched into Louis' room and snatched down Celeste's portrait. She made to rip it apart, but Louis stopped her in time and hid it away.

Briane's mother rushed back from Montreal to be with her daughter at this "happy" time. The only problem was that Celeste was unable to stay hidden. Louis had ordered her room to be in the garret upstairs, just beyond the stairwell. The morning after Desmoiselle Hubert's arrival, Celeste ran into mother and daughter on the stairs. Desmoiselle Hubert, beautiful with delicate features in contrast to her daughter's hawkish face, merely sniffed and turned her head as if Celeste did not exist.

Celeste later overheard the two women together in the parlor, with Briane wailing about the "abomination" of Celeste being allowed to parade around flaunting her bastard child. Desmoiselle Hubert soothed her daughter, telling her that she, too, had suffered a similar indignity. She simply reminded her daughter that she would always be the lady of the estate and her children will be the true heirs. Celeste knew that fact would not be enough to satisfy Briane's hunger to be the one and only love of Louis.

Knowing this, Celeste gathered the resolve to confront Louis about their predicament. She had worried herself nearly to death about the future, so Celeste decided that she would ensure her child's future. It was a difficult decision, but one that would be for the best.

She found Louis in the men's parlor. He was preparing his afternoon brandy. When she entered the room, he stopped what he was doing, perhaps surprised by her appearing to come to him for a change.

"Celeste, my dear, this is a surprise," he said. He beckoned for her to come to him. She approached him slowly, but would not sit when he gestured for her to do so.

He sighed. "Celeste, I do not feel like a fight today."

"Excuse me. I only need a moment of your time, Sieur Fontaine."

Louis rolled his eyes at the utterance of his title. "Yes, Celeste, what is it?"

"It is about our child," she said. "I would like to make a request."

Louis' eyes softened at the mention of their child. He had welcomed the news with great joy, and even had Evangeline order fine mother-to-be gowns. He'd spared no expense, and assigned Eulalie to attend to Celeste at all hours. Celeste would even admit that things were easier when Louis was around, for he kept Briane at bay.

"Celeste, anything you desire."

"Louis, I want you to sell our child."

Louis looked faint. He took a swig of his drink. It was a long time before he spoke. "Anything but that, Celeste," he said. "Why would I want to do a thing such as that?"

"Louis, you know that we both have to answer for our sins, but this child is innocent."

"There is no sin in love," he said.

"This is not love," Celeste said. "But I am beyond trying to convince you of that. I am concerned for this child coming into a house of hate. You and I both know that Briane would have me dead a long time ago. What do you think she will do to a child born of our union?" she asked.

Louis smirked and slammed his drink down on the table. "There will be no discussion of selling our child. I assure you, Celeste, I married that hag as a business arrangement only. But she's more trouble than she's worth," he added. "I've recently found out her family is near goddamn broke. They played me for a fool!" he said, wiping his forehead. "We have enough debt with the rising taxes and all, and now she's with child, against my wishes. I told her I did not want any children by her, but she got me drunk, I swear.

"No harm will come to our child, Celeste. I promise you."

"Ahem." Celeste and Louis turned to see Briane at the door. Celeste dropped her eyes and politely excused herself from the room. She could feel Briane's cold stare tunneling through her back as she left. Having heard Louis' contempt spoken aloud, there was no doubt Briane would be on the warpath.

~   ~   ~

Isabelle felt something slam against her chest. To her surprise, she awoke to find a grinning Ben on her chest. He had leapt onto her in a flurry of excitement. Looking over, she saw Michael stirring. He took note of Ben, then grabbed him.

"Come here!" The little boy squealed with glee as Michael scooped him up into one big arm, then flipped the little boy onto his shoulders. Ben clapped, and Isabelle was happy to see that he was not still terrified from the day before. Marie came through with a broom.

"I hope he is not bothering you," she said, flatly. She had done more than returned to her reserved ways; Marie seemed angry about something.

"No, Marie, Ben is no bother," Isabelle replied, curious.

After a few more moments of horseplay, Michael set Ben down gently on his two feet. The little boy skittered off elsewhere. Michael turned to smile briefly at Isabelle, and it caught her off guard. The smile turned sad, though, and Michael rose.

"I best be getting on," he said. Just then, Josie bustled in.

"Hot breakfast for everyone!" she chimed.

Michael gave his aunt a peck on the cheek. "Sorry Auntie, I must go."

Josie pouted. "You never stay anywhere long, do you?"

Michael chuckled. "Where's the fun in that?" he said softly, and was off. Isabelle heard the soft closing of the back door.

Isabelle followed Josie back to the kitchen, sullen, assuming Michael was rushing to get back to Diedre. *Well, at least he'd polite enough to stay with me last night,* she thought. She took Josie up on the offer of food, particularly after not having eaten dinner the night before. As she took a forkful of eggs, she contemplated yesterday's horrible events. Realizing that it would pain Josie, Isabelle regrettably brought up the issue of Ned.

"Josie," she said, slowly, "you do realize that Ned must have some involvement in what happened yesterday."

Josie paused at the stove, shaking her head. "I know what you are thinking," she said. "But just because that man mentioned the deed does not mean that he really has it."

Isabelle nodded. "That is a good point. He could have been lying." Secretly, she hoped that was true—from what she'd seen of the affable Ned, she could not believe he would cavort with the likes of that man.

"Ned usually stops in on Mondays for lunch," Josie said. "I will be hoping to see him later today. Then we can get to the bottom of this."

Isabelle dressed for the day. For once, she did not feel out of control. Regarding her mortal enemies—that being Mr. Beaufort and his henchman, at least; dealing with that burly Irishman was something real, something that she could see, and that others could attest to. Finally, Isabelle was not alone wrestling with unseen forces.

Descending the stairs, her thoughts turned to the music, the unfinished composition still ringing in her head. Her left hand began to ache, but this time it was more about a driving need to get to the piano, and quickly.

Closing the music room door, Isabelle quickly took a seat and began playing. She skipped all drills and formalities, going straight to the piece. As she played, she felt a warmth flow through her hand and arms, all pain gone.

Like always, the piece flowed like a river, one musical phrase pouring into the next, high notes and deep bass notes cascading towards each other; usually at this point, Isabelle would abruptly stop, blocked as to what should come next. Somehow, she knew this time would be different. Perhaps it was the frightening day before, or the sense of loss at Michael leaving her side this morning. Whatever it was, she realized that she had been resisting something that she did not want to face—it was there all along, waiting for her to claim it as her own, to tell the story. She closed her eyes. . .

~   ~   ~

For a brief moment, there was peace in the house. Louis was upstairs, asleep, and Briane was out in the gardens with her mother, surveying the fall harvests. At Evangeline's urging, Celeste took a moment to play a song or two. The keys felt loose, not stiff, under her unpracticed fingers. She sampled with the tune that had always been in her head since childhood; she'd always entertained the thought of finishing it one day, the day that she would be freed from life at Maison Fontaine. She played distractedly, however, as Jacques crossed her mind, the memory of him filling every note she played. Tears came unbidden, falling almost hard enough to strike keys on their own. Finally, she stopped playing altogether.

There was a commotion from the front of the house, a screech, then laughter. Celeste went to see and was surprised to find Suzette in the doorway, bags in hand. Evangeline was smiling. Upon sight of Celeste, Suzette dropped everything and ran to her. They hugged.

"Celeste, sister, I'm home," Suzette said. She was beaming, and Celeste marveled at how well Suzette looked, prettier than ever. She'd filled out somewhat, a little fuller in the face.

"Congratulations on finishing school," Celeste said.

"Thank you," Suzette said, "It was such a lovely experience," she began, breathlessly. "I wish you could have seen—" Suzette stopped mid-sentence, and took a step back from Celeste. She frowned.

"Something's different about you," Suzette said, frowning.

Celeste gave no response and turned away.

"No, wait," Suzette said, turning Celeste back to face her. Evangeline stepped between them.

"Come, Suzette, your brother will be waiting for you."

Suzette allowed herself to be led away, but she looked back at Celeste's stomach, and with dread, Celeste knew that Suzette had figured things out.

"How could you!" Suzette screamed from the parlor. Celeste and Evangeline listened from the scullery. Evangeline busied herself with preparing dinner. It had started to rain, and the thunder shook the house. Lightning temporarily lit the night sky. Suzette's voice rose above the thunder, however. From the sound of it, Louis said not much in return. He seemed to acquiesce only to Suzette, probably because she looked so much like their late mother, or just because of who she was. Pere and Louis had dealt with Suzette gently over the years, because she was the most innocent of them all, until now.

"You knew what Pere had said about you leaving Celeste be!" she wailed. "This is what we have slumped to?" she demanded. "Well, I want no part of it!"

"Where are you going?" Celeste could hear Louis demand weakly. There was shuffling in the front hallway. Celeste, Evangeline and another slave could hear a tussle, then the door opening and slamming shut.

"Suzette!" Louis yelled. Celeste boldly went to the front and demanded where Suzette had run off to. Louis dropped his head in shame, and he was crying.

"I knew she would be angry," he said, sniffling, "but I think she hates me."

Celeste did not say a word. Louis looked broken, but she felt nothing.

"Louis, where is she going?"

"Stupid girl trying to get to the fort," he said, "in the rain. She's going to look for her fiancé. She plans to elope with him. He is taking a new post in Louisiana." Louis looked up suddenly, alarmed. "She did not take her cloak, just her bags, she was so upset. The rain!" In a flash, Louis took off out the front door. Celeste could not remember the last time she saw him move that fast. She watched him running and calling her name in the near-frozen October rain, then he disappeared from view.

It was a tense night of waiting, with Evangeline pacing the floor. The storm raged nonstop all night. Celeste pulled a chair near the door, and sank down in it, weary. Eulalie brought Celeste a cup of water.

In walked Jacques, behind Eulalie. His clothes were wet. Upon seeing him, Celeste jumped from her seat to hug him. Evangeline watched them absently.

"Nothing yet?" Jacques asked. Word had spread quickly.

Celeste shook her head. Evangeline suddenly put her head in her hands.

"Mon Dieu," she moaned, rocking back and forth. Celeste felt her stomach drop; she had seen Evangeline like this once before, just before everyone discovered one of the infant slaves, Evangeline's favorite, died in her sleep.

"Oh, no," Celeste said.

Just then, the front door slammed open, the stormy winds howling in the distance. In walked a rain-soaked Louis, his face a horrified mask, his bottom lip slack. In his arms was a limp Suzette, her fine traveling gown in singed, muddy tatters.

Celeste rushed to her side, crying. With one trembling hand, she touched Suzette, who was already ice cold. Her smooth porcelain face was pale, but still so young. Her hair was tangled. Louis crumpled to his knees, Suzette still in his arms, and wept.

"The lightning got her. It's all my fault she ran out in the storm," Louis cried. "I ruin everything. Everything!"

Jacques squeezed Celeste's shoulder before walking back out of the house. Celeste looked down at Louis, almost pitying him. Evangeline was frozen in her chair, expressionless. They all stayed that way until the cold, overcast morning greeted them.

CHAPTER ELEVEN

Ben got Isabelle's attention. He was breathing in her face, hot, urgent little pants like a puppy. He looked worried, and that saddened her.

"It's alright, Ben," Isabelle murmured, gently pinching his fat cheek. He smiled at her, then climbed down from her lap. Isabelle looked down at her hands, which were suspended over the keys, then placed them in her lap.

She quickly jumped from the piano bench. Pacing the room, she forced herself to remember everything from her time "away." She now understood that Celeste was close to giving birth to Louis' child and that Jacques was still alive. Suzette, Louis' younger sister, was dead from being distraught over what had happened to Celeste. Knowing how much Louis loved Suzette, Isabelle could only imagine what he would be like in the days following. But what concerned Isabelle the most was the look that Briane had given Celeste on that day, a look Isabelle believed contained the key to Celeste's fate.

Isabelle rushed down the hall to find Josie. She was in her room, humming as she darned what looked to be one of Michael's socks. Isabelle hesitated in the doorway. Josie took notice of her, then motioned for her to join her on the side of the bed. Isabelle sat down on the hand-stitched quilt.

"What's on your mind, child?" Josie said, never looking up from her work. Isabelle knew Josie was trying not to appear too anxious, and that made Isabelle feel guilty yet again. She had discouraged Josie from talking about the strange things. Now she wanted her assistance.

"Josie, I know that you have told me about the legacy of this estate," Isabelle began, "and I didn't want to listen. But. . .recent events have changed my mind."

Josie's eyes widened. "You don't say," she said, but she still appeared to restrain herself from going manic. "Tell me, what's been happening?"

Isabelle told her some of the more disturbing elements of her near two weeks at Maison Fontaine, including the journal, her near-drowning and what the old Indian woman had to say. Josie listened, then nodded her head, as if it confirmed what she already knew.

"I am surprised about Barry, though," she said. "I never thought he would have a connection to all of this, but it fits. We always wondered who the woman was he was drawing, that is, till you got here. Your granddaddy looked scared the first time he saw the picture, but he ignored it after that, I'm sure because he would never believe it was her." Josie slapped her ample thigh. "I knew there was something amiss, just couldn't put my finger on it."

Isabelle took Josie's arm. "Josie, do you hear us? We sound insane. No one's going to believe any of this," she said. "I just wanted you to know what I have been experiencing. But we can't let anyone else know. I'm hoping that they are just memories that were triggered by my coming here, or something. In ghost stories from my childhood I've heard of shades who are merely a remnant of someone past, but that was a story for entertainment.

"Maybe," Isabelle reasoned, "this is something of that nature, a story that will eventually play itself out, then be done with."

"The only problem with that," Josie said, "is the problem started when you got here. Why at that moment? Also, what little I do know about your family history is that Celeste committed suicide shortly after the birth of her child. That story was passed down through the family, a shameful secret, but your granddaddy told me anyways. If you are seemingly not only rememberin' her life, but relivin' it," Josie reasoned, "then what's goin' to happen to you?"

Just as Josie assumed, Ned arrived at the house for lunch. Josie thought it better that she speak with him first, so Isabelle kept silent when he came through the door. Seated at the kitchen table, Isabelle was shocked to see Ned in such a poor state. He practically stumbled into the kitchen. He was hatless, and he looked as if he'd slept in his clothes.

"Ned!" Josie exclaimed. She helped him to the chair, but crinkled her nose. "You smell of booze."

"I'm sorry, Josie, so sorry," Ned slurred.

"Ned, what's got you like this?" she asked.

He shook his head from side to side. "Pure folly," he answered. "I came to tell you why," he said.

"Tell us why 'bout what?"

"About why Isabelle is so scared. It's my fault."

Isabelle could not keep quiet any longer. "Why do you think I'm scared, Ned? Why would I have reason to be?" she asked, growing angry. "The last time I saw you, Ned, you were trying to get me to sign over the deed to this house. But to my surprise, some mountain of a man threatens our lives and says he has the deed."

"I lost a lot of money," Ned said, simply. "In town, at the tables. They knew I had one resource left, the deed to this house. They tried to force me to get you to sign the deed over, but I wouldn't do it. They took the papers from me, but I'm going to get them back." Sighing, the old man ran a hand over his face.

Josie looked disappointed. "I thought you had stopped gambling long ago."

"I did!" Ned raised his voice, then apologized. "I'm sorry, Josie, dear. I was tempted some time back. You should have seen my luck!" He had a wild smile, then it faded. "Then my luck changed. I owe a large sum, and they want to collect. I was desperate, I tell you," he turned to look at Isabelle. "Poor child. I deliberately sought you out, not because of family ties, but because of what I thought I could get out of the house."

Josie nearly fell back. "Ned!" she wailed.

Isabelle was speechless. She could not believe what she heard.

Ned was tearful. He pulled out a monogrammed handkerchief to wipe his nose.

"Isabelle, I fear that the people I owe have been harassing you, trying to hurt you, to frighten you, because of me. I wouldn't be surprised if you've been watched ever since you left my office that day. Many people know about the ghost tales around the house, most of them laughable. Our assailants, however, decided to capitalize on that without causing you any great harm. They'd assumed you would be gone by now, being a woman and all, with no real interest in the place anyway."

She remembered the incidents she faced: the noose at the back door, the strange noises. These tricks were all the handiwork of some devious, cowardly minds, as far as she was concerned. As for the ballroom, it was just as she'd thought before, Barry somehow escaping Michael's notice and locking the doors. The incidents in her bedroom were just her own imaginings. She thought about seeing "Jacques" in the yard. Maybe they hired someone to stand in the yard, then her imagination took over after that, she reasoned.

Happy with her line of reasoning about the strange occurrences, Isabelle winced at Ned's belief that she had no real interest in the house. It was true that she came there out of idle curiosity, and as a way to get away from her problems. Since then, however, her feelings had changed. Not only towards the house, but towards a lot of things. But she would deal with those other things later. For now, she had to figure out how to save the house.

She reached out to touch Ned. "Ned, you did a terrible thing."

He sobbed. "I know, I know."

"But that terrible thing may have changed the course of my life," Isabelle added. Josie looked at her in surprise. "I want to tell you both that I do care about this house, and I'm not giving up. I will see to it that these jackasses are thrown in jail for what they've done."

Ned was nearly falling out of the rickety wooden chair, so the women helped him to the men's parlor, where they laid him across the couch and covered him in a blanket to sleep off his drunkenness. He did not struggle until he realized he was on the couch.

"Isabelle, there's more," he said, agitated. "I must tell you—" Isabelle shushed him, figuring he was going to repeat everything he'd already said, as so many drinkers do. She'd seen her own mother do that, in private, with repetitious ravings over why Isabelle's father left them.

Ned went right to sleep. Isabelle and Josie tiptoed out. Josie was tearful and said she would be going to lie down in her room for a while. Isabelle felt sorry for her, having been betrayed by a lifelong friend like that.

Isabelle's thoughts turned to strategy. Free now of believing in hauntings from the "hereafter," she could concentrate on this world. She would find the police headquarters bright and early in the morning. She would tell them everything Ned revealed to her; with his standing in the city as an attorney, she was sure to be believed.

She heard the front door open and close. Turning in the hallway, she saw Marie opening the door for Douglas. Watching from the parlor doorway, Isabelle made the rash decision to stay concealed. Marie leaned in to speak to Douglas in earnest. A surprised look came across his face. Isabelle was bothered. What would these two have to talk about? Ben ran up behind Marie, then sailed into Douglas with a hard kick in the shins. Douglas yelped in surprise.

Isabelle rushed out in the open, knowing that she could not hide after all that racket. But before he noticed her there, a dark look passed over Douglas' face, only to disappear in a flash. Marie turned to Ben and gave him a quick swat on his behind. She sent him to the kitchen. When Ben passed Isabelle silently, he gave her a sharp penetrating glance that seemed too old for a child of five. He was trying to tell her something.

Hobbling, Douglas noticed Isabelle. He gave her a sheepish grin. "Little boys," he said, breathless. He had a newspaper tucked underneath his arm. "They love to kick."

Marie, looking worried, excused herself.

Isabelle had to know. "Douglas, what was Marie talking about?"

Douglas leaned against the doorframe. "Huh? Oh, nothing, just thanking me again for helping get Ben back."

Isabelle nodded quickly. How could she have forgotten the kidnapping that quickly? She offered to help Douglas into the hallway chair, but he refused. As they moved on past the men's parlor, however, he stopped abruptly.

"What's he doing here?" Douglas asked. Isabelle could not help but notice the anger in his voice.

She shrugged. "Ned? He comes over on Mondays for lunch. But this time, he was drunk, which was a surprise to me. Apparently, he's had some issues with gambling and drinking in the past. I know Josie said he was no longer married. This is probably why. There are some other things he mentioned, though, that of great urgency."

Douglas looked up. "Such as what?"

Isabelle sighed. "It's good you are here. There are a few things I need to discuss with you. Let's go to the music room. I have a surprise."

In the music room, Isabelle took a seat at the piano, and Douglas pulled up a chair. Isabelle told him about how Ned was in financial trouble and had promised the deed to a group of ruthless men. Douglas looked shocked, then urged her to continue.

"As bad as it sounds, though, I'm somewhat relieved that it was not ghosts trying to run me off the place."

"Ghosts?" Douglas asked, his eyebrows shooting upward.

Isabelle chuckled. "Yes, Douglas, I have been going out of my mind since I got here. I thought I was seeing some people from the past around here, and I even had names for them. Jacques. Louis. Celeste." Isabelle paused at the mention of Celeste's name, forgetting that a Celeste had indeed existed in the past. The proof was in the journal.

"Turns out a Celeste did truly exist," Isabelle amended. "I found some of her journal entries. She is one of my ancestors, and I look like her. I found her painting in the attic. But the entries are just that, a part of the past, not my present."

As Isabelle spoke, Douglas seemed to hang on every word, eyes practically bulging out of his head. At the mention of the name "Celeste", he went pale. Isabelle wondered if his leg hurt more than he let on.

"Are you alright, Douglas? Is your leg smarting?"

Douglas shook his head as if to clear it. "No, I—that was an interesting story. I had no idea all of this was going on. I know that I have been away from you at long stretches, so you've probably been bored out of your head."

"No, not really," Isabelle corrected him. "I've even had a revelation about the song I've been working on for so long. You know, the one I can't seem to finish."

Douglas looked preoccupied. "Really," he said, flatly.

Isabelle nodded enthusiastically. She played an abridged version because Douglas was all too familiar with the song, and went into the new section. "This is the new part," she said as she played. "It is a melodic passage that has been in my head for years now, I realize."

Several seconds into the new section, Douglas turned pale and jumped out of his seat. Startled, Isabelle stopped playing.

"Douglas! What's wrong with you?" she asked.

"That—that melody," he stammered, pointing at the piano. "Where did you hear that?" He backed away as if the piano were a hissing cobra.

Isabelle was annoyed. "Douglas, I just told you this was a tune in the back of my head for a long, long time. I just didn't realize it would fit the song so well. I believe this will be the song that puts me on the world stage."

Douglas went for the door. "Isabelle, I'm just not feeling well. I've got to go."

Isabelle rose from the bench. "I'll see you out—"

"No, that's not necessary. I'll be back tomorrow. Goodbye, Isabelle."

Douglas rushed through the doorway, leaving a stunned Isabelle behind. She'd wanted to admit to him that she'd reconsidered her acceptance of his marriage proposal, that she'd realized that her heart did not lie with him, but she still wanted him to be her manager. But she took note about how Douglas had told her goodbye—it seemed so final. Looking down at where he'd just been sitting, Isabelle noticed that Douglas forgot his newspaper. When she bent to pick it up, the headline was hard to miss:

CASS FARM COMPANY FACES FINANCIAL CRISIS

Isabelle heard the front door open and close long after Douglas had let himself out. Thinking that he must have come back, she went up to meet him. She realized he must have been upset about the Company; the newspaper article said that because of several wildcatting bank failures, the national economy is slated to slow down by year's end. In Detroit, many of the new stores and hotels were already going into bankruptcy. She wanted to tell Douglas how sorry she was, going on with her own problems. Passing the men's parlor, she noticed that Ned was gone. In his shame, she thought, he must have decided to slip out. She'd let him worry if she was going to press charges against him.

Fixing herself an early dinner, then not eating it, Isabelle went up to her room. Josie did not come out of her room the rest of the day. Marie and Ben were long gone. Isabelle considered sneaking a quick drink to help her sleep, but cheerfully decided that she would not be needing that kind of help. The truth about the house was in the open, and there was nothing to be afraid of any longer.

Opening the door to her room, Isabelle spied something on her bed. The curtains in her room were drawn, and the days were getting shorter, so it was dark. Lighting a candle on the tallboy, she went over to the bed and picked up what looked like Barry's picture. When her eyes focused on the details, Isabelle nearly dropped everything. Covering her mouth, she stifled a shriek. The picture, presumably of "Celeste", was nearly complete. There were the turbulent water waves, and the hands of two men, but this time, there was another hand, larger than the other two, and it was sinisterly curled around the woman's neck; the nail on the thumb of that hand was long and twisted. The veins in the hand were raised, showing the force of the grip. The woman in the picture looked horrified, her eyes pleading for help. Isabelle could swear she felt the iron grip on her own neck. Falling to the floor, she choked.

~   ~   ~

Louis was too distraught to give his little sister a decent burial. He stayed in his room all day, drinking and smashing things. It was up to Evangeline to make for a nice burial; she even put a bouquet of wildflowers in Suzette's hands, making her look like a young bride who was simply sleeping. The town undertaker was brought right away, and Father Daniel presided. Suzette's pine coffin was carried by Silas and Caleb to the family graveyard out back, and she was gone.

Evangeline took Suzette's death to heart. Celeste knew that in many ways, Evangeline had been like a mother to all three of them. Once Suzette was buried, Evangeline stormed back to the house, up the stairs, and into Louis' room. Louis would not open his door, so she kicked it in. Celeste and Eulalie, who were on Evangeline's heels, were terrified, never having seen her behave like this.

Without warning, there was a severe banging from in the room, and Evangeline's voice could be heard over the racket.

"You son of a bitch!" she screamed. "You killed her! And what you did to Celeste!" There was a resounding slap.

The two young women dared not look into the crashed-open doorway, but they heard everything. Not once did Louis fight back, nor did he say a word. After a while, Evangeline tired, and she quietly walked from the room. Wiping her eyes on her sleeve, she took no notice of the girls. She went to the kitchen, back to work. Louis could be heard sobbing softly. Celeste and Eulalie went back downstairs.

The next week was deathly silent, with Louis remaining in his room and never coming out, not even for his drunk friends. A couple of days into his absence, Evangeline had pity and took a plate of food to leave outside his door. He never ate it, however. It went unspoken, but Celeste was sure everyone (except, perhaps Evangeline) were breathlessly hoping that Louis would die. They all used to be afraid of having a new owner, but not anymore, having lived under the whims of a self-indulgent manchild. Once Briane and her mother returned to the Fontaine and learned what happened, they barged into Louis' room, having an indifferent Caleb break down the door that he had just repaired the week before. When found, Louis was indeed close to death, but not quite close enough. The doctor was summoned.

It was during this time that Celeste and Jacques saw each other freely, out in the open. They took long walks together and watched the few slave children frolic. They talked of being free of Louis once he was dead, and Jacques planned how they would leave the farm and fetch his sister, for Louis would no longer have a hold over her. It was then that Jacques proposed to Celeste, who burst into tears when he got down on one knee, in front of the slave quarters. The women who used to torment Celeste had finally come to accept her, pitying what happened to her. They looked on with smiles as Jacques slid a silver ring etched with three wavy lines onto her third finger.

"*The river brought me to you, so I had this made in remembrance,*" he had said. "*You are mine forever, Celeste.*"

They knew not when or how a ceremony could be held, but Jacques was determined. Sadly, Celeste did not believe it would ever happen, but she was happy to see Jacques happy.

Briane nursed Louis day and night, and her mother assumed the management of the farm, as harvest time was upon them. Desmoiselle Hubert looked surprised to see work had been going on, just as before—everyone had a stake in the farm's success this year. Too consumed with Louis, Briane left them all alone, for a while.

At the very least, Celeste was sure Louis had finally seen the light and would not object to her being with Jacques. She was wrong. Instead of regretting what he had done to her, to all of them, Louis kept a tighter rein on her as soon as he could speak again. When Celeste saw Louis propped up for the first time in the music room, she was disturbed by his gaunt frame and haunted eyes, but found herself completely cold; she could have cared less. She would never have believed this about herself, but after Suzette's death, Louis' only redeeming quality died with her. There was no one to save him now, and even though he had not died yet, his appointment with hell was set.

When Celeste entered the music room as summoned, Louis' empty face said that he knew he was damned as well.

"*Bright Eyes, it is so good to see you,*" *Louis said. She could barely hear him. Louis motioned for her to take a seat at the piano. Their baby kicked Celeste hard right at that moment.*

"*Play for me,*" *Louis said,* "*The song Pere loved so much. That one.*"

Without a word, Celeste began to play. The song was from their childhood, an original song Celeste composed to impress Pere. They all loved it. Suzette had said that she would have Celeste play it for her wedding someday.

Louis pulled his quilt up to his neck. He closed his eyes and leaned his head back. Not knowing if he had fallen asleep or not, Celeste continued to play. She played not for Louis, but for herself, and for Jacques. She could see Jacques in her mind right then, knowing that he could hear from wherever he was on the farm. In her mind's eye, Celeste saw him stopping his work, wiping his brow, cocking one ear to hear better. She could feel whenever he thought of her, and he could sense her feelings, usually dark feelings of despair. This time while she played, she sent him her feeling of brief contentment.

She played on for a long while, losing touch with her surroundings. Lost in the music, she did not immediately see Briane looming in the doorway. The new bonnet, required of French wives, was lopsided atop her curls.

"What's this?" she asked, her face feigning innocent inquiry, but Celeste could feel the menace from where she sat. Briane sauntered in confidently, not so awkward this time. Celeste realized that with Louis nearly helpless, Briane had the power.

"Briane, don't you dare," Louis warned. He could barely lift his head.

Briane had a tight smile of triumph, and Celeste felt her heart drop into her shoes. Briane yanked a struggling Celeste off the piano bench. Celeste's thigh painfully scraped the corner of the bench. With a man's strength, Briane dragged Celeste down the hallway by her collar. Celeste reached up in vain to free herself, but Briane's grip was final.

Briane was muttering as they went down the hall. Everyone was outdoors, working on the harvest.

"I've had enough of you," Briane said. "If I take your child now, Louis would hate me forever. If I kill you now, I know I will lose him as well. So, what to do?"

Celeste ceased clawing at Briane's hand, which had thin streaks of blood running down from her wrist. They reached the scullery, and Briane went for the butcher block. Celeste's eyes widened as she realized what her enemy intended to do.

"No!" Celeste wailed only once. She would not give Briane the satisfaction of hearing her beg.

Briane swiveled around. As Celeste tried to roll to one side, Briane clamped one foot down onto Celeste's arm, pinning her to the floor. Briane swung a butcher's blade in a downward arc to connect with Celeste's left wrist. Celeste's delicate hand was severed in one clean chop. The blade was embedded so deeply in the floor its hilt wagged and vibrated. Too stunned to scream, Celeste lay in a puddle of her own blood. The last thing she saw was Briane standing over her, dissatisfied.

"You won't even scream," Briane said, bemused, her face covered with Celeste's blood.

~   ~   ~

CHAPTER TWELVE

Isabelle moaned. Her left hand was throbbing, but now she understood why. In the past, Briane had taken Celeste's hand to ensure she never played the piano again. Panicked, Isabelle looked down to convince herself that she still had her own hand. Everything had felt too real to be some elaborate dream. These disturbing realizations set Isabelle right back on the path she'd so desperately wanted to leave behind, the path of true belief about Celeste, about everyone. Rising and dusting herself off, Isabelle picked up the picture from the floor and hurried to Barry's room.

He must be trying to tell me something new about the picture, Isabelle thought. She rapped on the door quickly, then swung it open.

"Barry, I—" Isabelle stopped cold upon sight of Barry unconscious on the floor of his room, just as she had been, moments, or hours, before.

Falling to her knees beside Barry, Isabelle found him cold to the touch. His lips were blue. She felt for his pulse, which was thready. Dashing for the top landing of the stairs, Isabelle yelled down.

"Is anyone home? Quick, Barry needs help!" she called. By the time she went back to check on Barry again, heavy, uneven footsteps could be heard from the staircase. It was Michael.

"Michael," Isabelle breathed, relieved to see him. Michael removed his jacket and went straight to work on Barry.

"Barry? Can you hear me?" he asked. There was no response. Michael checked his pulse. "His pulse is weak, but steady. He was like this when you found him?" he asked.

Isabelle nodded. "What's wrong with him?" she asked.

Michael sat back on his heels. "I'm not sure. Can you go down and fetch my bag?"

Isabelle rushed down the stairs. Josie was just coming back in the house from out back, so Isabelle told her what was going on. Josie rushed up to Barry's room. Isabelle opened the door to Michael's room. It was sparse, but neat. On his dressing table, Isabelle could not help but notice a beautiful

Chinese fan splayed partially open in the bottom of a velvet gift box. In the dim light, the ruby-studded handle of the fan glittered. Thinking of the Oriental fashion sense of the mystery woman at his office, Isabelle guessed this must be a gift for her. Pushing that thought out of her mind, she grabbed his black bag from the top of his dresser to rejoin him upstairs.

Barry was on his bed, under a blanket. Some color had returned to his lips, and he appeared to be breathing deeply. He looked asleep. Michael thanked Isabelle for the bag, took out his stethoscope, and listened to Barry's heart.

"Heart sounds good," Michael said. "His pulse has slowed down. But I can't explain why he is unconscious. It's like he's in a deep sleep, the kind after someone has a seizure."

"A seizure?" Josie asked, afraid. "Will he come out of it?"

Michael nodded. "Most people do, after a while. It depends on the severity of the attack. No one really knows why they happen, but it's odd that Barry would suddenly have one."

Isabelle was still clutching Barry's picture, which was now crumpled. She knew that his "attack" was related to the picture in some way, but she did not want to reveal that to Josie and Michael just yet; she wanted to think about the connection for a while.

"I'll sit with Barry tonight," Isabelle said. She climbed into bed next to him and held his clammy hand.

Michael pulled up a chair. "Of course, I'll be here, too."

Josie nodded. "Fine. I'll get supper started, then I'll bring somethin' up for everybody." She cast one more worried look, then left.

Isabelle and Michael sat together, both in their own thoughts. Finally, Michael spoke.

"Isabelle, there's something you're not saying about Barry," he said, simply. "What is it?"

Isabelle shrugged lightly, hoping he would not persist, but his look said he was not through yet. "It's nothing, really," she added, nervous. She'd forgotten about Michael's piercing perception.

"Might as well tell me."

"It's—it's about the pictures Barry works on. I think I know why he draws the same face over and over," Isabelle confessed.

Michael looked intrigued. "Really? I always wondered about them. He stays so focused on drawing them, but he always destroyed them, saying they were not right. The little I know about nervous conditions is that patients with artistic inclinations tend to draw the same scenes over and over, or," he said with a mischievous smirk, "play the same song over and over."

Isabelle took one of the extra pillows on Barry's bed and threw it at Michael. He ducked, then chuckled a little. Looking down at Barry, Isabelle sobered and resumed her story.

"Barry says that he's been drawing Celeste all of these years."

"Celeste?" Michael asked.

"She's my ancestor, it turns out," Isabelle said. "One of the people I told you about. You know, the ones from the past."

"Ah," was all Michael said in return.

"You can imagine my surprise when Barry and I finally talked about having this woman's image in common. She is his ancestor, too. But there's more. He claims she 'tells' him to draw the picture. The picture seems to be telling a story. The two times I've seen it, it's changed, and not for the better."

Michael motioned for Isabelle to show him the drawing. After he studied it for a while, he frowned.

"This is disturbing," he said. "This Celeste person appears to be under siege, no doubt. Three different people wanting her for some reason."

"The other thing is," Isabelle paused, "I have a sense she died a horrible death. Not by suicide, as my family history suggests. It is no coincidence that Barry's picture progressed at the same pace as my vision, that is, a forward progression to some final moment."

"That moment being Celeste's death?"

"I think so," Isabelle said. "Through my dreams I am remembering scenes from Celeste's life, to tell myself what happened. I met an old woman during the boating trip who seemed to know what I was going through. I paid her little attention, but I recall her telling me that I was 'chosen' to remember, simple as that."

"I sensed you were special, Isabelle, but not like this," Michael said.

For the second time that evening, Celeste noticed Michael had made a witty comment. She was curious. "Michael, you almost seem to be in a light mood," Isabelle said, warmly. "Why now?"

Michael shrugged. "Just trying to brighten our situation. Besides," he added, "it's fun having you all to myself for a while," he gestured to the sleeping Barry, "so to speak."

Isabelle's heart beat faster. "Michael, there is something I do want to tell you about my engagement—"

Her statement was interrupted by Barry's stirring. Immediately, Michael leaned over him to check his pulse again. "Barry, can you hear me?" he asked.

Barry screwed up his face as if he had tasted something terrible, then his face relaxed. He opened his eyes. Isabelle noticed they were strangely clear again, like the other day.

"Isabelle," he said, his voice strong. "I don't know how long I can hold them back. I think they've done something to me, to stop me from finishing the picture."

"Barry, who are 'they'?" Isabelle pressed. Michael did not move, so as not to distract Barry.

Barry squeezed Isabelle's hand, and she could feel the urgency. "You are out of time. The picture reveals all. Somehow, they found me."

Isabelle shook her head in frustration. "Barry, I can't follow you. I don't understand it all. I know that Celeste was murdered, I'm sure of it. But what happened to Jacques?"

Barry looked lost. "I don't know of any Jacques. Only her. And them. They'll be coming for you, now. I wish I could have done more. I knew the picture would tell the truth once I was able to finish it. When you arrived here, I felt the change, as if a door was opened. The rest of the picture came to me then. But now that the truth is out," he paused, his voice growing raspy. "They went into action before I could think of what else to do. I've been so helpless all of this time, but did not know why," he started to cry, and Isabelle wiped away his tears with her own hands.

"Shh, Barry," she crooned. "Don't cry. I have made it this far. You and I will push on together. I've just found you, and we have so much to catch up on."

Barry turned on his side, away from Isabelle. "It would be grand to get to know you, dear Izzy," he said, "but our time has to be cut short. There's one thing I know I can do to stop it all." With that, he went back to sleep.

Isabelle rose from the bed and went into Michael's waiting arms.

Several hours later, Isabelle and Michael ate Josie's light supper of leftover chicken stew. Barry refused to eat at first, but then took a few bites. His eyes seemed to cloud over once again, and he was lost in his own world. As the night wore on, Michael discussed the reality of Barry going to a hospital after this family situation was resolved. Feeling defeated, Isabelle agreed after Michael promised he would find the most caring place, maybe even in Canada, so that he could be near her. Isabelle froze at the mention of Canada, having almost forgotten that she'd ever lived there.

"I know of someone who might be able to help you," Michael said. "He has an unorthodox approach, but this is more of his specialty. I would like to take you to him early tomorrow morning."

Isabelle agreed, glad at this point for any help whatsoever. She thought about what Michael said about her and Barry in Canada in the near future. The thought had not occurred to Isabelle that once all of this was over, she would probably never see Michael again.

"If Barry and I are in Canada," Isabelle hedged, "where will you be?"

Michael went silent in the darkness. "Isabelle, I'll be anywhere you want me to be."

At that, Isabelle smiled. Michael caressed her arm, and their shared silence spoke volumes. The silence was broken, however, by Josie bustling into the room with a lit lantern, her Bible, and a quilt. She was going to join them for the night. Michael and Isabelle looked at each other, then laughed. Josie looked up in surprise.

"What?" she asked, innocently.

Eventually, Michael and Josie were fast asleep. Isabelle yawned several times, and pulled up the quilt around herself and Barry. She did not fear going to sleep; she needed to know what would happen next.

~ ~ ~

Jacques was thrown into the Fort's stockade for several days after what he did to Briane. Surprisingly, Louis had not ordered the arrest; he was furious enough with her to kill her himself. It was Briane, with a severely bruised face and missing tooth from Louis' beating, who pressed charges against Jacques for trying to strangle her.

Celeste learned from Evangeline that Jacques had stopped working out front the day of Briane's attack. He had sensed something was wrong and barged into the house with no concern over what Louis would do. When he found Celeste on the floor bleeding to death, he called for help, then ran back in to wrench the knife from Briane's hands. He then proceeded to choke the life out of her, but Caleb and Silas pulled him off, not wanting him to be executed. Louis had practically crawled down the hall only to find the gruesome scene. He went to Celeste's side, and, summoning some miraculous strength from within, picked her up to carry her to Evangeline's bed. He did not bother to help Briane.

Evangeline had quickly wrapped Celeste's hand and sent for the doctor. Briane's mother went to the fort. When she returned with four soldiers, Jacques was taken into custody. Louis spoke in Jacques's defense, but his bad reputation for drinking and "whore-mongering" with the notorious slave Celeste hurt his credibility. Once he saw that Celeste was being cared for, Jacques went without a fight.

Celeste slept for many days. In her dreams, she could see Jacques, shackled by the ankle in his cell; he communicated to her that he would be with her soon, he promised. When she awoke, it was to the sound of a baby's cries. She opened one eye to see a swaddled infant right next to her in a bed. It looked like Evangeline's room.

"So, you're awake," she heard Evangeline say. "Your baby arrived the night you were attacked. You had already lost so much blood, but Mon Dieu, you lived. That stands for something," Evangeline said.

Slowly, Celeste looked all around, then remembered her hand. Hoping it had been a dream, she was bitterly disappointed to see her slender arm ending in a bandaged stump. She dropped her head, realizing she would never play the piano again.

Evangeline sat on the side of the bed and rocked back and forth with a crying Celeste. She too, cried freely. "All of my life, I've seen one tragedy after another," she said. "My own enslavement. The enslavement of my children. I don't even know where any of them are. My husband being shot. At least when I found myself here, I thought I could live out my days in some little kind of peace, even though I had lost all my loved ones.

Then here you come, like the sun, too radiant for us all to withstand," she went on. "It's not because you are pretty and can play the pianoforte so nicely—everyone already knows that. There's something else about you, something that makes everyone want to possess you for their own. Just like your name, you are from the heavens. And that was your undoing. But it wasn't your fault. Never was."

Her head down, Evangeline went on. "But don't worry. I won't let anything happen to your child. This I can do something about. I'll guard your child with my life."

Celeste nodded before drifting back into a laudanum-induced slumber. Celeste knew that Evangeline would keep her word, no matter what happened.

Jacques was set free about a week later. Even though he was an slave, he was respected as the famous boat builder and was treated well by the Commandant.

"Besides," Jacques said, when he was able to sneak in to visit Celeste, "they know all about the deranged 'lord of the manor' and his hawk-faced, gangly wife."

It was obvious that Jacques was trying to make Celeste laugh, but it did not work. She was sitting up in a chair in Evangeline's room, and the baby slept on the bed for the moment. Briane, who had not dared come near Celeste since then, was gone with her mother to Mass at Ste. Anne's. Evangeline had said that Louis had a setback for a few days, but he'd said he would die before he let Briane touch him again. Briane stayed out of his way, and watched him sullenly from across the room. Her mother tried to make peace, but Louis ignored her.

The baby stirred and cried weakly like a little kitten. He had his father's eyes. Jacques gently scooped up the infant and rocked it. Celeste let herself pretend for a moment that the child was theirs, and they were in their own home on a lazy afternoon.

"She's not through with me," Celeste said, matter-of-factly.

Jacques' eyes darkened. "That pitiful hag will not harm you again, Celeste."

Celeste said not another word about it, because she knew that Jacques could not guard her day and night. She took out her journal, which Eulalie had fetched for her, to make a few last entries. Briane would pounce like a cat on a mouse, when no one was looking. It was just a matter of when.

~   ~   ~

For once, Isabelle did not wake up panicked or terrified, now that she understood some of what had happened in the past. Isabelle was now able to pay attention to more details within that mysterious world, to take in the sounds: the cackle of chickens out in the yard, the clacking of Evangeline's spinning wheel, the *ting* of the butcher blade as it severed her hand. . .Isabelle shook her head violently to dispel that last gruesome sound. She could hear Jacques' heart beating through his chest when he held Celeste back then, much the way she heard Michael's in the now, strong, steady, adoring.

She looked around for Michael, but he was not in sight. Isabelle was not surprised, for Michael was always on the go—that was his problem. Josie was gone from the room as well, but from the smell of bacon cooking coming from downstairs, Isabelle knew what she was up to. Barry was still sleeping peacefully, so Isabelle felt he had passed through the worst. She knew that Josie would keep an eye on him until they returned.

As she rode side by side with Michael in his carriage, Isabelle was bewildered by what sort of person would be able to help her. She was sure that her case was one of a kind. They went north of Jefferson, to Lafayette, where a cluster of stately homes lined both sides of the street. Most had white picket fences surrounding them. When Michael pulled the carriage to a halt, he disembarked and helped Isabelle out. She followed him up a paved walk to the front door of one of the houses. After a couple of Michael's raps on the door, it opened.

A white woman with light hair gave Michael a smile. "Michael, do come in," she said. She was in an expensive silk gown, a dark peacock blue. The woman eyed Isabelle closely for a moment, then stepped aside to let her through after Michael. The front parlor was cheerily designed, with flowered wallpaper and white furniture. A gold colored parrot was in a rounded cage suspended from the ceiling.

The woman gestured for them to take a seat. "My husband will be out in a moment." She left out and disappeared down the hall.

In walked Dr. Innis. In his forties, he looked kindly enough, with brown suit and spectacles. His blue eyes assessed Isabelle.

"So, this is the beautiful young woman you told me about," he said, taking her hand and giving it a quick kiss.

"It is a pleasure, Miss Fontaine. I'm Dr. Innis. Come to my office, both of you."

The three went down a short hall, then entered a room on the right. Dr. Innis gestured for Isabelle to take a seat in a leather high-back chair. Michael was instructed to sit in a chair behind her out of sight, near the door. Dr. Innis pulled up a chair to Isabelle's left.

"Now, Isabelle," he began. "Michael's told me that you have been having visions."

Isabelle was about to deny the whole thing, then thought better of it. From the sincere look on the man's face, he seemed to already know what she was going to say.

"I, well, sometimes, yes," she stammered. "And it feels as if I know these people. I'm in the shoes of someone named Celeste. I live through whole days in her life, I feel her pain."

Dr. Innis started taking notes on a small tablet. "Do go on."

Expecting to be rebuffed or mocked, Isabelle was surprised by how open Dr. Innis appeared. She went ahead with her story, comfortable in sharing her experiences, even in front of Michael. Blushing, she also told about Jacques, and the sometimes overwhelming feelings for him that enticed, confused, and frightened her all at the same time. She felt Michael's eyes on her back, but she told everything—it was best if he knew it all before they went any further.

Once Isabelle finished, Dr. Innis sat back, astonishment on his face. He then looked rather elated.

"My Dear," he said enthusiastically, "this is the most detailed case I ever heard. You have a very deep involvement in this past history. An involvement," his face fell suddenly, "I fear that is far too deep."

After taking a deposition from Michael about what he'd seen happen to Isabelle, including her near-drowning in the river, Dr. Innis frowned. When Isabelle handed him Barry's drawing, he went pale. "I don't like this at all," he said. "People dream and wake up sure they have been in contact with a relative long dead—that happens more often than many of us think. The things you speak of, however, are unlike anything I've heard, and I've been in this business for twenty years.

"I had my own experience with the supernatural, you see," Dr. Innis continued, "as a young man. I distinctly remember hearing my departed younger brother, Milton. He died out there on the river, one Sunday when we were crossing over the ice from Canada. The ice gave way, and he drowned, despite my family's best efforts to save him. We were distraught for quite a while, none of us wanting to go on. But Milton reached me, one bright, glorious morning, he called my name, just as I was about to awaken for the day."

"Did you believe it was truly him?" Isabelle asked, intrigued.

Dr. Innis shook his head. "Of course not, not at first. I loved studying science, and had planned to be some great scientist. How would hearing from my dead brother fit into my way of thinking? I ignored the voice, for days, weeks, but he persisted. Finally, our youngest sibling, Henry, a three year-old, went missing. He had wandered off. My mother was fainting, and my father was frantic—they could not take losing another child. In desperation, I listened to Milton's voice when it came to me, because he told me where to look for Henry. Just as he'd said, I found Henry two streets over, in someone's backyard. He was seated and looked to be holding someone's hand, but there was no one else around.

"As I took Henry away from there and back to our parents," Dr. Innis continued, "he cried because he didn't want to leave his friend.

" 'A friend?' I'd asked."

"'Yes,'" Henry had said, "'Milton. He said we are friends.'"

"Needless to say," Dr. Innis said, "my attitude towards things like that changed dramatically. I did become a scientist, but my focus is on things out of the ordinary. I have found a strong connection between electricity and the occurrence of 'ghosts'. Hundreds of case studies, people all over the world having similar encounters. Lately, I've gone into a new field of research, and that has to do with what I think you are experiencing."

Isabelle held her breath. "You think you know what this is?" she asked.

Dr. Innis nodded. "It's called ancestral memory."

"I am of the firm belief that death is just the beginning for us," Dr. Innis explained. "Our bodies wear out, but our soul endures. Most of us go on ahead to the proverbial light you always hear about," he said, "but some of us don't go right away. They hang around because of some unfinished business, or, in your case, to warn others. This Jacques, I believe, means you no harm. He never went on to the other side. His desires for revenge and to protect you are too strong. Desires can be so powerful as to outlive death itself. Jacques believes you are his long-lost Celeste. The other thing keeping him here is, well, you, I'm afraid."

"What?" Isabelle and Michael asked in unison.

"The theory of ancestral memory," Dr. Innis said, "has to do with certain memories being passed down through generations. For some reason, this is the particular time that memories have been awakened within you. My guess is that Jacques was that spark. You are unique, Isabelle, because you are most undoubtedly a 'sensitive,' that is, someone who can communicate with the dead. You share a common bond through music, as well. But you also possess your ancestor's memories of her time with Jacques. You are caught in the interplay between these forces. I, and some other scientists, believe that certain cycles in time repeat themselves, for whatever reason. If you look at the nature of life itself, you can see the circle—the rotation of the same four seasons, the cycle of life, death, and birth again. In the East, the Indians talk of a rebirth. I digress, but what I'm saying is that the soul does not die.

"The problem is, though," the doctor said, rubbing his chin, "is how to free yourself, before it causes you harm."

"It's already too late for that," Isabelle said. "I've seen my fair share of harm since I've been here."

"No, there's a greater harm," Dr. Innis said. "Because Celeste came to a bad end, you are practically doomed to repeat her fate."

"Doomed? What kind of talk is that, Dr. Innis?" Michael interjected. "Nothing's going to happen to Isabelle, I promise you that."

Dr. Innis gestured for Michael to simmer down. "Hold on, Dr. St. Vincent. What I was going to say is that I see the roots of your survival already. You mentioned your cousin Barry, who is assuredly a sensitive actually seeing your ancestor, not living her memory. He has a small part of what you are able to see, but it has nearly destroyed him. I would almost say that he is the key to your surviving this, but I have the feeling I would be wrong. His completion of that picture reveals Celeste's killer; this is yet another warning."

"Another warning of what, exactly?" Isabelle asked, feeling faint.

"That someone is going to kill you."

Back in Michael's carriage, Isabelle tossed Dr. Innis's extravagant theories around in her mind. The theories seemed to explain things, but they were so outrageous. She put a hand on Michael's arm.

"Thank you for trying to help me," she said, as the carriage swayed on.

Michael kept his eyes on the road. "I don't know if I was much help to you, but I know that Dr. Innis is a good man. He believes what he's talking about."

In spite of her own dire situation, Isabelle could not help but think about Diedre again. Michael had promised he would explain everything, but Isabelle didn't know if she could stand the wait. She forced herself to stop thinking about it.

"Before we go back to the house, I'd like to find the local police headquarters," Isabelle said. "I'm still going to press charges against Ned, so that he'll be forced to get my deed papers back. Douglas told me the day of the kidnapping he'd reported that crazy Irishman to the foot patrol, and they're still looking for him. Perhaps he and Ned can share the same cell."

The police headquarters was abuzz with activity, mostly pickpockets that had been picked up. Douglas had told Isabelle that along with the overwhelming growth of any city comes its fair share of crime. There was an increase in streetwalkers as well; several of them were bound together, plumes of feathers on their dainty hats matching their showy dresses. They watched Isabelle closely as Michael helped her out of the carriage. They admired Michael as he strode by, and Isabelle was reminded of how handsome he was. She couldn't imagine why he had not married yet, but chided herself for letting her thoughts drift to him again.

As they took the first steps of the building, they were stopped by two Negro men who surrounded them. One of them had a pistol, and it was shoved into Michael's back.

"Come with us, please."

"This is between us," Michael said. "She has nothing to do with it."

The other men surveyed Isabelle, and not too politely.

"I don't know," one of the men said, closing in on her, "she's sort of pretty. We could have some fun together."

"Try it, and you die," Michael said. The finality of his words made the man step back quickly.

A stunned Isabelle was forced to walk down a block or so with Michael. They then turned the corner. They found themselves in a narrow, dank alley, all light blocked out by the buildings behind them. On the far end, people could be seen walking to and fro, oblivious to their predicament. Isabelle wondered how Michael knew these people and how they were going to get out of this.

The leader of the pack stepped aside to allow another man, presumably their leader, to come through. He was tall, like Michael, but not handsome at all. His mouth was permanently twisted to one side. He walked slowly up to them, a gold pocket watch dangling from a vest pocket.

"So, Dr. St. Vincent," the man began. Isabelle could swear she felt his seething hatred for Michael. "Finally come home to get what you deserve?"

CHAPTER THIRTEEN

"Maurice, I should have killed you then," was all Michael said. His words chilled Isabelle. *How did they know each other? And why would Michael want to see this man dead?* she wondered.

The man took notice of Isabelle for the first time. "I think I know why you had the gall to return to the city. She is pretty, prettier than Diedre, I suppose. Certainly lacks the, er, worldliness, though."

Isabelle was insulted. "I don't know who you are, sir, but—"

"Whoa!" the man said. He did not look to be that much older than Michael, but to Isabelle, whatever he had been through made him look that way. "Mike, your little celebrity is not afraid of the big bad wolf, I see."

Michael looked alarmed. "How do you know who she is?"

The man rolled his eyes in mock boredom. "I find out what I need to find out, particularly when money is involved."

Isabelle looked up into Michael's face; it was unreadable. "Michael, what is he talking about?" she asked.

"Your dear doctor," Maurice said, "is an old business partner of mine."

"We were never partners," Michael countered. "You traitor!" He made a move for Maurice, but two of his men stepped between them.

"Well, if you see it that way," Maurice said. "I thought we were partners, but then that explains why you left me to die."

"Everyone knows the truth about you now," Michael said. "I'm surprised you would show your ugly face around here. Does Diedre know you're here?" he asked. The question seemed to infuriate the man. He had two men grab Michael by the arms, then he punched Michael squarely in the jaw.

Isabelle screamed. Michael looked up, and one corner of his mouth was bloodied. She rushed Maurice and slapped him as hard as she could. Caught off guard, Maurice stumbled back, and the other man grabbed a hold of Isabelle.

Rubbing his jaw, he grinned. "She's a hellcat, Michael. Would not have thought it from first glance. I'll deal with you later, Miss," he added, ominously. "Where's my money, Mike?" he asked.

"Don't have it. I gave every last dime to charity," Michael said, then spat out some blood not too far from Maurice's shoes.

Maurice's black eyes widened. "I hope that's not true, Doctor," he said. He gestured for Michael and Isabelle to be brought along behind him. "Come on."

Isabelle and Michael were thrown into a waiting carriage nearby. The curtains were drawn, so they could not see where they were going. Isabelle was placed next to Maurice, who smelled of stale cigar smoke and whiskey. Michael was seated between two men directly across. He looked like a caged lion, biding his time. After a long while, the carriage stopped. They looked to be on the farthest end of the warehouse district. Tall grass surrounded them, but Isabelle could hear the river's waves and the seagulls.

Pushed out of the carriage, Isabelle and Michael were taken inside a small house and shoved into two chairs. It seemed to Isabelle they were in there at least an hour.

Maurice circled their chairs. Twirling a wooden 2" x 4 ", he paused beside Isabelle. Before she could see what he was doing, Maurice had one man hold down her arm at the wrist, spreading her fingers wide on the arm of the chair. Maurice made to swing the board down onto her hands to crush her fingers. Isabelle's eyes widened. She could hear Michael yelling, seemingly from off in the distance somewhere.

Maurice stopped mid-air. He laughed.

"Well, I certainly know the value of things, don't I?"

Michael took a deep breath and closed his eyes. "Maurice, you do that again," he said, his eyes still closed, "and they won't be able to find all of the pieces of you."

Maurice blanched and set the board down.

"Mike, I didn't want things to be like this. You forced my hand. And I didn't mean for you to find out about us the way you did, back then."

Michael looked Maurice in the eye. "Maurice, I will not discuss the past with you. That part of my life is over. I'm starting anew, and you will not be a part of it. For the last time, your cargo is long gone, somewhere in Canada. The last time I saw the boat was when we were all there together. Let Isabelle and me go now, and I'll forget I ever saw you. I suggest you go on with your life as well."

"It's a lot harder to go on without any money," Maurice said. "You've cost me an incredible amount—you had no idea, of course, but all the same. . ." Maurice's voice trailed off as he pulled out a pistol to aim at Michael's head. Michael did not flinch. Isabelle shifted in her chair, worried for Michael's life, waiting for any opportunity to rush Maurice.

"Sorry, old friend," Maurice said, dejected, lowering the pistol. "I guess I do believe you don't have it. You always were honest. Now what to do with you?" he asked. "I can't leave behind witnesses to my resurrection." He motioned for the back door. "Stand up, both of you. We're going out back."

Isabelle and Michael were marched out the back door. They were in another alley. Isabelle looked for a way to escape, but the alley was closed off by high bushes on both ends. Feeling trapped, she looked at Michael, who was quiet, yet watchful. He leaned on his cane. One man was still inside the house.

Maurice held the gun level with Michael's heart. In a flash, Michael reached up, knocking Maurice's arm to the right. The pistol went off, and it struck the other big man right in the chest. He fell and did not move. Before Maurice could aim again, Michael brought his cane up, and, holding it mid-hilt, knocked Maurice across the face. Pouncing, Michael proceeded to beat Maurice.

In a fury, Michael rained blow after blow upon Maurice's body. Maurice did his best to cover his head with his arms, rolling from side to side. Each explosive blow was stronger than the last. In a daze, Isabelle watched absently as Michael unleashed what looked to be years of anger upon Maurice.

"Arghh!" Michael gave a guttural, wordless cry. With every blow, Isabelle could see the years of pent up rage release itself upon this man. Most of the rage was well placed, but Isabelle was also witnessing a young Michael, who'd failed his dead mentor, and the even younger Michael, a boy cradling his dying mother in the rain. Isabelle tried to pull him back, but Michael managed to hold her back behind him with one arm. Finally, when she knew Michael would kill Maurice for certain, she screamed his name.

"Michael! Please! He's had enough." With these words, Michael stopped beating Maurice. Panting, he stepped back, and handed Isabelle his cane, whose top half was dark with Maurice's blood. Isabelle held it by the bottom; the cane was nearly split in half. Michael turned to clutch Isabelle in an embrace. He was shaking.

She rubbed his back to soothe him. She looked down at Maurice. He was lying still in the dirt, but he was breathing. Maurice's other henchman rushed out, but Maurice held up one trembling hand to stop him. Isabelle stooped beside him.

"Maurice, if you can hear me, this is the end, do you understand?" Slowly, without turning to face them, Maurice nodded, choking on his own blood. She returned to Michael's side, and took his hand.

"Come on, Michael, let's get out of here."

They sidestepped the back door of the house to make it to the front, where they took Maurice's carriage. Riding back to the police headquarters, the two went inside to make a report on Maurice. Michael, who was respected by the police, reported that Maurice, the famous smuggler, was back in town. He left out the details surrounding Diedre. The chief of police sent out a wagon to the address provided.

"Thanks for the information," the chief said. "I'll be glad to catch the man involved in so many unsolved murders in the black market."

In the melee, Isabelle had nearly forgotten why they had come to the police in the first place. After she mentioned that she wished to tell him something about Ned duRoy, the chief looked baffled.

"Attorney Ned duRoy?" he asked. "He was just here, about an hour ago. He came to report some papers stolen from his office. We're supposed to be looking into that—it's got scandal written all over it," he whispered conspiratorially. "Some bigwigs might be involved. Is that what you're talking about?"

Isabelle decided to back off of the accusations against Ned, considering he seemed to be hard at work trying to fix the mess he put them all in. After leaving Maurice's carriage in police custody, Isabelle and Michael returned to his own carriage and headed back to Maison Fontaine.

Before Isabelle could say a word, Michael started to explain.

"Isabelle, I'm so sorry about what happened back there. The thought of him hurting you, I—"

"It's okay, Michael, nothing happened," she said. "Who is Maurice, and why did he say you were partners?"

"We never were partners," Michael said quickly. "But I made the mistake of trusting him. I knew him when we were children, but Auntie said he was not going to amount to anything good." He frowned. "I guess she was right. Maurice liked to steal, and I almost got arrested because he told the candy store owner it was my idea to steal. After that, Auntie forbade me to play with him. Years went by, and we met again a few years ago. He was well known in town as the man who made it big. He approached me about my plan for the clinic with your grandfather. He said he'd made a fortune from importing and wanted to give something back to the community. He talked me into considering building an entire hospital—he said he had the connections for investors."

"How did my grandfather feel about that?" Isabelle asked.

"He didn't like the idea, and with Josie going on that she'd heard Maurice was into shady business, there was no way he would approve. Like an idiot, though, I thought I was a good judge of character, and planned to go on without your grandfather. He was very hurt, and we didn't talk for weeks."

Isabelle was outdone. "How does Diedre fit into all of this?"

Michael never took his eyes from the road as he talked. "Diedre was special to me back then. She was a Chinese art dealer, having been a child of privilege from New Orleans. She went to fine schools and traveled the world. She particularly loved Chinese art and wanted to show it in the West. She'd been an acquaintance of Maurice for some time, at least that what's she told me." He paused for a moment. "Maurice made the introductions, and like a fool, I fell for her. We spent six glorious months together, but I had no idea she was also Maurice's woman. They played me."

Isabelle felt sorry for Michael, but she did not want him to stop talking. She wanted to know the whole story. "Michael, go on. It's best to finally tell it all."

He pulled the carriage over to the side of the street. The twilight air was crisp, and fallen leaves were lifted on the wind, being carried to new destinations. There were no other carriages in sight. Michael turned to face Isabelle, and for the first time, she could really see into the depths of his eyes. He was trusting her, and it felt good.

"They pushed me into going into business with Maurice, but I didn't know they wanted to use the hospital for shipping ill-gotten artifacts and art disguised as supplies. When I became involved with the Blackburn escape plan, I helped by securing the boat that would take Mr. Blackburn to Canada. I needed more money, so I asked Maurice. He was happy to oblige, but I didn't know he had an ulterior motive. I thought he sincerely wanted to help the Blackburns, considering this affects us all here in the city. I thought he was my friend.

"When the day for the escape came," he continued, "we went to secure the boat. He was anxious when I met him at the rendezvous point, and he had Diedre with him. I was still too dumb to see what was right in front of me," Michael said, slapping the top of the carriage door. "He then revealed just about everything about the smuggling. He had run afoul of someone on the black market here and needed the boat that day to hide in Canada for a while. Turns out he'd already loaded the boat with some valuables, which were hidden in a hollow space."

"Then what?" Isabelle asked. "I know that Mr. Blackburn made it across the river. So what happened?"

"I made sure that Mr. Blackburn got on that boat," Michael answered. "I told him that he'd have to get through me first to get at that boat. We fought, and I had Maurice pinned to the ground. I turned to Diedre, who shocked me by going over to help Maurice. It was then I realized they were involved with each other.

A handful of men started running towards us, and Maurice scrambled away. The men were after him, and they had guns. Maurice took off down the road the other way, and called for Diedre to follow. She hesitated, but only for a moment, and ran after him. My heart sank, but I knew I had to stay focused on the Blackburns' escape."

Michael looked exhausted. "Just then, a man ran up to tell me something was wrong back where they were transporting Mr. Blackburn to the jail. The people were standing in the way of the sheriff, and it was probable that Mr. Blackburn would be broken out ahead of schedule. He told me go back and see what I could do to help, and thanked me for securing the boat. He told me that he was the 'friend' from the Canadian contingent."

Isabelle teared up. "Richard," she breathed.

Michael smiled. "Yes, I had the pleasure of meeting your brave fiancé, just for a moment. But I don't know what happened to him after that." His eyes darkened again. "When I got to the ruckus, the sheriff had already been shot. In the madness, we were able to get Mr. Blackburn out. The foot patrol showed up and started arresting people. I helped a young girl to get away from a patrolman. I was much taller than he was, so he clubbed me repeatedly in my leg. I stumbled and hit the ground, and he kept hitting me over and over. I knew my leg was shattered, but they hauled me off to jail with everyone else. I was in there for several days, until your grandfather and Ned were able to get me out. I tried to set the leg myself, but couldn't. They had me in a cell by myself.

Isabelle's face was soaked with tears. She hugged Michael. "I'm so sorry! You must have been in agony. No one there to help you."

Michael hugged Isabelle for a brief moment, then pulled away from her. This time, however, his eyes did not harden, nor did he turn away from her.

"I learned Maurice was back in town after he hid out in Chicago with Diedre for close to three years. According to her, he has been waiting for the right moment to get back at me and reclaim the fortune he lost. Maurice heard I was back in the city, and he was coming for me. Guilty about what she'd done to me, Diedre revealed all to her family and was disowned. She left Maurice and tried to get to me first, to warn me. Fearing I would reject her, she sent a prized fan I once admired to my office as a signal."

Isabelle nodded, remembering the fan in his room.

"By messenger we arranged that she would come to my office. She was leaving when you saw her there. I thanked her for warning me, but told her I could offer her little else. She told me how sorry she was, and that she really did love me, but she was tempted by greed at the time. She says she's a changed person. I hope so," he added.

Isabelle wondered what Michael planned to do now that Diedre was back in his life, and she'd changed her ways. Also, because she was broke.

"Will you be seeing her again?" Isabelle asked, holding her breath.

Michael looked surprised by the question. He shook his head. "Never, Isabelle. Never, I tell you. I realize now that I did not love Diedre. I was caught up in her exotic allure. Deep down, I suspected she was with Maurice," Michael confessed, "and I liked the challenge of trying to take her away from him, to out-do one of the most powerful men in the city."

He took her hand. "Isabelle, I've had so many past betrayals," Michael explained. "After some of the things I've seen in my life, I've been close to losing my faith in humanity. But then I look at you," he smiled, tears welling up, "and I see the beauty in the world again. Your lovely face. Your graceful walk. Your courage. Your music. Your kindness to others. And the way you looked at me, even when I gave you a hard time."

Isabelle reached up to caress Michael's face. "What look?" she asked, curious that she'd given away some secret without knowing it herself. "And all this time, I thought you hated me."

They both laughed, then Michael took her hand from his face to kiss the inside of her palm. Isabelle felt her stomach flutter.

"Hate you?" Michael asked. "Never. I've loved you from the minute I saw you on the ferry, so lost looking, but so beautiful. You blended in with that sunset, a burning glow coming from you that called to me. I prayed that I would see you again, but dared not hope.

"Then I found out you were with Douglas," Michael said. He dropped his head. "I don't believe that Douglas is the man for you. There's something—"

Isabelle stopped Michael from talking by giving him a deep passionate kiss. Michael sighed, then crushed Isabelle's body to him. Leaning in, Isabelle placed her hand on the knee of Michael's shattered leg, as if to heal it with her love. He covered her face with hungry kisses, his smooth hands running up and down her tingling spine.

"Don't worry about Douglas," Isabelle said between kisses, almost forgetting Douglas' name. "I am breaking the engagement."

At that news, Michael pulled away for a brief moment, as if he could not believe what he'd heard. He then pulled her to him again. In his arms, Isabelle never felt more alive.

After shocking several passers-by with their fevered display of raw passion, Michael and Isabelle broke apart long enough to resume their trek back to the house. The closer they got to the house, however, the worse Isabelle felt. Any feeling of happiness or optimism faded. Having forgotten her troubles in Michael's arms, Isabelle remembered what was awaiting her at the house, some unseen force directing her life, and her future.

As they turned onto the road leading to the house, Isabelle noticed that the air looked hazy. Thinking at first that it was just the night rolling in, she felt unsettled as the haze grew more dense. Her nose picked up the smell of smoke.

"Michael," she said, tugging his arm. Smoke was hovering above the trees.

"Heyah!" Michael urged his horse forward. They reached the house within minutes. Isabelle jumped from the carriage, Michael fast on her heels. They paused on the steps, surveying the house from end to end. The smoke was coming from the first floor, the ballroom.

"Barry!" Isabelle screamed, then made for the house. Michael grabbed her.

"No, Isabelle, wait here," he said. Eyeing the upstairs, Michael charged into the house through the front door.

Isabelle paced for a few moments, wondering where everyone was. She rushed to the back of the house. Alder's wagon was not there, and the back door was closed. Hearing footsteps running behind her, Isabelle spun around to see Ben there. He had black smudges on his cheeks and his clothes smelled of smoke, but he looked unharmed. She scooped him up and kissed him.

"Ben, what's happened?" she asked.

"There's a fire," was all he said, looking up into her eyes.

"How did you get out?"

"My mommy is not here. She went with Mr. Douglas for a while."

"Douglas?" Isabelle asked, confused. "Why would she be with Douglas?"

Before Ben could answer, Isabelle heard a loud crash from within the house. She set Ben down.

"Ben, I need to go inside, but you must promise to stay right here until I get back."

Ben nodded, and Isabelle ran through the back door. The kitchen's air was clear, as the smoke had not reached that part of the house. She ran into Josie's room, but no one was there. Working her way up the hall, she called for Josie, but there was no answer.

When she reached the stairwell, she saw the cause of the crash. There was Michael, heading for the doorway. The writing table had been knocked over. In his arms was Barry, but the young man was unrecognizable. He had been burned in the fire, and his hair was singed.

"No!" Isabelle howled, then fell to her knees.

"Isabelle, help me get Barry out," Michael panted. He was limping, and about to lose his balance holding Barry. Isabelle gathered her wits and ran to them. The front of the house was dark now, as the hot smoke filtered out of the ballroom. Taking one of Barry's arms over either shoulder, Isabelle and Michael dragged Barry out through the back of the house.

Reaching fresh air, Isabelle, Michael, and Barry fell in a heap out in the cool grass. Michael was coughing, but he was already at work on trying to save Barry. Michael had a panicked look on his face, and Isabelle knew that he was afraid he would not be able to save him. Looking down at Barry, Isabelle felt the sad certainty that he was not going to live. His breathing was shallow, and most of his body was charred. She fought back the urge to wretch at the smell of burnt flesh. Gently, she motioned for Michael to let her speak to Barry.

"Barry," she said, touching the one corner of his hand that was not burned. "I'm here. Can you tell me what happened?"

Barry opened his eyes. A startling contrast to the black ash covering his face, his eyes were clear.

"Izzy," he tried to smile, but couldn't. "I've saved you."

"Saved me?" Isabelle asked. "What do you mean?"

"The house is coming down," he said. "I put an end to it all." He choked for a moment, but was determined to continue. "I snuck out so that everyone would come out of the house to look for me. That was the only way to get them all out at the same time. I knew you and Michael were already gone, so I seized the opportunity."

He coughed again. "This was the best way to end the story," he said. "When I finished the picture, she came for me, so I knew there was not a lot of time left. With the house gone, she will be gone, also. It's the only way." Barry's voice trailed off, then he opened his eyes one last time.

"Pretty lady, pretty Izzy," he said, then with one last great breath, he was gone.

"Michael, he's gone," Isabelle wailed. "He's gone!" As she slumped over Barry's lifeless body, Michael tried to get a pulse, but to no avail.

They heard a scream behind them. At first, Isabelle was too stunned to turn around, but when she heard the scream again, she turned around where she sat on the grass. Up ran Marie, who looked terrified.

She screamed again, dragging Ben behind her. "It wasn't supposed to be like this. Ben is not a part of this."

A chord strummed through Isabelle's body as she contemplated the unimaginable. She rose and stormed over to a huddled Marie. Curiously, Ben had turned his body away from Marie, and was fighting to break free of her embrace. Isabelle wondered why a scared child would not reach for his mother.

"Marie, what have you done?" Isabelle shrieked.

Marie looked up slowly, guilt wracking her young face, transforming it instantly into the haggard old woman she would become.

"Ever since you got here," Marie said, her voice turning hard, "everything changed. We thought you would not be a problem, that you would run back to Canada the minute you got here. But you stayed," Marie's venomous tone was shocking. "We had to think of another way to get you out of here."

"Who's 'we'?" Isabelle asked, but Marie started crying again.

"But Ben was not supposed to get hurt," Marie continued, her eyes taking on a faraway look. "I tried to kill you myself, once," she admitted.

Isabelle felt faint.

"I was going to smother you where you slept, but I couldn't do it. When Barry started telling you things, I had to put the poison in his meal—it was easier to let the poison work, rather than smother someone."

"But, Marie! Why?" Isabelle implored.

"To tell you the truth, I'm not quite sure," she answered, looking dazed. "He said that it was important that you, then Barry, were out of the way, then we could be together."

"Who would tell you such a thing?" Isabelle demanded, grabbing Marie by the collar.

"Douglas," Marie said, with a twist of her mouth.

Shortly after that stunning confession, Isabelle heard the ringing bells of the fire brigade in the distance. Having no idea how long she'd stood over Marie, Isabelle was startled by Josie screaming in her ear, asking her if she was alright. Absently, she nodded and Josie practically knocked her over hugging her.

Remembering Michael, Isabelle turned to see her beloved being attended to by a volunteer fireman offering him a cup of water. Josie ran over to Michael and knocked the fireman over; the cup of water went flying into the air.

Isabelle turned back to find Marie still standing there, not having run off to evade arrest. Isabelle saw that she wouldn't have to hunt Marie down herself, but she would have taken great pleasure in doing so.

"Tell me the rest," Isabelle commanded.

Marie looked at Ben, who had come to stand beside Isabelle. Nodding, Marie seemed to be making a decision about something. "Before I tell you the rest," she asked, "would you consider taking care of Ben for me?"

Isabelle was taken aback, but did not hesitate. She was quite fond of Ben, and it would be years before his mother would be released from jail. He'd be alone in the world.

"Of course I would. I would love him as my own."

At that, Marie exhaled, relieved. "I'll start from the beginning."

CHAPTER FOURTEEN

The fire brigade was able to save the house. Isabelle watched them use a chain of buckets from water pumped from the well out back. Josie and Alders arrived shortly afterward. They saw the smoke on their way back from looking for Barry and backtracked to get help. The fire was contained within the ballroom, and there was some smoke damage in the front hallway. The foot patrol arrived shortly afterward, and Marie willingly went with them. They were not quite sure what they were arresting her for, but Isabelle corroborated what Marie told them, that she'd tried to kill two people. She also told them about Douglas.

"Once I told him that Barry was still alive despite the poison, Douglas turned on me," she whispered. To Isabelle's alarm, Marie had a small knife cut on her neck to prove it. "Me," Marie repeated, "the one person who really loved him. Not the self-absorbed diva who ignored him all the time."

Isabelle blushed at the rude description, wondering how much of that was true about herself.

"He told me he loved me," Marie said, looking down at the browning grass. "I met him last year at my sister Gamelin's house."

Isabelle gasped. "Gamelin is your sister?" Then she saw Marie's resemblance to the old woman, Gamelin's grandmother, their grandmother.

"Gamelin married well—I didn't," Marie said. "When Douglas came along, I thought I had a future again. He promised that once the house was his, we'd get married. I just had to do a few things for him at the house, because he had a plan. He was looking for something around the house, something that belonged to him. I failed him, but then he tried to kill me." She burst into tears. "I managed to escape and ran all the way back here for Ben so that we could leave Detroit. Poor Gamelin and her husband didn't know anything about this, but I'm sure Grandmother suspected something," Marie sneered, "she always said I was trouble."

As he listened in, the patrolman confided in Isabelle that he knew of the people Douglas was with. Some of them were involved in a lot of nefarious practices, but it was unlikely any of them would ever be implicated. "Too much money floating around these days," he said in disgust.

Alders had invited everyone to come stay with him at his house a few miles away until the smoke cleared out, but Isabelle wanted to stay at the house, to keep watch. She was relieved that the fire and police patrols had not pressed her about who owned the house, with the deed in jeopardy, such as it was. They smiled when she spoke of Ned, so she knew she was among friends, at least for a while. Whomever hired the Irish bully would sniff blood and come running the minute they heard about the fire.

Michael said he would stay with Isabelle as well, so Josie and Ben went with Alders. Ben gave Isabelle a hug before he climbed into Alders' wagon. Isabelle had asked him how he'd known to get out of the house when it was on fire.

"My friend told me," he said.

"Who?" Isabelle asked.

Ben giggled. "You know who, Miss Isabelle," he said. "He says to tell you he's waiting for you." With that, Ben took off running for the wagon.

Those words left Isabelle with a chill. Absently, she watched the fire patrol load Barry's body into the wagon to take to the undertaker, for a fee of course. Isabelle had to postpone her grief, or she might be joining Barry in the hereafter sooner than she'd planned. *I must find a way to communicate with Jacques*, she thought, *to tell him I'm not Celeste.*

Michael joined her as she watched the wagons pull out of the yard. He was limping heavily. His stylish suit smelled of smoke. The forlorn look on his face broke her heart; she knew he was still thinking about Barry.

"So, what now?" he asked her.

She shrugged, fighting tears. "You need to rest for a while. "Let's go in the carriage house."

Michael gave a small smile, then winced in pain. "Just you and me? That's sounds very good."

Once inside the carriage house, they made two makeshift beds of blankets and straw. The horse was currently hitched to Alder's wagon, so they were all alone in there. Everywhere was dim except where sunlight poured in between the wooden slats of the door. Michael sank down on the blanket. Isabelle asked if he needed more water; she could get some from the well.

"No, just would like to close my eyes for a while," he yawned. "You should do the same. There's nothing else we can do until perhaps later today, until the smoke clears."

Isabelle had not noticed that it was early morning already. They'd arrived in the night, and in the chaos of worrying about the house and hearing the devastating news about Douglas, she'd lost track of time. Michael must have sensed that she was worrying again. He gestured for her to join him on his mat.

"I'm sorry to hear that Douglas has something to do with all of this," he said. "I still don't understand exactly how."

"I'm not sure, either," Isabelle said. "Why would he want me out of the house, even dead, for that matter?" she asked, hurt. "We've known each other for quite some time. He proposed to me. What could I have done to make him want me dead?"

Michael held her close. "Believe me, Isabelle," he said, fiercely, "there's nothing in this world or the next you could have done to make anyone want to harm you."

After a few moments, Isabelle was unable to keep her eyes open. Michael was already snoring beside her. His arm was stretched over her, and it was heavy.

~   ~   ~

Celeste awoke, the memory of Jacques' embrace the other night still with her. Donning a dressing gown, she tiptoed over to the baby's crib. Little Rene was sleeping peacefully. Jacques had helped her choose a name for her son, suggesting his name, "reborn" might be a good omen. Celeste still could not believe she now had a child of her own. Now she was fighting for two lives.

When she joined Evangeline in the scullery, they were hard at work on preparing for the upcoming harvest dance next week. Word had come that the Intendent himself was coming to town to assess Louis' progress with the boat building and to collect the taxes, which were six months overdue. She'd heard Briane and her mother wanted to make a good impression, so they decided to use the annual harvest dance to celebrate the success of the crops and honor their visitor, no matter what the cost.

Evangeline watched Celeste closely when she entered.

"Is there something you need?" she asked. Ever since the "incident," Evangeline treated Celeste more kindly then she ever had in the past.

"No, Evangeline, thank you," Celeste answered. "What needs doing next?"

Evangeline stopped chopping vegetables for a moment. She looked worried.

"Celeste, it's best you stay out of sight when you can. I've got Eulalie, and with Briane's mother here, the workload has been lighter."

"How long can I hide?" Celeste asked, angry. She held up her stump, and Evangeline looked away. "There's no hiding from this—they did it to me. I—"

Briane's mother walked in. She was carrying a tray with a teacup. She looked scared. Ignoring Celeste, she went to Evangeline.

"Can you fetch the doctor, Evangeline?" she asked, quietly. "There's something wrong with Briane, with the baby, I fear."

Evangeline rose and went to the back door. She called for one of the young men to run to the fort for the doctor.

Glancing at Celeste for a moment longer, Desmoiselle Hubert slowly went back down the hall and up the stairs.

Celeste had returned to her room and was nursing the baby when Eulalie burst in a few hours later. The solemn look on her face told Celeste everything. Briane let out one solitary scream from upstairs.

~   ~   ~

Isabelle was awakened by the sound of someone calling her name from a distance. She turned over to see that Michael was still asleep. Gently lifting his arm so as not to wake him, she rolled over, then stood. Tiptoeing to the door, she peeked out. Ned, shaking and stumbling, could be seen calling out desperately. She went to meet him.

"Oh, Child!" Ned cried out when he caught sight of Isabelle. When she reached him, he hugged her. "I was worried about all of you," he said.

Isabelle could feel Ned's distress, so she held in any angry words. "We're all fine, except for Barry. Ned, he didn't survive."

"No," he said softly.

Isabelle decided against telling Ned exactly how Barry came to die in the fire. The trust between them was broken, and she did not wish to reveal the whole story just yet.

"How much of the house is damaged?" he asked.

"The ballroom. We can save the house," Isabelle answered. She liked those words.

Ned nodded. "Good, good. Well, you're going to be needing this." Ned gently placed a scroll in Isabelle's hands. She could tell by the worn pages that it was the deed.

"I got the papers back, and I told the police who was behind everything,"

Ned said. "You can get these filed again with the Register of Deeds."

Isabelle was relieved. "Ned, that's good news. Come inside. The kitchen door was left open. Hopefully, it's clear enough in there to put on some coffee."

As they entered the doorway, Isabelle could smell the faint scent of smoke, but it was nothing like the night before. The room was clear. Ned took a seat as she prepared the coffee.

"I'm certain that the Cass Company was not responsible for this," Ned said, "just Beaufort and that other maniac. I've had Beaufort arrested. In exchange for my testimony, the police will keep me out of jail, but I will lose my license," Ned said, sadly.

Isabelle stopped for a moment. "I'm sorry, Ned," she said, without turning around.

"No, I'm sorry for everything. And for not telling you about Douglas. I—" Ned had stopped mid-sentence. Isabelle heard a gurgling sound, then a crash. Turning, she saw Ned slumped in his chair, blood flooding from his neck. She looked up to see Douglas standing there, holding his blade.

"Douglas, what are you doing?" she asked, horrified. Douglas looked nothing like the man she knew; his clothes were dirty, and his hair was wild. The most disturbing difference was his eyes, which had a dark gleam in them. Before Isabelle could react, Douglas leaped over Ned and put the blade at her throat.

"Not another word. Come with me," he said.

"Douglas, why?" Isabelle asked again. Keeping the blade at her neck, Douglas forced her through the house and out the front door. They stumbled on the steps, but Douglas made her press on towards the river. He pushed her to the far end of the property, a grassy bluff. Douglas shoved Isabelle over and she wound up rolling down the slope to the sand below. Regaining her feet, she looked up, afraid that Michael would not be able to see her from above.

Down there was a shovel, and a deep hole in the sand. At first, Isabelle thought Douglas had dug a grave for her, but the hole was too small for that. She heard Douglas land behind her. Choosing not to run just yet, Isabelle wanted to see what Douglas was up to.

"Look down in there, whore," Douglas said. Isabelle blinked at his choice of words. Dropping to her knees, she peered down into the hole. At the bottom was a small tin chest.

"Pull it out," Douglas said, panting. "I want you to be the one to open it."

Slowly, Isabelle reached down the length of her arms. Curling her fingers around its bottom, she pulled it out. The box was slightly dented, and sand poured from one corner. Coming in contact with the box, that strange thrumming sensation, like at the church, came over Isabelle. She fell to her knees.

"What is this?" she asked, panting. She was finding it hard to breathe.

"You'll see," Douglas said. He seemed to relish in her distress. "Good, you are remembering," he said.

Isabelle looked up, alarmed. "How would you know—" Before she could get out the rest of her question, the world went dark.

~   ~   ~

The night of the dance, everyone was gloomy. The weather was dark and rainy, and it was obvious none of the guests wanted to be there. The string quartet music was muted and forced. Out of propriety, some of the neighbors and friends came, dressed in their finest, to help the pitiful Louis, who had just lost his child and was in danger of losing his farm. Most came to see the bizarre comedy of Louis and Briane's marriage. Slaves from other farms, Indian traders, and soldiers from the fort gossiped freely about the goings-on at the Fontaine farm, and word had gotten around.

"The King's Gardens are dreadful!" Celeste heard one bejeweled woman comment.

Celeste thought the harvest display, at least, looked beautiful. On a large table in the ballroom was a representative sample of the crops. Tight, round, black and red bunches of grapes, dark purple plums and large ears of yellow corn were piled high at the center of a table. The best beaver pelts, though sparse, were strung up in one corner of the room. Fresh deer carcasses were being kept cool in a small shed out back. The new bateaux, ten so far, had been dragged up to rest just beyond the front porch.

"Ladies and gentlemen! The Intendent Giles Hocquart!"

All the guests made way for the Intendent, appointed member of the Sovereign Council of New France, standing on either side of the room. The Intendent, followed by attendants wearing high white wigs secured at the nape with black ribbons, strolled through the party with much pomp. He was bedecked in jewels, and all of the royal visitor's waistcoats were trimmed in gold braid with heavy embroidery, leather shoes fastened with silver buckles. With his eyepiece, he inspected the spread, and after several moments of silence, sniffed his approval. The crowd, which had been waiting expectantly, cheered.

"So, I take it that we did well." Celeste smiled before turning around. Jacques was directly behind her. She stepped out of the room to greet her lover with a kiss in the men's parlor.

"Congratulations, Jacques," she whispered. "I hear that the Intendent is impressed with the boats. He's planning to send word to the king about your skills."

Jacques shrugged. "It only matters if you like the work, Cherie. I will take you out one day on a boat I'll build just for you." He gave her one more kiss. "I should go before I'm seen. I love you," he said, then walked off. It was hard for Celeste to watch him walk away.

Teary, she returned to spying on the festivities from the doorway. Some of the guests recognized Isabelle and beckoned for her to play their favorite songs. With reddening faces, however, they remembered what Briane had done to her.

Celeste planned to stay in her room all night, but Louis insisted she made an appearance. He'd had a deep red silk gown ordered from Paris for her, and that was the final insult to Briane, whose own olive green gown had to be sacrificed for a crow-black mourning gown.

Louis was determined to have his way, and as always, everyone complied. He ignored Briane, even in the wake of the loss of their own child. Evangeline said Louis told Briane he would never forgive her for what she'd done to Celeste. He ordered fine clothes for Celeste's baby, and did not share Briane's terror over her baby's fate after dying before a christening. Days before the dance, he'd had Rene christened and given his name in the church, without Briane's knowledge. Robert Navarre, the appointed Royal Notary, was there to witness, and he did not look happy. Celeste was not so sure why Louis rushed to do this, then she found out why the night of the dance.

"Everyone! I have something to announce!" It was Louis, and somewhere in the room, someone groaned. Celeste muttered a quick prayer. "As you know, there has been a joyous birth recently. Raise your glasses in a toast to my new son, Rene." The crowd followed suit, lifting their glasses of wine in salute to Louis' illegitimate son, mum about Briane's stillborn daughter.

Wavering on his feet, Louis continued. The Intendent had sipped some wine, loaded several casks into his wagon, and was gone, presumably to give a good report to the king. Louis still looked gaunt from his illness, but it did not stop him from drinking.

"I would like to announce that Rene has been christened Sieur Rene Fontaine, inheritor of all that I own." There were gasps from every corner of the room, and some dropped glasses that shattered on the floor. Briane's mother fainted; Evangeline sent Eulalie for the smelling salts. All eyes fell on Celeste, who was still standing in the doorway. The looks of scorn and confusion came to rest upon Celeste's head, and she felt buried under the weight. The deepest look of scorn came from Briane, who was holding a plate of food. Her hand was trembling, and the food was tumbling to the floor.

She pitched the plate to the floor, where it broke in half. Shrieking, she ran up to pound Louis on the chest.

"How could you?" she cried. "What about me, your wife? Our future children?"

Louis shoved Briane, who slipped and fell. He sneered at her. "I've made the biggest mistake marrying you, but I'm about to change that. You and your mother are to leave my house at once! Go back to your broke father." He gulped the last of his wine, then ordered the quartet to resume playing. Under the strained string music, Briane gathered the shreds of her dignity and dusted herself off. Standing tall and straight, she said one last thing.

"Louis, I curse you and your miserable family. Even if it takes a lifetime, I will reclaim everything due me, and your whore's going to pay with her life. I also curse her to suffer in the hereafter!" Louis ignored her, waving her off. Briane gave all the guests one final glance, then rushed out crying, her mother following. Celeste ducked out of the doorway before Briane and her mother ran out.

She was next met in the hall by Evangeline, who had the next course of the meal, roast pheasant and pig, on steaming platters.

"Caleb said to come outside right away," Evangeline said. "I told him I didn't have time to see what he was jumping up and down about. I've got to get this food in there before the party is ruined any further."

The closer she got to the back door, the worse Celeste felt. Something was very wrong. She swung open the door to see Jacques in the arms of two large white men. She ran out.

"What's happening?" she asked, her stomach in knots.

Up walked Monsieur Duchene. "Your mistress sent for me to come tonight. Apparently, she wished to sell someone back to me. It's odd, though, because your master had written to say he was well pleased with the work."

The ground under Celeste's feet seemed to give way. "No," she wailed. She ran to Jacques, who was struggling against the two men. "Let him be!"

Duchene laughed. "Sorry, fille, this is business. Wish I could get you too, in the bargain. So pretty." He walked off into the growing darkness, Jacques in tow.

"Jacques, I'm going to get Louis right now," Celeste said.

Jacques gave her a sorrowful glance as they dragged him down the path towards the road out front. He dug in his heels, but the two silent men were giants. Celeste ran for the door, but never took her eyes off Jacques.

With one loud cry, Jacques raised up seemingly in mid-air, breaking free of the men. Touching the ground, he made for Celeste. The men jumped him, and Duchene rushed up with rope. One of the men hit Jacques on the back of the head with a nearby rock. His body went limp, and blood sprayed everywhere. Screaming, Celeste ran back to the men, where she was quickly knocked to the ground. The wind knocked out of her, Celeste gasped for air, staring at the twinkling stars in the sky. The wagon carrying Jacques away from her arms forever was long gone before Celeste could regain her feet. Crying, she ran for the back door. Maybe Louis could catch them in time, maybe—

She was met at the door by Briane and her mother. They both were breathing heavily, triumphant in their defeat.

"How about that, Celeste?" Briane asked. "He's been sold to the deep south. I gave Duchene extra to kill him if he tried to escape along the way. And we all know he will try to escape, to get back to you." She had a gleam in her eye. Her mother put one hand on her daughter's shoulders in praise, clenching a length of rope in her other hand. Her eyes, too, had a wild gleam as she shared in her daughter's madness.

"If he does survive his escape, imagine the look on his face when he finds his woman has taken her own life out of grief," Briane added.

Mother and daughter pounced. Celeste was crushed under their weight. Her hands were bound. She was dragged by her hair to the farthest end of the estate, out of sight of the house. Pushed over a large bluff, she rolled, dirt filling her nostrils. As she tumbled, Celeste closed her eyes and dreamed of a happier time with Jacques, a secret place where they were free together, free of this world. Heavy rocks were tied to her ankles. Mother and daughter dragged Celeste into a canoe, where they rowed out into the middle of the river. She could see the lights from the party twinkling from the windows.

"Are you his forever?" Briane taunted. "The river will tell."

Celeste only struggled for a moment, realizing that without Jacques, she did not want to live on. He had been her only light in this world of darkness.

She prayed for the future health of her child in Evangeline's care. As she was thrown overboard, Celeste welcomed her coming freedom. Briane would never realize that she had done Celeste a great kindness, after all.

~   ~   ~

Isabelle shook her head violently, thinking she was underwater. Her vision cleared, and she found Douglas staring at her.

"So, now do you remember everything?" he asked. "I remembered a long time ago, before we ever met. I realized it was my duty to make things right for my family," he said.

Isabelle could still not believe that Douglas was a part of this, that he'd known the entire time. He believed he was avenging a past wrong to his great-grandmother Briane, or worse, perhaps he thought he really was her.

"Douglas," Isabelle said, her hand up to ward him off. "There's much to be explained about what you have been feeling. These are memories, nothing more, and we should not make the same mistake again. Briane murdered Celeste."

"Celeste got what was coming to her. You look just like her, you know," he added, the gun trained on her heart. "That's your damned bad luck." He pointed to the box. "Open it. Before my ancestor was forced from her home, she buried a box of something very valuable to her out here." His eyes were glinting in the light.

"She went back home to Montreal to find that her father had died of a heart attack days before," Douglas continued. "She and her mother were penniless for years, then her mother died of tuberculosis. She then married a lumberjack who resented her so-called privileged past. She bore him one child, out in the wilderness, then died. Her letters said she left a prize at the Fontaine to ensure that her promise to Louis was kept.

"The man she married hated being left with a child, so he gave it away to the orphanage. And that is the story of my family line. Until now," Douglas said. "When I first remembered, I couldn't believe it. I'd stumbled through life, the descendent of broken and impoverished people who were cheated out of their legacy.

"Over time," Douglas said, "I embraced my new memories, knowing that they were meant for me, that my time had come. I've been chosen to turn things around. There's something valuable here, and I came to claim it, along with her house."

"That's why you were trying to get me out of here," Isabelle said.

Douglas smirked. "I was going to marry you to get the house, kill you, then sell it," he said, coldly. "I didn't expect you'd be so hard to budge. You were so pathetic back in Canada," he added. "It was as if you gained strength when you got over to this side of the river."

Isabelle felt so foolish for trusting Douglas with her innermost fears, crying on his shoulder so many times, whining about her future. He'd been there, all that time, seething, hating her, and she didn't know it.

"Then there was Barry. I thought he was a simpleton, until Marie told me about his sketches, about how much you looked like them when you got here. I had her report on the pictures, and when they were shaping up to be Celeste's whole story revealed, I had to stop him from completing it."

"He died in a fire trying to warn me about you," Isabelle said, bitterly.

Douglas shrugged indifferently. "I didn't know he was going to do that. He just did my job for me. I couldn't let him finish that picture."

Isabelle lunged forward, her teeth bared, but Douglas shoved the pistol in her chest.

"You were willing to kill Ben, too?" she asked.

Douglas looked troubled, but only for a moment. "No, I didn't mean for that to happen," he said, softly. "Beaufort, du Roy and I were partners on the side, outside of the Cass Company. Our acquisition of the Fontaine would have given me the money I needed, then I was going to do away with Beaufort and du Roy. du Roy brought you into this in the first place, arranging for you to come here, even after I failed to get you here from Canada myself. Desperate to pay his debts or be killed by his gambling compatriots, he was sure you'd be no problem.

"du Roy had no idea what Beaufort and I wanted to do with the house," Douglas said. "Beaufort only wanted to scare you into signing the deed, but I paid Bart O'Shea a little extra to rough you up to make sure you signed. I didn't know that idiot was willing to harm a child. My miscalculation," Douglas said. "It all worked out, though, thanks to me."

"My God, Douglas," was all Isabelle could say.

"I decided that a boating accident would be clever, but when the storm suddenly rose up, it felt like destiny. It was so much easier helping you overboard in those raging winds, than trying to drown you on the shore as a suicide in the night. I still don't know how you made it back, though."

Isabelle could barely focus on his words, with the gun pointed at her, and the throbbing in her body that was turning into a roar in her ears. She couldn't take it.

"Then came the damned song you wrote."

"What?" Isabelle asked loudly, the pulsating sound overcoming her.

"I could not believe my ears," Douglas said. "The same godforsaken song that Celeste used to play for simpering Louis, that imbecile. The day you played it for me, something came over me, so many memories flooding my mind at once. I couldn't concentrate, nor carry out the rest of my plan. The song just played over and over in my head.

"After that, I decided I was willing to give up the house, considering what I am sure is a great wealth in this chest," Douglas added, tapping his foot against the chest. "Great-grandmother was forced out on the spot, with only enough time to snatch this box from her room and bury it. I'm sure she hid something of incredible value here."

Isabelle rubbed her forehead. "Douglas, I think you are going to be disappointed," she said. "I have a feeling there are no valuables here, I'm afraid. Just put the gun down, then we can talk—"

"No!" Douglas shouted.

"This is the only way I can get the right kind of money, fast. Open it."

Slowly, Isabelle made to open the box. The weak padlock practically crumbled in her hands. The chest was etched in French Louis XV flowered designs. Lifting the latch, Isabelle's body thrummed with heat covering her from head to foot. She pushed the creaking lid back, only to reveal a tattered piece of silk covering something underneath. Isabelle pulled it back, already aware that something horrible had to be inside.

When the box's contents were revealed, Douglas fell away in disgust. He wretched.

In the box was a small hand, a blackened skeleton. On the third finger was a silver ring, etched with three wavy lines. Isabelle dared not touch it, but she knew to whom the hand belonged. Nausea swept over Isabelle. Celeste's hand turned out to be Briane's most prized possession in the world.

"I'll not be denied again!" Douglas wailed. He trained the gun back on Isabelle. "At least I'll put a final end to you both. Your memories will die once and for all."

Just then, a chilling breeze overtook them. The winds came from every direction, all at once. Sand blew in their faces, and Douglas was unable to keep the gun fixed on Isabelle. She made for the bluff to climb back up, but Douglas ran up to pull her back down again. She fought him as best she could, slapping at his face.

"You fool!" she yelled over the wind.

Douglas' eyes bulged, then, and he started choking. He rolled off her, his tongue hanging out of his mouth. In the sandstorm, Isabelle could make out the bright form of a man standing over Douglas.

It was Jacques, in all his glowing glory. It was apparent that Douglas could see him as well, for he gagged and rolled from side to side in agony and anger. Jacques stood over him, pointing silently at Douglas' heart. A noose hanging from his neck again, Jacques was a fearsome sight to behold.

Her knees shaking, Isabelle heard Douglas mutter, "You," before taking a last gasp. She knew without looking down that he was dead. Jacques reached out to her.

"Celeste, My Love, come." His lips never moved, but Isabelle could hear his reedy voice carried on the wind.

She shook her head. "No, Jacques," she said, pointing at the box.

Jacques followed Isabelle's pointing finger and leaned over to look into the box. When he looked up again, he no longer had the noose around his neck, and his eyes were the same peaceful ones from her dreams. He finally understood.

Isabelle smiled at him gently. "Jacques, it's time to go," she said. "Celeste has been waiting for you for so very long. Thank you."

Jacques' eyes returned the smile. With a slight bow, he turned and walked away from her, down the shoreline, then faded from view.

Isabelle knelt and closed the box. She left it beside Douglas' motionless body. Just then, she could hear Michael calling for her in the distance. She climbed back up the bluff to greet him.

He held her tightly. Looking down over the edge, he saw Douglas' motionless body. Isabelle told him quickly what happened and why Douglas tried to kill her.

"It's still hard to believe all of this," Michael said, "but as long as you are safe. You know, I seemed to have my own dream this time," he said. "It was a man. He was in white clothes. Knowing what you told me about Jacques, I listened to him carefully. He told me wake up and come save you."

Isabelle looked up into Michael's beautiful, loving face. She kissed him deeply. "And you did just that, Michael. You did."

EPILOGUE

Isabelle sat on a bluff overlooking the river, her legs curled beneath her. It was morning, and the sun was still on the rise. The water was still and clear. Watching the multitude of ships and ferries floating past, she waved occasionally to the passengers. The number of ships grew every day. Detroit, once a little fort in the wilderness, was now a thriving city.

In the year since her arrival, Isabelle had never been happier in her life. She and Michael had been inseparable since that last day of chaos and terror. They were married right on the grounds, in the orchard, by the pastor of the new Second Baptist. It was cold that day, but no one cared. Dr. Innis and his wife came to the wedding. Dr. Innis was delighted over the nuptials, but he was more interested in whether Isabelle's family ordeal was truly over. Isabelle assured him that it was, as the visions and the voices were gone.

Returning to Amherstburg long enough to attend Bess' wedding and to pack, Isabelle brought Michael and Ben with her. Her mother was speechless when the three arrived on her doorstep, grinning. Rosalie and Michael did not get along, as Isabelle expected. She especially loved Rosalie's distress over telling her friends and neighbors she now had an Indian grandson. Rosalie was clearly hurt over Douglas' betrayal, though, and Isabelle appreciated her mother's hug. Isabelle chose not to reveal the mysterious elements of her ordeal at the house, feeling sure that it was only meant for her alone. Regarding Barry, though, Isabelle berated her mother over being careless with his heart so long ago. When she heard Barry was dead, Rosalie did cry sincere, guilty tears, and cried harder over her father's death.

Returning to Detroit without a backward glance, Isabelle was finally home. Roaming the Fontaine freely, all doors were open to her. She closed the door to Barry's room by her own choice, however, as it would only be used as a guest room. It still pained Isabelle to walk past his room, and sometimes she imagined a flicker of dim candlelight from under the door. Her breathless exploration of the garret revealed just an old bed frame and a quilt, the only evidence of Celeste having lived there.

Until I arrived, that is, Isabelle amended.

Listening to the UNITED's distant wail from the Griswold dock, Isabelle plucked a crumbling red leaf from the grass. The horrifying showdown with Douglas had nearly destroyed her. Collapsing in Michael's arms right there on the bluff, Isabelle finally buckled under the weight of history. Her history. Douglas' history. The Fontaine's history. Detroit's history. All of these rivulets of destiny had swirled into an eddy inside Isabelle's heart and mind. She was the one chosen to dispel the vortex that had ensnared so many people. Briane's dark soul had sought out Isabelle in order to destroy Celeste. All the while, however, the entirety of Jacques's essence survived one hundred years to prevent this second tragedy. Jacques' love and protection saved Isabelle, but it almost killed her. She realized that she had saved Jacques in return, for she helped him understand that Celeste was dead, that he was dead. Letting go of the past out there on the shore, Jacques was finally able to rest. A small hand on her shoulder made Isabelle turn around. It was Ben. He sat down next to her. They watched the sparkling fresh water together with no need for words. Since the turn of events last year, their silent communication was stronger than ever. They were witnesses together, witnesses to one of the greatest dreams of love that ever existed, the love between Jacques Benesche and Celeste Fontaine.

Isabelle absently twirled her wedding band, ever grateful to be free of the gnawing pain in her hand. Her playing was better than ever. Free of Celeste's haunting melody, Isabelle was finally able to write new songs.

"Good morning, Dear Family." Isabelle smiled when Michael joined them. He set down his cane and sat down behind Isabelle and Ben. Wrapping his arms around them both, Michael kissed them atop their heads. "Josie says breakfast is ready."

The sun's bright rays engulfed islands in the distance, then swiftly came to rest directly above them for a lingering moment, then moved on towards the end of the shoreline. Isabelle, Michael, and Ben paused, remembering that on this day one year ago, Jacques' soul was finally set free.

On that terrible day, Douglas' body had been taken away by the patrol, and that was last of his story. Before he died by Douglas' blade, Ned du Roy had gotten his will updated, having a funny feeling about how his former business partners would treat him after telling on them. The will specified that his eldest son, Edmund, an attorney in Chicago, take over the house's affairs, including any future renovations. Including a clinic.

In the wake of his father's death, a stunned Edmund, Jr. told Isabelle what his father had shared with him as a boy about the Fontaine family history. Back then, he had never believed those stories. Until now.

"Most of the guests left after the showdown between Louis and Briane, and there was enough gossip to last them for years," Edmund Jr., began. "Early the next morning after Briane's embarrassing exit, Celeste's body was found floating in the river, after a frantic Louis searched all night for her. No one knew why Louis had Celeste buried as an unknown, but I guess it was to ensure she could have a proper Catholic burial on church grounds. In his grief, Louis freed all of the slaves, and arranged for Therese to be sent home. "Two days later,"Edmund Jr. said, "one of Duchene's two men was found near death on a road heading south by one of the Indians who traded at the Fontaine. Before the man died, he choked out that Jacques had overtaken them and snapped Duchene's neck. The two slave catchers shot Jacques in the back, then hung him from a tree. As his eyes bulged from the tight noose, it was said, Jacques still looked determined to reach Celeste."

Edmund Jr. told Isabelle he'd also learned from his father that after the men robbed Duchene's dead body they were stopped that night by someone looking like Jacques. This fearsome, glowing man with a noose around his neck killed the partner with only a look. The lone survivor had crawled away, helpless, with Jacques clawing at his heels. By the time the accursed slave catcher finished telling his story to the Indian in the icy dawn, his last words were, "Jacques, I'm sorry."

Edmund, Jr. had given Isabelle the rest of the family records from his father's office, dusty papers in a large leather bound ledger. Isabelle read that Evangeline and Eulalie had stayed on to raise Rene. Brokenhearted, Louis died just a few days after Celeste's burial. Tabor du Roy honored his family's promise to watch over the farm and all of the descendants, including, at Louis' dying request, any descendants of one Celeste Fontaine.

Most of the former slaves signed on as paid workers, and the farm survived, barely. Isabelle learned that once Caleb and Silas finally had the chance to cultivate grapes, a choice wine emerged that enriched the farm for years to come. In the decades following, Rene grew up and married, and had children of his own.

Isabelle heard Scout barking in the distance. Alders was back from the farmer's market. Isabelle, Michael and Ben rose and walked back up to the house, their home. Michael had some patients coming in early.

The three stopped mid-stride as a chilly October breeze caught them by surprise. They paused, waiting to hear a reedy voice calling out. None came.

"We'll start your piano lesson after breakfast," Isabelle told Ben as they started walking again. He smiled as he skipped up the walk to the porch, Michael laughing heartily on his heels.

Isabelle wanted to get in a few extra lessons before she and Michael set off for a two-week concert tour in Chicago, at Edmund Jr.'s urging. Her haunting song, Isabelle and Celeste's song, was the talk of the music world, a tour de force.

Isabelle turned to look back at the river. Deep within her heart, she knew Jacques and Celeste were finally together.

At last.

Select Bibliography

Blum, Stella. *Fashion and Costumes from Godey's Lady's Book.* New York: Dover Publications, 1985.

Burton, Clarence M. *When Detroit Was Young: Historical Studies by Clarence Monroe Burton.* Edited by M. M. Quaife. Detroit: Burton Abstract and Title Co., 1912, 1953.

<http://www.colonialdetroit.homestead.com> (21 March 2006)

DeRamus, Betty. "Straight of Detroit Shaped Our Fate." <http://www. detnews.com/history/river300/0529a.htm>

The Detroit Almanac: 300 Years of Life in the Motor City. Edited by Peter Gavrilovicki and Bill McGraw. Detroit: Detroit Free Press, 2000.

Doten & Boulard. *Costume Drawing.* New York: 1947, 1956.

Dunbar, Willis F. and George S. May. *Michigan: a History of the Wolverine State.* 3rd revised edition. Grand Rapids: Eerdmans, 1995.
Farley, Reynolds, Sheldon Danziger, and Harry J. Holzer. *Detroit Divided.* New York: Russell Sage Foundation, 2000.

<http://www.geocities.com/michdetroit/michhist/landclaim.html> (21 March 2006)

Hivert-Carthew, Annick. *Cadillac and the Dawn of Detroit.* Wilderness Adventure Books, 1994.

Kuclo, Marion. *Michigan Haunts and Hauntings.* Thunder Bay: Thunder Bay Press, 2003.

Leigh, Brian. *Frontier Metropolis: Picturing Early Detroit, 1701-1838.* Detroit: Wayne State University Press, 2001.

Oxford, William. *The Ferry Steamers: the Story of the Detroit-Windsor*

Ferry Boats. Boston: Boston Mills Press, 1992.

Phillips, Betty L. *Unmistakably French.* Salt Lake: Gibbs Smith ASID, 2003.

"Sovereign Council of New France." (18 July 2006) <http://www. en.wikipedia.org/wiki/New_France_Sovereign_Council>

Telling Detroit's Story. Detroit: Detroit 300 Commission, 2001.

Wilson, Moira Z. *Revolutionary Fires: A Tale of Indians on Erie.* Vol. 1. Haslett: MZW Ink, 2005.

About the Author

Heather Buchanan is a native Detroiter, and has always been fascinated with her city's history. Inspired by a series of articles about the little-known truth of slavery in Detroit and the reality of an unknown dead slave woman, Heather embarked on a ten-year odyssey to bring *Dark River* to life. An award-winning publisher and film producer, Heather is the author of the historical fiction novel *Victors: A Novel of Love, War and Jazz* and producer of an accompanying musical, *Love, War and Jazz*. She resides with her husband in Detroit and is hard at work on a sequel to *Dark River*.

9 780099 852789 5